taken by the night
STOLEN HEARTS
BOOK 1

JASMINE P. DANE

Copyright © 2025 by Jasmine P. Dane

All rights reserved.

No part of this book may be reproduced in any form or by any electronic or mechanical means, including information storage and retrieval systems, without written permission from the author, except for the use of brief quotations in a book review.

about the author

Jasmine P. Dane pens dark & smutty contemporary mafia romance & erotic horror with dangerous MMCs and the objects of their obsession. **Join me** @ GothikaBooks.Com to access free WIPs, early releases, extended editions & swag!

volume one

PRETTY WHEN YOU SCREAM

author's note

This is a dark, erotic horror romance. Trigger warnings: stalking, abduction, dubious consent, bondage, gore, murder, gun and knife violence, and knife play.

Note: before being released to retailers, the subsequent books in this collection will continue exclusively as WIPs @ **GothikaBooks.Com**

spotify playlist

Scan me

prologue

I WAS in the wrong place at the wrong time, and that's when I saw him in the act. Worse, he saw me, too.

His dark gaze burned into me from behind his white skull mask.

He's the reason I've been afraid to sleep at night. You could say I became obsessed with the killer. I couldn't get the image of him slashing that guy from my head—one of the town assholes, but to see him get sliced up like that? So much blood.

When I close my eyes, I see the mask. When I open my eyes, I see the mask—in the shadows, watching. Towering, broad-shouldered, and dressed in black. He is there and gone in an instant. Or is it just my imagination?

There are theories about who he could be, but the worst theory is *mine*. It's a dark secret, and I haven't told a soul.

Around Halloween, I attended a costume party and did something I'd never done before: I had a one-night stand. The thing is, I never saw his face. His one condition when he stole me away into a dark room? That he kept on the white skull mask.

ONE
bethany

HE'S WELL over six feet with round, solid shoulders, long arms, and long legs, and dressed in black. He has a distinctive swagger—confident and athletic but unruly, as if he doesn't like staying between the lines. He seems to need space, as if maybe he's angry about something.

I walk, gawking en route to the party at the Hollow Inn, wondering who he is. He looks back several times, piercing me with stormy eyes that cut through the holes in his white skull mask. It's Halloween, so that part isn't weird. But everything else about him is strange, and goosebumps tingle my spine when he looks at me again.

I reach the rope leading to the party inside the old Victorian, a popular B&B venue for costume parties near the old lighthouse on the Hudson River.

Skull motions me ahead.

"Ladies first," he says in a low, deep, slightly graveled voice.

"Thanks," I mutter, avoiding eye contact. I pass him and look back after the security guy lets me inside. Skull is gone.

Did he come inside? I look around, but it's hard to see beyond the wall of machine-induced fog.

I'm supposed to stay near the entrance to meet my girlfriends, but after coughing in a cloud of smoke, I search for cleaner air. Reaching the red-lit patio area at the back of the building, I text Albi and Mary to let them know my location before ordering a blood-orange-pomegranate sangria.

I check my phone, but no reply. Maybe they hit traffic. They're traveling from New York. I'm the only one in my friend group who returned to Sleepy Hollow after college. I just wasn't cut out for the major city. As a borderline autist, New York was overstimulating for me. Too many people, cars, colliding smells, and dizzying buildings block the sun and fresh bay air.

I always felt a bit better when I was in Central Park or near the water, looking toward Brooklyn. I thought that I could get used to it there. But the architecture, history, and endless array of places to see still weren't home. Even the jaw-dropping libraries and bookstores weren't enough to keep me, and that's saying a lot for this bookish girl. I guess I'm just not one of those make-a-new-home types of people.

My phone beeps. Finally, a response from Albi. But, shit... It's bad news. There was a big accident, and they won't be here for at least two hours. The outlook of them making this party with me is not good. My shoulders slump with disappointment. I guess I'll people-watch while sipping my drink and then go home.

Scooting back in the chair with a sigh, I observe the costume-clad groups of people quickly filling the patio. My costume consists of smoky eye shadow, a black baby-doll dress, and thigh-high stockings. I turn my head toward the already drunk and loud people to my right, dressed like characters from Beetlejuice. One has a shrunken head whipping from his wrist on a string as he makes dramatic hand gestures, laughing hysterically.

Speaking of overstimulation.

When I hear the show announcement over the speakers, I remember why I paid extra for tickets. Jumping up from my seat, I sift through the crowd until I reach the striped walls of the sitting room converted into a theater with a "show time" sign hanging above the open door. I shuffle between shoulders, facing the pop-up stage at the back near an antique piano. Most chairs are already taken, so I stop behind the first row. The lights dim, and my eyes widen in disbelief as a hand slides over my mouth. I gasp, startled as hell.

"Shh," he says with hot, minty breath, his lips grazing my ear.

I jerk my elbow backward into his firmly muscled torso. "Let go," I hiss, muffled under his large hand. His fingers are warm and strong.

"Somebody is going to die tonight, Bethany."

He knows my name, and his dead-serious tone sends my heartbeat racing. I thrust my elbow into him. "Get off!"

"With you? Gladly," he whispers. His voice is sexy enough to make my body respond in ways that it shouldn't. I guess it's been too long since a man touched me possessively—never this possessively.

"You need to leave this room, Beth. It isn't safe." He kisses my earlobe, sending heat through my core. Damn, get a grip, girl.

"There will be a lot of *blood*. Understand?" I nod my head.

"Good girl," he whispers in a deep tone that manages to make my panties damp. It defies logic, but he has a sexy, commanding voice thick with male prowess. With a voice like that, it's hard to imagine that he isn't drop-dead gorgeous.

His hand releases my mouth as the stage lights filter brighter, and the show begins. I turn around and look up, and the man in the white skull mask nudges his head toward the hall. He takes my hand, and I follow him just far enough to get some answers before yanking my hand away.

"What the hell is going on?"

He cocks his skull head like a predator eyeing its victim. "There's a killer on the loose, Bethany."

The coldness in his tone sends a chill down my spine. "What? How do you know my name?"

At first, when the screaming begins from behind, I think it's part of the show. But then people start running from the room, and I almost get knocked over. Skull grabs me by the wrist and tugs me away from the rush. He leads me upstairs, and I resist, trying to pull away, but he grabs hold of my arms and pivots me forward with a push. "Move," he orders.

He drags me into a room at the top of the stairs, where he shuts and locks the door. From there, he orders me into another room, using a key to open the door.

"We'll wait it out in here," he says coolly.

I pull my phone from my pocket, and he snatches it. "Calling the police won't help," he snickers. "Not in time."

"Hey, give that back! What is going on?"

He places my phone high on a shelf out of reach between storage boxes. "Trust me."

"Tell me what the hell is going on!"

"Where's the fun in that, Beth?"

Screams rise from downstairs, and I bring my hands to my mouth, horrified. "Oh, god. What...is happening?"

"What needs to be done." He takes my hand and leads me to the bed. "Sit. Relax."

"They sound like—"

"They're being slaughtered? Not all of them. Just the important ones."

"Are you fucking kidding me? How do you know?"

"I know things," he shrugs. "But I want to distract you from the chaos."

He sits on the bed beside me and turns me so that we are facing each other. I reach for his mask, but he snatches my hand and kisses it.

"No looking," he warns.

"What are you hiding?" I mutter as he trails his lips down my hand. His kisses are slow and deliberate.

When the gunshots ring out, I begin to cry. He gently pushes me back on the bed. "It's going to be okay," he says in a low, soothing voice.

He throws off his black hoodie, revealing his muscular chest beneath a fitted tee. Then he climbs between my legs, kissing slowly up my ankles through my black stockings. Wanting so badly to tune out the horrid noise, I let myself get lost in the soothing feel of his lips on my skin when he lifts the lower part of his mask, exposing his squared jaw with the divot at the center and a perfectly masculine mouth.

He trails up my legs but stops before his masked head is within reach of my hands. I realize he has a black rope when he gets up on his knees.

"I can't take the risk," he says, scooting between my legs and gathering my hands above my head.

"What the hell!" I snap, tugging my wrists, but it's already too late.

He has me tied to the bed as he grabs my knees and lifts

my legs into a bent position. I jerk my head toward the loud banging commotion beyond the room. "This is insane," I mutter as he ducks down between my legs.

"Do you want me to let you go?" he says.

Before I can answer, I'm struck with the overwhelming sensation of his mouth caressing my thighs. *Fuck, that feels good.* A moan escapes my lips as he pulls my panties aside and slowly circles my clit with his tongue, gently sucking.

I shouldn't be here. I shouldn't want this invasion of privacy as much as I do. But damn, he knows what he's doing...

"I knew you'd be wet, baby," he rasps, the vibration of his mouth tickling my pussy as his tongue slips inside me. He's a stranger, but he talks like he knows me. He touches me like he fucking owns me.

My head knocks back against the bed frame in startled pleasure. Oh, shit, I'm in trouble. The sound of commotion rises from downstairs as he thrusts his tongue back and forth inside me—am I getting off while people are...dying? No, people aren't dying. It's Halloween. It's just part of the show. Skull is playing his part. I want to believe that.

I greedily rock my hips against his mouth as he fucks me with his tongue, pressure building in my pussy with each stroke. Getting close to the edge of release, I wish I had free hands to hold his head in that perfect spot while I— *ohh. Yeah, just like that.*

"*Mm.* You taste *so* fucking good, baby. I knew you would."

"Oh...god," I cry out, my body flushing hot as I tumble over the edge, my pussy spasming. The man behind the mask goes quiet. He cocks his head, watching me as I catch my breath.

Is this the part where he kills me?

I gasp when he lifts to his knees and pulls out his thick, beastly cock. "Now suck my dick like a good girl," he says, tapping the fat tip of his erection against my lips. Admittedly, it's a turn-on.

I want to grab his hard, swollen erection in my hand, but with my hands tied, all I can do is open wide as he shoves himself inside my mouth. He ruthlessly thrusts back and forth, his shaft sliding over my tongue and hitting the back of my throat repeatedly until I finally choke.

"Do you want me to fuck your pussy, Beth? I promise to pull out," he rasps.

I hesitate, wishing I didn't want to say yes so badly. I'm about to tell him to free my wrists so I can wipe my mouth, but he doesn't wait for an answer. He lifts my legs, supporting his weight with long, strong arms as he lowers his hips between my thighs. When the tip of his cocks smacks my clit, I moan in pleasure.

"Is that a yes?"

I nod with a pant, wanting more.

"I thought so," he rasps, penetrating me with one hard thrust. My mouth slackens, and my eyes roll back in my head as he fucks me slow, deep, and hard. *God, yes-s.*

The frame of the bed slams against the walls as he pounds inside me, each thrust gaining in urgency as his huge cock fills me up completely. I can see a hint of his ass in the moonlit mirror across the room, the tension in his muscles as he thrusts back and forth inside me.

The frustration of being unable to grab onto his strong arms only adds to the desperate need building inside me as I reach the edge again. This time, it feels like I will fall so hard that my whole body burns hot with pressured angst. I try to muffle my scream as I come so hard I could die. But I can't stop myself from screaming as his pelvis slams my clit, and the tip of his swollen erection knocks against my cervix. The high pitch of my release fills my ears, and I gasp for air, barely catching my breath as he pulls his cock from me.

He comes all over the bed with a deep groan, and I stare up at him with mixed emotions. This is so far out of my character that I'm in shock. I don't even know his name.

"We need to hurry," he rasps, untying me.

"Why?"

He doesn't answer. He puts on his hoodie and takes my hand, helping me out of bed. I change clothes, and he hands me my phone before rushing me into the hall, where another set of stairs leads down to a mudroom.

We escape out a back door, and I try to keep up with his pace. My heart races amidst the sound of police sirens as he firmly holds my hand for the two blocks it takes to get to my townhouse.

"How did you know where I live?" I ask, but he doesn't answer.

He lifts the mask just enough to kiss me, then bites my lip as he looks into my eyes through dark slits. His stormy gaze is cold and unreadable as he pinches my chin between his fingers.

"You're fucking pretty when you scream," is the last thing he says before leaving me alone in the night.

* * *

I lock every door and window in my house and turn on the radio, listening to the news about the "murder spree" at the Hollow Inn.

Three people were killed: males who attended the party together. The skeleton-masked assailant in dark clothing used a curved, claw-like dagger, a cross between a knife and a sword. Somebody shot at him, but he got away.

My stomach drops as I fall back into a chair, bringing my shaky hands to my face. People were murdered while I was having sex with a stranger in a room upstairs! He knew what was about to go down and warned me about it before forcing me upstairs.

When I asked what was happening, he replied, "What needs to be done." Which means…he's likely an accomplice to murder.

Everything happened so fast that I barely had time to think. I let him convince me that I deserved a distraction. I'll never get the image of him while he fucked me from my mind. Half cast in shadow and moonlight, his stormy eyes were fixed on me through the slits of his mask, the muscles flexing beneath his fitted tee as he thrust his body into me, and the visual tease of the corded muscles in his solid arms that I couldn't even touch as I came.

The sight of him in that mask, grabbing his huge dick in hand and spurting his semen all over the sheet and red bed quilt, I'll never see anything like that again.

Unless…

My heartbeat speeds at the thought of him knowing my name and where I live. Will he visit me, expecting sex? Should I report this to the police?

I should.

But the thought of telling a cop what I did is mortifying, and I can't bring myself to do it. I need time to think it over.

So, I take a hot shower and try to sleep. When I close my eyes, I see the mask, and when I jolt up in bed in a hot sweat, I see the white mask just through the cracked blinds outside my window.

I jump from bed, my heart racing as I part the blinds,

peering into the darkness. He's not there now. Did I imagine it? It dawns on me that he had a key to a room inside the Hollow Inn—a big, brown, historical-looking skeleton key. Where did he get that?

I throw on a robe and head to my small desk. If there is one thing I'm good at that can help me get out of panic mode, it's doing research. I majored in research in college while working as a local librarian.

I type in Hollow Inn on my laptop, reading about its history in search of any possible clues as to why Skull would have a key. The room was only accessible from another locked room off the main hall, which seemed to be being used for storage. There were boxes stacked near the bed.

He could have stolen the key. But...what if there's another connection?

I've named this dark riddle "Skeletons."

A skeleton mask and a skeleton key. What is the connection, and why did people die? Is this the start of something or the end?

Then, that memory I tried so hard to forget from a year ago flashes into my mind. The murder. The man in the mask. Blood. So. Much. Blood. The killer looked right at me before I ran.

No, I can't think of it!

I look up with a jolt to a tapping sound at the window. My stomach jumps as I get up, and my heart thuds in my chest when I reach the window. Slowly, I open the blinds to find a piece of paper taped to the glass with red writing.

Shh. I'll be watching you, Beth.

TWO
bethany

I FLIP the window sign to Open and unlock the front door, then look around with a sigh. Beth's Books could use a makeover, but my little "new and used" bookstore is on a limited spending budget. It's my first year in business, and my profit margin is relatively low.

A woman appears outside the door, and I head to the counter and open my powder compact to check my face in the mirror. I have bags under my hazel eyes and should have put on some mascara or maybe a dab of eyeshadow. It's too late now. At least my mess of dark hair is tied into a neat ponytail.

April ducks in wearing a wet raincoat, letting the door slam shut. I need to fix that door. A waft of cool air gives me a chill, and I tighten my grey cardigan over my chest.

"Morning, Beth," she chirps, far more awake than I'll ever be today.

"Morning," I say, stifling a yawn. I don't do well without sleep, and today will be rough.

Three things kept me awake—coffee, anxiety, and adrenaline.

The anxiety came from knowing people were dead and that I was indirectly involved. The coffee, of course, facilitated my research, which was the source of my adrenaline. I always get a buzz when researching, but the topic was on a whole new level this time. As tired as I am now, I was wide awake until four a.m. Life has never been more disturbingly exciting or excitingly disturbing—either way.

Mostly, I'm mortified over what happened, but somehow, I don't feel my life is totally in danger. But maybe I should. In the meantime, for my sanity and coping, the research scientist in me has made this into a project. I will find answers.

April meets me at the counter, looking both ways before she speaks.

"Can you believe it?"

I shake my head, averting eye contact while sorting through a box of books. The last thing I want to discuss is what everyone will be going on about forever.

"Like clockwork," she says, and I look up. "What do you mean?"

"Oh. Forgot you were away at college. But didn't your mom mention the serial killer?"

Chills tingle my spine as I return to sorting, trying to keep cool.

"She...mentioned an uptick in crime," I say.

She puffs out air. "I think it's more than that. Last November, two guys were cut to pieces on the riverwalk. Then, a few days later, they found that guy up at Tower Hill outside the Rockefeller Preserve. His neck was nearly severed."

"Yeesh, that's terrible. You think it's all related?"

She nods. "I'm not the only one who thinks that. Sara Luton's husband is a cop, and he thinks the dead victims were killed with the same weapon. The wounds look like they were gashed with a meat hook."

I cringe, making a face.

"Whoever this guy is, he isn't using the typical slasher weapon. The news said one of the survivors described it as a claw-shaped dagger."

"Yeah, I heard. Long and curved; a cross between a knife and a sword."

So, everybody thinks this is a one-person job. But I know otherwise. When Skull said, "There is a killer on the loose," he wasn't just talking about one person. For all I know, they operate as a group, maybe even a network.

God, did I have sex with a serial killer?

If he's a serial killer, why did he force me away from the scene of the crime? Just because he wanted to fuck me?

He was forceful, but he wasn't violent. He didn't hurt me; he made me orgasm so hard that I screamed. It felt like I was outside myself listening to the high-pitched sound, and I was too overwhelmed with coming all over his giant cock to stop myself...

I hear his deep, gravelly voice on repeat in the back of my mind. "You're pretty when you scream."

But I wasn't the only one screaming that night. People screamed in pain while I screamed in pleasure. People died while I was getting off upstairs with a masked stranger.

I feel like I'm guilty by association.

I've never been the kind of girl to have many skeletons in my closet to feel ashamed about. I follow the rules and live a quiet, bookish life.

But now.

Now, everything has changed. I have the worst kind of skeletons imaginable, and they aren't the kind that stay hidden in the dark confines of locked-up secrecy. These skeletons jump out from the shadows when you least expect them. One of them knows where I live, and one is watching me.

It darkens outside, thundering, and big drops of rain hit the windows as the lights flicker inside my shop. It's getting late, and the shop will be closing soon. Only a dozen people have come in today. Each time it's a tall or tallish male, I analyze him a little too much, looking for any resemblance to Skull.

After reheating a cup of coffee in the microwave, I return to my laptop, which is open on the counter near the cash register. I sit on a stool and finish the article I was reading about the local legendary mansion. I don't think it has anything to do with my research; it only popped up in the search results because it has "skull" in the title.

The Greylinn estate is known locally as "Skull Hill" because its massive 45,000 sq ft old-world mansion sits on the hill by that name. A large skull-shaped boulder is at the bottom near an old well where people would get water back when.

Stretching over one hundred twenty acres, the Greylinn estate is legendary. We used to go there when I was a kid, and we'd walk the lush, perfectly manicured grounds for hours. That was before they closed it to visitors. The Greylinns moved to Calabasas, California, and their kids, all adults now, moved out. But the estate is still in the family and closed to visitors. Seems crazy to maintain a palace like that with nobody living in it. At least, I don't think anybody is still living in it. I can't begin to understand what having that much money is like.

But what does this have to do with the murders? Nothing. I'm more interested in the history of the Hollow Inn and why Skull had a key if he didn't just steal it, which he may have.

But wait a minute...

At the end of the article, it says that, like a few other historical buildings in town, the Greylinns also own the Hollow Inn. Hm. Weirdly, this adds another skull or skeleton to this dark riddle--how many skeletons are there to find? This... can't get any more surreal.

Jarring me from my thoughts, the thunder cracks loudly, startling me. The lights flicker again, dimming. I sure hope the power doesn't go out. I reach into a drawer, find the flashlight, and flick it on to ensure it works.

When the front door opens, I look up. A tall guy in a black hoodie ducks his head, comes in, and briefly nods in my direction before disappearing down an aisle. The way he walks straight back suggests he knows where he is going, but I don't recall seeing him before.

"Can I help you find anything?" I call out, but he doesn't answer. Maybe he came in to find a bathroom with no intention of looking at books. People do that sometimes, as if my shop is a gas station. But I guess when you gotta go, you gotta go. I haven't bothered keeping it locked. Seems rude.

I hear his words: *There's a killer on the loose.* Maybe April's right and the murders are connected, which would mean the killer(s) live nearby.

"Just let me know if you need anything," I call out again, trying not to feel suspicious about the unknown man I'm alone with.

I shouldn't be paranoid, but how can I not be? He's not the only operator; these guys could be anybody.

With a sigh, I turn to grab my water bottle from my bag

when a book slams down on the counter behind me, making me jump before spinning around.

"Jeez, that was loud," I say, and the hooded guy on the other side of the counter smirks at me. Despite his attitude, he has a gorgeous face, even if it's half-shrouded by a hood.

"Didn't mean to scare you," he says in a low voice, causing me to pause, my heart quickening. His voice isn't as deep as Skull's and not as gravelly, but it's similar enough to creep me out. He has intense eyes—bluish-grey. Maybe in the moonlight, they look stormy like Skulls.

I nervously fumble with the book on the counter, The Damnation Game by Clive Barker.

"Horror books are half off right now for Halloween," I say.

He taps his finger on the counter. "Yeah. I saw the sale sign."

His tone isn't friendly, but it isn't quite unfriendly. He has an aggressive edge about him. He's so tall, with intense eyes looking at me directly, which makes my cheeks flush. I'm pretty sure I wouldn't be so easily flustered if I had slept last night.

I straighten my posture, smiling professionally. "Did you find everything you were looking for, or may I help you with something else?"

"You may help me with ringing up that book," he says in a low, measured voice, handing me a crisp, new hundred-dollar bill. But his book only costs $2.99. Most people pay with credit. Luckily, I always start the day with some change in the drawer.

I open the register, gather his change, and start counting it back to him on the counter.

"So, who do you think did it?" he interrupts, and I pause, looking up at him. He must be a local if he's talking about the murders. Or maybe he's an out-of-town journalist. His poker face is unreadable, his grey eyes intent upon me. I swallow thickly.

"No idea," my voice nervously wavers. I return to counting.

"A lot of rumors," he interrupts again. This time I don't look up. My heartbeat speeds as I continue counting.

"I...don't know anything," I say, feeling defensive. "You sure about that?"

Is it just me, or does his tone hint at being accusatory? I look up, and our eyes lock for a few long seconds. He's vaguely familiar--*oh, god. Is it him?* The thunder crashes, and the lights flicker.

"Do I...know you?" I mutter, my heart beating in my ears.

He shrugs.

I hand him the book, and his thumb slides over my hand as he takes it, raising the hairs on the back of my spine and sending a shot of heat through my pounding chest.

He slightly bows his head before turning away.

I watch him leave in silence. A familiar swagger to his walk sends chills down my spine. No. I'm just imagining it. Not him.

God, my mouth is dry. I chug my water bottle before going to the bathroom to splash my face with cool water. It's time to go home.

I pass through the horror aisle on my way back from the bathroom, and that's when I see it. A message written in red letters on a big white piece of paper stuck to the spine of a book.

My heartbeat pounds in my ears as I pull it down. Without reading it, I rush to the front of the store and grab my things before locking up. I want to get safely into my car before it's dark. My car is right out front, and the moment I sit in my seat with the doors locked, I pull the paper from my bag and read the letters written neatly in the shade of blood.

Be a good girl, Beth.

After listening to the news and learning that some of the survivors of the "murder spree" are in the hospital due to being trampled in the commotion, I turn off the radio and attempt to go through my usual evening routine.

I'm so tired that I feel like a zombie as I go through the motions: eating, showering, and brushing my hair and teeth. I water the plant, tie the trash bag off, and put a new bag in the can. I'm too afraid to take the trash out in the dark, so I set it by the front door inside the small foyer. It can wait until morning. Being afraid of the dark is part of my new routine.

Over the next hour, I continue doing routine things, but mentally, I'm somewhere else, the memory of the night of the murders piercingly pinned to my brain like a Polaroid picture. It's all I see, and the repeating mantra of the riddle is all I hear: *skeletons. Skull.*

The idea of sleeping seems like a sick joke. But I already feel like shit from pulling an all-nighter, and if I don't get some sleep tonight, I will become physically ill.

I check the locks on the doors and windows and then recheck them before turning out all the lights. I usually find the dark peaceful. Not tonight. I turn on the kitchen light before finally going to bed, where I try in vain to clear my mind enough to sleep.

The only thing that makes me feel better also makes me feel worse. That I was protected from the scene of the crime. I wasn't trampled or killed because Skull insisted that I leave the room before forcing me upstairs.

I try to focus on the part of that equation that makes me feel better: that he didn't hurt me then, and so why would he hurt me now? This means that even though he might be out there stalking me, I can safely sleep. I tell myself this as I take deep breaths, imagining a peaceful meadow where deer are frolicking.

I think I'm asleep when I see something lurking in the shadow of the woods like a predator. The deer don't seem to notice—why don't they notice? A tall, dark shadow appears at the meadow's edge, but they don't hear it. What is wrong with these deer? When the shadow lunges forward, they all look up, but it's already too late. The menace descends, flattening over the scenery like an inkblot. When the shadow retreats, only skeletons remain.

Jolting up in bed, I try to calm my pounding heart. "Shh," hums a distinctively male voice. Low, deep, and steady.

"Who is it?"

"You're dreaming," he says, and I lie back down, confused. I'm delirious, that's all. I must sleep.

I wake again in a cold sweat and check the time on my phone. It's 3 a.m., and I crashed around nine, so I've been sleeping a fitful six hours—at least, that's something. I try to go back to sleep when a thought occurs to me, and my research brain is activated.

So, I get up and go to my desk, looking for more articles on Skull Hill. I want to know more about the family, especially the kids. They didn't go to public school, and I never saw them around.

I do some more digging on the family and learn that Lindsay and Landon Greylinn are twins, three years older than me. They went to Groton boarding school near Boston, which would explain why I never knew them. I zoom in on a picture of them together. They are identical twins: tall, dark-haired, with greyish-blue eyes. Their parents, Charles and Blythe, were known philanthropists. However, when they relocated to the warm beaches of Southern California, they stopped allowing the public to visit and use the lower part of their acreage as a community park.

The twins are heirs to their parents and grandparents' billion-dollar oil fortune. Lindsay Greylinn is engaged and lives in Manhattan, but Landon…lives at the family estate in Sleepy Hollow! He's twenty-five years old, unmarried, and has no kids. Wow, somebody is living up there alone on the hill all this time?

Skull Hill.

It's only called that because of a stupid rock, so I need to focus on other details.

Skull had a key. He could have stolen it, or…

How tall is Landon Greylinn? I do some more digging before learning that Lindsay is 5'8" and Landon is 6'3".

God, what is the probability that the tall, slate-blue-eyed, billionaire heir, Landon Greylinn, is part of a murder gang? Practically nil. He has everything in the world he could ever want and would have no reason to kill people. Unless he's just crazy and doing it for the thrills.

I zoom in on a picture of him at a charity event with his parents when he was seventeen. It's a garden party amongst the hedges, flowers, and perfect lawns of the Greylinn estate. Everyone is wearing white and bright colors—except for him. He wears a dark blue shirt rolled at the sleeves, a Rolex on his wrist, and black jeans. He doesn't smile for the camera, and his intense eyes stand out. He has the kind of intriguing look in his eyes that makes you want to know what he's thinking. He's probably thinking something very different from the people around him.

He reminds me of that guy at the store who reminded me of--oh, hell. Did I have sex with Landon Greylinn?

No freaking way. It cannot possibly be him. That's crazy.

When my phone suddenly rings at 5 a.m., I jump, startled. Shit.

Why is April Fetzer calling me this early? I didn't know she had my number, but our moms are friends, so that's not hard to come by. This has to be about recent events.

I gather myself before answering. Just play it cool.

"Morning, April."

"Oh, hi. Sorry to bother you. Did I wake you?" "No. It's okay."

"I just wanted to give you a heads up. Sarah Hamilton said the police were doing rounds with any locals who attended the party. Tiff said you were there, and I just wanted to check in with you."

My stomach drops. "Yeah, I was there."

"Why didn't you tell me when I came into the shop? I guess you're okay, then."

"Yeah, I'm fine."

"Okay, well. Just letting you know that the police will probably come by your house or shop."

"Thanks for letting me know, April."

"No problem. I'm here if you ever need to talk to someone about what you went through. Just putting that out there." Even though she's probably already heard it from so many other people by now, I can tell she wants me to tell her my version of that night. But there is no way I'm getting into that with her or anybody else.

"Thank you, April. I...should go." "Okay. I'll talk to ya later, hon." "Bye."

I go to the kitchen and make myself a fresh cup of

coffee, nearly dropping it when I hear a door slam shut. I freeze, my heart thudding. Okay, calm down. All the doors are locked, so it must have been an inside door. The heater may have kicked on and caused a draft or something.

Listening for any more sounds, I turn on the lights around the house and recheck the windows and doors. Everything is as it should be--how long will I be living in a state of paranoia?

When I get to my room, I audibly gasp, bringing my hands to my mouth. A piece of paper with red writing is attached to my laptop screen.

Holy fuck. It's him. In my house!

The blinds rattle over my bedroom window, and I realize it's open. That's how he got in! I rush to the window, slamming it shut and locking it. He might still be out there. The dream of the deer flashes into my mind. I woke up, and a voice lulled me back to sleep—a man's voice. Oh, god. Was he here the whole time?

With my phone in my hand, I pace the room, deliberating if I should call the police. My head is spinning so fast that I fall into the chair. The blood-red words stare back at me like a vital warning: *Good girls never tell.*

THREE
skull

WHEN I EXIT my silver Mercedes Humvee, the moon is low, and the ocean downhill looks flat and grey, with a hint of light on the cloudy horizon.

Ace cocks his head, pinching the tip of his blonde beard. "Your parents ever fucking home?"

I leer at him. "Funny. And this isn't my home."

He and Banks look at me like I'm crazy, but they already know that about me.

"What about the gardener?" jokes Banks, pulling his mask off and running his hand through his dark curls.

I crack my knuckles. "Landscaper is in dreamland. Now get the fucking body out of my vehicle before it starts to smell."

"Sir, yes, fucking Sir," Banks drawls over his shoulder as they disappear around the back of the vehicle.

Ace has the black body bag slung over his shoulder when they reappear. "He's a lightweight. I've got this."

"They finally reported him missing," scoffs Banks.

I shake my head. "Interrogating a druggie rapist isn't

my cup of tea. He was too numb to feel pain. At least we got the names."

"Three dead, and they call it a massacre?" snickers Ace.

"They like to exaggerate," says Banks.

The guys follow me down the trail to the old family cemetery, surrounded by hedges and massive oaks, where a freshly dug hole awaits the dead bastard inside the body bag.

Ace squats before he lugs the limp body from his shoulder, tossing it in. It hits the dirt with a heavy thunk, and I step forward, looking down into the hole. An image of the last time he was alive flashes into my mind, with deep, red gashes on his chest and arms.

"It's nothing but maggots for this one," says Banks, grabbing one of three shovels, and we all pitch in until the grave is covered. Next comes the sod and rocks sprinkled with twigs. This no longer looks like a grave but a stretch of grass between headstones.

I crack my neck. "I need a fucking whiskey."

Banks gives me a hard stare. "What about...that girl?"

My jaw tightens. "What about her?"

"You deviated from the plan," he shrugs as if that means something needs to be done about it.

I narrow my eyes. "My plan. I can't deviate the fuck I want. Remember who pays you."

"Shit, I don't need the money," Banks spits on the ground, and I crack an evil grin.

"I know you do it for the love, you sick, preppy fuck."

We smirk at each other.

"Are we staying over? I'm tired as shit," yawns Ace.

I run my hand through the back of my hair. My scalp is sweaty, and it's time for a hot shower.

"Whatever," I say. "Just don't touch anything that's not in the kitchen. I'll be in and out before dawn. Let's go."

Bank's eyes me suspiciously, getting under my skin.

"Where you off to, Skull?"

"None of your fucking business."

We return to my Mercedes, and I drive up the paved road until I reach the sprawling mansion. This place was never a home for me. Now, it's just somewhere to bury the bodies.

Inside the marble foyer, I head to the nearest walk-in shower.

As the hot water pours down my back, I think of that lovely, innocent girl named Bethany and how much I enjoyed defiling her. How could I not? When I saw her walking to the party, I was already making plans for her. Then when I came up behind her and grabbed her pretty mouth in my hand, her reaction made my cock so fucking hard.

She was alarmed, and she fought back a little. But just before she delivered a few blows of her pointy elbow into my muscled stomach, I felt her mouth relax under my hand as my lips grazed her soft earlobe, and a delicious little moan vibrated against my palm. I knew her pussy was already getting wet for me.

I'm thinking maybe, just maybe, Bethany gets aroused when she's scared. That is… So. Fucking. Hot. Yeah, I want to scare her some more.

I smile as I wash myself, thinking she is a neglected little thing. She may not have admitted to herself when I first touched her skin, but she needed somebody to finish the job I began. When I got her upstairs, she was putty in my fucking hands. God, I loved the taste and feel of her sweet hot pussy, and when I got my dick wet inside her--mm--yeah, fucking her juicy cunt was pure heaven.

Without a doubt, I am not done with that pretty little thing.

If she only knew the savage things I had planned for her, Oh, I'm going to make her scream again; she doesn't know it.

FOUR
bethany

I LEAVE my house two hours early because I'd rather talk to the police while I'm in work mode at the bookshop than inside the privacy of my home, where I'll feel more vulnerable. If I'm going to be lying through my teeth, I should do it with confidence.

There is no way to interpret Skull's notes and breaking into my house as anything other than a threat.

I'll be watching you, Beth.

Be a good girl.

Good girls never tell.

Because of him, I know certain things that others do not, and he wants me to keep my mouth shut.

I know that the killer didn't act alone. I know that more than one of these guys wears a skull mask. Even though it was pretty dark in the room that night, and Skull kept his shirt on, hiding any tattoos, I know his dimensions. He's over six feet tall and built like an athlete. His eyes are greyish.

God, why the hell did he bring me into this? Now, he's

watching me like a hawk and has no qualms about breaking into my home. This shit is whack.

Nerves rattle my gut as I close and lock the front door to my shop. The store doesn't open until 9 a.m., so I don't bother flipping the sign yet. I've never lied to a police officer before, and I'm not looking forward to it.

If I tell the truth, I'm afraid it will make me an accessory to murder. I could tell them that he forced me upstairs. That part is true. But I can't claim innocence over having sex with Skull while knowing that people downstairs were being hurt and that he was a part of it, which makes me part of it.

This isn't the only reason I must lie. I'm afraid of what Skull will do to me if he learns that I ratted him out. He didn't hurt me that night; he protected me. But that could change if I don't do what he wants. Was it really worth it to him to tip his hand in this way so that he could fuck me? Now I'm this problem on his hands that he must stalk and scare into submission? Or...is this his idea of a game?

If I could go back, I wouldn't have gone with him. Then again, I could have been one of the ones trampled or killed. Hindsight is such a bitch.

I busy myself finding solace amongst the stacks of books piled haphazardly on the book cart, reading the spines and placing them on the proper shelves. The scent of books and the sounds they make when I flip the pages, shut them, and stack them are always calming. Being surrounded by books is my idea of heaven.

I always linger the longest in the mystery aisle—it's probably the most organized section in the store because it's my favorite genre. The next aisle over is horror, which reminds me of *him*.

I stop at the gap between the spines, a missing book

below where I found the taped note. This must be where that strange guy got the Clive Barker book he bought, near where the note was left. Coincidence?

Maybe he just bought it to buy something, as an excuse to ask me a few questions, see if I'm keeping his secrets safe. There is no way to know why he bought it or if that was even *him*.

Sighing, I grab a misplaced book lying flat atop the row. I flip it over. My heartbeat picks up as I read the title: *The Damnation Game* by Clive Barker. *What the hell?* There shouldn't have been another. I looked it up in my records after that guy left. It's an old book that I got in a shipment bundle. So, where the heck did this one come from? Did that guy slip it back in here? There is no sticker price on the back.

Admittedly, I get so many used bundles dropped off from locals that my inventory records aren't always accurate. Either way, I've decided not to sticker this. Since I'm highly suspicious that the strangely gorgeous, hooded guy who came in here is my masked stalker, I will keep this copy to read, hoping to pick his brain a little, whoever he is.

Somebody knocks on the door, startling me. I take a deep breath, preparing myself to speak to the police. But it's only April here *before* the store is open. She's becoming a new fixture in my life, not in a good way.

Begrudgingly, I unlock the door and let her inside. A cold draft follows her in, giving me the shivers. I pull my black cardigan tighter around my chest.

"Morning, hon," she smiles.

"Morning. Mind locking that," I say before heading to the counter perpendicular to the large window near the entrance. I lift a box onto the counter, pulling out books. Maybe she won't stay long chatting me up if I appear busy.

"*So,* have they talked to you yet?" she asks, getting straight to the point.

I glance up at her. She's wearing a burnt orange sweater with a collared shirt underneath, and dark curly hair frames her overly curious facial features. I can tell she's utterly engrossed in this mystery, like me. But it feels like we are on two different sides of the coin. It's an isolating feeling worming deeper inside me by the day.

"Not yet," I say, wiping a smudge from a book cover.

"Well," she sighs. "I went ahead and stopped by the police station this morning."

I look up, brows pinched. "Thought you weren't at the party."

"I wasn't. But Maddy Johnson was. I helped her with the catering menu. She told me something that rang a bell with me. She thinks copycat murders are going on. We have two weeks left in October, and so many people are wearing these skeleton masks, it's hard to tell the real killer."

I put down the book and stare at her. "You don't think they've already thought of that?"

"Well, Sarah Hamilton said she'd be at the station this morning, so I just dropped in to talk to her about it. Her husband's--"

"A cop. Right, I remember you said that." I sigh. "Well, I have much sorting to do, so..."

"Yeah, I should go. I have a hair appointment."

"Thanks for dropping in," I lie.

"Feel free to give me a call anytime," she says over her shoulder.

When she leaves, I lock the door behind her and turn down the lights. I'm going to give myself one hour of peace before opening. If the police come, I'll ignore them. They won't know I'm here.

I head to my reading chair tucked away behind the counter. I open the horror novel by the light of my small, portable reading lamp. I get one page in before I stop cold, heart-jumping from my chest. Red ink is splattered inside the cover around the words *Damnation Game*, and underneath, scrolled in ink, are the words: *Good girls play by the rules.*

I study the warning in red, wondering how I got unlucky. Something tells me that I should read the book—I mean, what if the rules he's referring to are inspired by it? Or maybe I'm reading too much into it, and this is just another way of telling me to keep my mouth shut.

I don't make it past the first page when somebody knocks on the front door. I snap the book shut, grab my phone, and check the time—thirty minutes until opening. I wonder if April told the police I was here.

I rise just enough from my chair to peek at the door. Whoever is on the other side is wearing dark clothing. I sit back down, ignoring it. When the person knocks again, anxiety rattles my nerves. I don't want to know who is on the other side.

Determined to hold my ground until opening hour, I settle back into the chair and flip past the threatening words to the first chapter.

The story is set in war-ravaged Eastern Europe. The main character is a gambler hellbent on beating this rumored, ominous champion who has left a trail of victims. Gambling against him is like a Faustian type of deal with the devil.

This reminds me of something I glimpsed when I was researching the Greylinns. I pull my laptop from my tote bag and open the labeled "Skulls" folder with the saved articles. I click on a few until I find the one about the

Greylinn fortune. Early on, the family made money in oil, real estate, and later casino hotels. The current generation is among the wealthiest casino chain owners in the U.S. Wow.

My phone beeps, letting me know it's time to open the doors. God, can't I hide out all day reading and doing research? At least it's raining again, so today will probably be slow. Then again, it isn't customers whom I'm avoiding. The dread I feel over speaking with the police is only slightly less than seeing him again, here in my store, leaving me another message to find.

I think of the guy who bought this book. But is he Landon Greylinn, and is Landon Greylinn *Skull?* My instincts are leaning toward yes.

When another knock hits the door, I jump with a yelp before getting up and heading that way with a sigh. I hold my breath as I unlock the latch, realizing that the closed-and-open sign is facing the wrong way. How did that happen? That explains the early knocking.

Whoever it was is gone now.

My phone beeps inside my pocket, and I read the text from the National Hurricane Service. So, the Hurricane Watch issued yesterday has now become a Hurricane Warning, with expected high winds and heavy downpours to hit in a couple of hours, followed by a severe storm surge. Great.

There will be zero business today, and I could get stuck in the weather if I don't leave now. Looks like I'm going home.

After grabbing my bag and locking up, I catch a tall, dark figure out of the corner of my eye as I get into my car. He disappears into the alley, and my stomach does a deep dive over fears that it's *him*.

Not just fear. Or I should say, it's not the kind of fear that others may have over a masked man linked to a murder spree. My fear is rooted in my mixed emotions. Curiosity, awe, and shameful arousal are among the feelings that I shouldn't have but do.

Regardless of the context of how we met, he made me feel so…well…

When he tied me up and filled me up, fucking me so hard—*damn*. When I came all over his big, thick cock, it was the most intense physical pleasure I've ever had in my life. I can't just forget that part of the equation.

As deranged as it may be, Skull took me to a place I didn't know existed. I hate the part of me that wants to feel that way again. My mind knows it can't be healthy.

If only my body felt the same.

* * *

When I get home, I push through the wind gusts and heavy rain, hurrying inside, drenched to the bone. After tying my hair with a towel, I peel off my clothes and put on my warm grey robe. Then, as has become my new habit, I check the locks on every window and door. All secure.

Or so I tell myself.

After answering Mom's call regarding my "safety plans" for the storm, which consist of a battery-operated radio, a nearly empty box of matches, two candles, bottled water, and blankets, I turn on the living room space heater and look out the window with a sigh, hoping this hurricane dies out fast and that I don't suddenly see a tall man in dark clothing lurking behind the sheets of rain. I think of that man I saw going into the alley. He still can't be out there in this weather. No way.

I scan the small, puddled front yard and the street, water streaming fast beneath parked cars. Nobody sane is out there. Everybody who hasn't left town is hunkering down.

The thunderous sky is darkening fast. Leaving the window, I turn on the lights and the radio to listen to storm updates. The sky cracks, and right on cue, the lights flicker before going out. *Damn.*

I get up from the sofa and open the blinds, letting in streaks of cloud-filtered grey light. The treetops bend severely in the heavy wind as the rain pummels the windows.

Grabbing my tote bag, which still has my packed lunch for today, I settle into a corner of the sofa, listening to the "Category Three" announcement while eating my turkey and kale sandwich. "Winds of 111 to 130 mph...storm surge 9 to 12 feet above normal tide...structural damage to small buildings...mobile homes may be destroyed."

Same-ol-same-ol, I shrug, pulling out my laptop and checking the internet connection. My shoulders slump with disappointment at the zero bars. No bars, no research. I wanted to read more about the casino business that the Greylinns are into. It's too much of a coincidence that this horror book has a gambling theme. As hard as it is to believe, Landon Greylinn must be Skull.

Nobody would ever think the killer(s) are connected to the wealthiest family around. I can hardly believe it myself.

Pulling the paperback book from my bag, I stare at the red ink, imagining Landon's hand scrolling it. Is this sharply slanted horror movie font his usual writing style, or did he do this for effect, part of his game? A game I am unwittingly caught up in.

It's so dark in the room now, the grey streaks of light

mottled with deepening shadow, that I get up and light both of my candles before settling back down and covering with a blanket, ready to read. I turn off the radio, and the relentless backdrop of wind and rain only seems to serve the creepy vibe of the book. I get lost in the slow-burn, classic literary style for a few pages, but my stomach starts to turn when I get to the part about the woman with no lips.

There's a weird noise coming from the attic. Is the roof falling in?

I try to focus on the book, but when I think I hear the fridge open and shut, I jump up, startled. *What the hell?*

I grab my phone, trying to ignore the din outside the house so I can hear the strange noise from within. It can't be the fridge. That makes no sense. The power is out, and the home should be silent.

When I get to the kitchen, I feel a dark energy, and this needling feeling crosses my scalp like static electricity raising my hair. I blink at the surreal sight of two foreign, black-colored wine glasses, half-filled with liquid, sitting on the counter. *Whose?*

I jolt my head, my panicked gaze finding the strange, large picnic basket on my dining table. A dizzying, dissociative feeling flashes through me like I'm in somebody else's house or like I'm dreaming that I'm awake, but I'm not.

Blinking my eyes, I gasp when a warm, masculine hand slides over my mouth.

"Remember this, Beth?" he whispers, with a familiar voice, his lips on my ear as he pulls his body tightly against mine from behind.

The hard bulge pressing against my ass is unmistakable, and it's like I'm back in that Victorian house again, feeling a rush of fear and arousal. He holds my waist firmly while he reaches his other hand around, sliding down my thigh before cupping my pussy, thinly covered by cotton leggings.

"Did you miss me?" he rasps, sucking my lobe while rubbing my dampening sex as he grinds his erection against my ass.

"Why...are you in my house?" I pant, attempting to twist out from under him. He surprises me by letting me go, and when I quickly turn around, he silently towers, staring at me with grey eyes through the skull mask. He cocks his head slightly to the side, reminding me of Jason from the movie, Halloween. I can't decide if he wants to fuck me, kill me, or both.

FIVE
bethany

THE THUNDER HAS DWINDLED while the wind continues to rage, shaking the rain-beaten boards of the house. A dozen black candles light the kitchen—not my candles. He planned this right under my nose during a goddamn hurricane? Now he has me right where he wants me. Trapped. Again.

It takes me a moment to realize that my hand is empty. The bastard took my phone.

He takes one step toward me, and I match his step backward, my heart racing. "What do you want?"

"You know what I want." His Hollow eyes twinkle darkly, and I imagine him smirking beneath the mask. But he could be sneering viciously, for all I know. Is that Landon Greylinn beneath the mask? Oh, god... This is fucking insane.

He takes another step forward. "Just as I know what *you* want, Beth. Admit it. You've been quietly waiting for me like a good girl. Isn't that right?"

I open my mouth, but nothing comes out. He holds my

gaze with such intensity that I feel transfixed. His eyes are like a beautifully violent maelstrom coming at me, sucking me in, threatening to tear me to pieces.

"People died," I frown.

"Happens," he shrugs.

"And you're...part of it?"

"I merely said I know things, and that's all *you* need to know, Beth."

"You...can't just take over my life," my voice cracks, and he cocks his head again.

"I'm in the habit of doing whatever I want in this town."

"Why's that?"

Because you are the billionaire who owns half of it? I want to confirm this by asking, but I don't think tipping my hand will do me any favors. This crazy guy doesn't want his identity known, and I don't know what he'll do to me if he knows that I have him figured out.

"It's just the way it is, Beth. Would you like a glass of wine before I fuck you?"

My mouth and eyes widen in unison as a heated alarm courses through me. I can't believe he just said that to me. I resist the rogue memory of him inside my body and how good he made me feel.

Buying myself time, I answer with a nod.

He nudges his head toward the table. "Then, sit."

I walk a few steps, pull out the chair with a shaky hand, and then sit. He hands me a glass of wine, then sits kitty-corner from me, head wrapped in thick black and white fabric, white bones and teeth, black where his nose should be.

"Petru, Pomerol," he says with a convincing French

accent. "It's a fine Merlot. Over four grand per bottle," he adds.

"You must be very wealthy," I say, and he shrugs.

"No. But my *enemies* are," he says sharply.

Admitting that he is filthy rich would blow his cover, but he can't contain the unfiltered violence in his tone when he says the word *enemies*. There is no doubt in my mind that his enemies are real.

He lifts the mask above his mouth before holding up his glass. "To my Lady Luck," he says with a wink, his tone lighter around the edges as he taps my glass before sipping.

My brows furrow. "This is all a game to you."

"I'm just getting started. Drink your wine, Beth."

I stare at him, feeling unable to move.

"Go ahead. It's delicious," he says with a velvety, encouraging tone, just like he had that night in the bedroom when he convinced me to let him distract me from the chaos. His words.

The fruity, silky wine goes down smoothly, warming me inside.

"Good?" he says, a smile beneath the mask just reaching his eyes.

"Yes, very," I admit.

"There is more in the basket for you, Beth."

I jump, nearly spilling my wine, when something crashes against the exterior wall, and the window above the kitchen sink cracks, folding around an intruding branch. "Shit, the tree fell!"

"This house is made of fucking tin," he says, standing and towering above the table. His piney masculine scent wafts as he reaches into the basket, pulling out a roll of black tape.

My heartbeat quickens. "What is that for?"

"Presently? The window. Where are your trash bags?"

"Huh? Oh. Under the sink," I point.

"Don't worry. I'll let you finish your wine before I tie you up," he snickers before going to the sink.

I feel outside myself as I finish the wine, watching him break the branch with his bare hands between glass shards and adeptly tape the plastic bag tightly over the window gap. Has he done this before?

He turns toward me, and my breathing pauses.

"You want to know what else is in that pretty picnic basket?"

I swallow thickly. "Not so sure about that."

"But I want to play with you, Beth. You've been reading that book I left?"

"Was that *you* in the store who bought the other copy?"

He slowly shakes his head, then returns to the table.

"Nope," he says, bending and taking my free hand.

My heartbeat thuds anxiously as he tugs me from the chair.

"Finish your glass," he says, impatience thinly veiled. "I want you in your bed."

My glass is nearly empty, but I stall.

"What if I say no?"

"You'd be lying. Tell me. When you fantasize about what I did to you, what do you call me in your mind?"

I shake my head. "Nothing."

"Don't lie to me, Beth."

He takes the glass from my hand and presses it gently to my lips until I tilt my head back to finish it. When he sets down the glass, his arm wraps quickly around me, spinning me until my back is to him. He holds me there.

"What are you doing?"

"Shh," he says, grabbing something from the basket. I slam forward into the chair as I try to pull away, but he quickly tightens his grip on my wrists, binding them. I twist, shoving past him, and he doesn't stop me. I get halfway across the kitchen, looking at the black zip ties tightly around my wrists.

"Dammit! This isn't fucking necessary!" I yell.

"I can't trust your roaming hands."

"I'm not going to take your stupid mask off!"

"Such a pretty little liar," he says, blowing out the candles.

He follows me into the living room, where dark grey wavering daylight streams from the open blinds, and the two lit candles pool with hot wax. Under the weight of the storm, a pinned branch repeatedly taps the window behind the sofa.

"It's not letting up," I say with a shiver. The heatless house is getting cold fast, and my shoulders are chilled.

He pinches the two flames of candlelight between his fingers, extinguishing the remaining flicker of light in the room. Now, it's just us in the dark of the storm. He looks out the window.

"The water is rising fast. *Damn*. A fucking car is floating away."

"And you've trapped yourself inside my little tin house. This is no mansion on the hill," I snipe.

Shit. I shouldn't have said that.

He turns around and stalks toward me.

"True. But aren't you glad you aren't alone in this nightmare, Beth?" His voice is low and graveled, making my heart speed up.

"You are the nightmare," I mutter as he reaches me, clutching his hand around my bound wrists. He tugs me toward him, then grasps my chin firmly between his fingers.

"But I'm the kind of nightmare that makes your pussy wet," he rasps.

SIX
skull

I PULL my prize by her bound wrists, leading her out of the living room, down the hall, and into her dusky bedroom, which is decorated in shades of lavender and floral accents. I'm looking forward to sullying her in this feminine room.

Releasing her wrists, I shut the door behind me. She goes to the chair by her desk and sits in it as if it will keep her safe from reach. It's cute.

"Have you ever had a man in here before?"

She shakes her head, and that warms me a little inside. My mouth cracks a tiny grin beneath the mask.

"What's that on your desk?" I ask, and she picks up the object beneath her hand. Ah, it's the book. So, she brought it home with her then.

"You've been doing your homework," I say approvingly.

"Why did you give me this?"

"Mm. You'll have to figure that out. How far have you gotten?"

"Far enough to know that the main character is a billionaire who sells his soul."

I bring my hand to my skeletal-looking chin. "Yes, but he's not the most interesting player."

"The villain, the one that he sells his soul to—"

"Is more like me," I say.

"So, you're the villain in this game," she mutters, and this time, I fully smile beneath the mask.

"What do your instincts tell you, Beth?"

I walk to her and step between her legs, parting her thighs with my knees. I grab her chin, tilting her face upward to look into her pretty eyes. Her breathing gets deeper as her lips part, and I'm betting right now her pussy is getting moist for me.

"Yes," she hisses defiantly.

"Your instincts aren't wrong."

Her eyes water. "You're going to hurt me?"

Peering down at her through the mask slits, I nod.

"I'm going to make you bleed a little, Beth. I want to mark you because you are a treasured game piece I've claimed."

I pull a zip tie from my pocket before dropping to my knees, and when she tries to kick me, I grab her ankles before binding them.

"Why?" she cries out.

"Shh," I tell her, lifting her bound ankles into my lap as I sit on my boots. I slide off the sock on her right foot, admiring how delicate her toes are, before I pull out the razor blade.

She gasps, tugging her legs, but I tighten my grip on her ankles.

"Just a few marks. Hold *very* still so I don't mess up your pretty foot."

"You're fucking crazy!" she cries, and I snicker.

Lifting her foot in one hand, I hold the blade like an ink

pen in the other, creating a red line as I slash a thin diagonal mark deep enough to leave a scar.

"*Ouch!*" she whines.

"Almost done." With a flick of the wrist, I slash another red line.

"Please, *stop*," she grimaces.

"X marks the spot."

"What the hell is that supposed to mean?"

I release my grip, and her ankles drop into my lap.

"You are my found treasure. Don't forget that."

Putting away the blade, I stand and pick her up from the chair, cradling her in my arms with her bound wrists and ankles. Her face is pouty and tragic.

"It wasn't even that bad, baby. I'll make you feel better now."

I lay her on her side on the bed with her back to me, and when I lay down behind her, tightly spooning her body, she shudders before relaxing into me.

"See, I'll keep you warm during the storm," I say, lifting my mask enough to kiss her neck. The scent of her skin and her hair on my face makes me fucking wild inside, and my dick instantly fully hardens. I shove down my jeans and then tug on her leggings until her ass is fully exposed. Spooning her, I slide my dick between her thick thighs, holding it there to see how she responds.

I can already feel the moist heat radiating from her pussy, and it's fucking maddening to not shove inside her. I continue kissing her neck with my dick resting between her thighs. When I start sucking her lobe, she loses composure, thrusting her hip backward, creating much-needed friction over my wanton cock.

I respond by thrusting deeper between her thighs,

sliding back and forth over her pussy and clit until she's drenching wet.

"What do you want, Beth?" I say, forcing her to beg.

She rocks her hips without responding, but I retreat my dick.

"Answer my earlier question. What do you call me in your mind when you're imagining me fucking you?"

She lasts a few seconds before relenting. "I call you... Skull."

"What do you want me to do to you, baby? Say my name when you ask me."

"I want you to..."

"Yes?"

"...*fuck me*, Skull."

I thought my dick was fully hard, but I was wrong. Now, I'm so painfully swollen that I'm ready to unleash inside her. I'm going to give a new meaning to the term *skull-fuck*.

"Raise your wrists above your head," I say, giving her warning before I rock her onto her stomach, then lift her ass into the air until she's on her knees. I spread her thighs wide and grab the sides of her plump ass cheeks firmly in my hands before seating the tip of my head inside her juicy cunt, hitting her g-spot.

"Oh, *fuck...yeah*," I groan, with a forceful thrust, shoving deep inside her tight heat.

Her face hits the bed between her bound wrists, and her muffled moans make me swell even more inside her. Her pussy clamps around my shaft as I fuck her so deeply that the head of my dick repeatedly smacks against her cervix.

The sound of her panting and gasping emboldens me. I squeeze her sumptuous thighs in my hands as I stroke inside her pussy, growing more urgent with each forceful thrust.

Her thighs begin to tremble as she screams into the bed, and her pussy clamps tighter, sucking and swallowing my cock as she comes all over it. This sends me over the fucking edge, and I barely pull out in time to spray white cream over her ass cheeks. I grab my dick in hand, finishing myself until every last drop has dripped down over her supple flesh, like vanilla icing on a pink angel cake.

Her knees buckle, and she collapses onto the bed before rolling herself over. I spread her thighs until they fall flat, exposing her red, swollen pussy, and with her ankles bound, her legs form the perfect shape of a diamond—my newfound treasure.

SEVEN
bethany

"AREN'T you going to untie me now?"

He doesn't answer. The wind howls in the background as he towers over the bed, in black clothes with his head slightly cocked, his grey eyes framed in shadow, and his white, skeletal mouth seems to smile at me in the darkness, but I know it's only the illusion of a lipless face.

I push off my feet, moving backward like an inchworm until I'm at the bed frame, then shoving myself into a seated position. I lift my half-clothed legs to my chest and drop my bound wrists over them.

Skull raises his phone to his ear, listening. He goes to the window, muttering something. When he turns around, he pulls something from his pocket. I recoil when he sits on the bed and has that little blade in his hand again.

The power comes back on. A light appears in the hallway, and the radio is playing.

"...crime spree...this sleepy community..."

"Hold still," he says, taking my feet. He lifts the mask over his chin and mouth, reminding me that a handsome face is hidden under the scary mask as he kisses the sore spot on the top of my foot.

"X marks the spot," I repeat, disbelieving his words.

He looks up, and the edge of his mouth lifts. He has a divot on his chin.

"That's right, baby. I made my mark."

"You've...branded me. You think I'm yours."

He flashes perfect white teeth framed by an uneven grin.

"I *know* it," he says with an ironclad conviction that tightens around me like a chain. I blink my eyes, baffled. His conviction is to be my imprisonment.

He runs his finger down my foot before gently massaging it with his fingertips. He kneads my foot so adeptly that my lids grow heavy. He moves to the other foot, singing to me.

I open my eyes, watching his mouth move.

"Hush, little Bethany...don't say a thing; Papa's gonna steal your diamond bling. And when that diamond bling don't shine...Papa's gonna steal your heart and mind."

I shake my head. "You're crazy," I mutter.

"The winners always are," he says, lowering the mask with a nod before sliding the blade between my ankles. I yelp as he cuts upward with a jerk, releasing my conjoined limbs.

He stands. "Be good, babe," he warns before leaving me. The wind has quieted, and a streak of sunlight cracks through the clearing clouds out the window.

Sighing heavily, I get up and pull my pants up before turning on the light. I sit in the chair and raise my foot to my thigh, examining the marks that form a red X, the slashes reminding me of his handwriting. The cuts are deep enough to scar.

I imagine myself showing my foot to the police. How humiliated I would feel, and how hard it would be to explain this ordeal. Even if I leave out the bit about how much this twisted guy turns me on, how hard he makes me orgasm, it's still going to look suspicious. Like, I'm the crazy girlfriend of an accomplice to murder.

Is that what I'm becoming? His crazy girlfriend? *Fuck.*

A brutal reality pits inside my gut. Every day, I'm sinking deeper into this madness. He's absorbed me into his game, and there seems to be no escaping it.

Me, his "prized game piece."

His stolen treasure.

EIGHT
skull

SQUEEZING a man inside an unfinished sheet metal cabinet meant for a slot machine is a slight challenge. This is mainly because a panel is three-quarters down, which separates the would-be coin tray from the rest of the machine. This is where I place one foot of the limp body. As for the other foot, there is a narrow opening where the bill mouth goes, and the money pours into the money chamber. I extend his leg and pull off his dress shoe, chucking it before shoving his foot down the hole.

When I finally slap him across the face, his eyelids twitch as he slowly wakes to find himself tied in place, secured by zip ties through the screw holes, wishing he could stretch his bent neck and crouched body. I walk away and leave him there. His voice croaks as he realizes he's trapped.

"What the...shh-it...FU-U-CK!"

The slamming of the metal echoes through the large factory as he struggles.

"You won't...fucking get away with this!" he yells.

The ones who think they're important always say that.

The ones who don't go straight to begging. But he'll be begging soon enough. Everybody begs, eventually.

Banks and Ace are in the break room, devouring a pepperoni and onion pizza. I grab myself a slice, my thoughts drifting to a feeling like I forgot something. Puzzling for a moment, it dawns on me. Though my lips briefly enjoyed the pleasure of Bethany's delicate skin, I left without tasting her mouth or her pussy. Shame. Feels entirely remiss.

I'll have to use my time better when I see her again.

Ace looks up from his pizza. "Somebody shut that fucker up."

"Bout to," offers Banks.

"Police are making the rounds again," says Ace. "Heather was at the party. She says they think it's a lone operator."

Banks shoots me a look. "Speaking of girls. How about *Bethany*?"

My eyes narrow. "How the fuck do you know her name?"

He looks at Ace.

"Some chic named April rattled off to Heather a list of everybody in attendance at the party. When the commotion started, someone saw Bookstore Bethany go off with a guy. She only saw him from behind; it looked like he wore a black ski mask. *Bookstore Girl*. I knew I recognized that bitch."

"She's none of your fucking business. I'm handling her."

"You're not going to share in the spoils?"

He and Ace exchange a lustful glance.

My face flattens as my eyes harden into a cold stare.

"My apologies, boss-man," he says, standing. I keep my hard gaze fixed on him as he kicks back a beer.

"Stay the fuck away from her. *Both* of you," I warn, making my opinion clear.

I don't expect these dicks to see the whole picture as I do or to understand how Bethany plays into the game. Regardless, they need to know that I'm not sharing this girl; this one I'm keeping for myself.

I pound my fist on the table.

"I'll kill anybody who fucks with her! Remember that."

I've never been so dead serious in my life.

NINE
bethany

LIKE A DARK AND LINGERING VIOLATION, I can still smell and feel him inside my house and body. My wrists, ankles, thighs, pussy, and the top of my foot, are all sore. He says he left his mark. In more than one way, he's not wrong.

My mind is a hot mess!

This experience is single-handedly the most insanely twisted thing ever happening to me, and I'm terrified.

Will I be good at lying to the police? Can I be the good girl Skull wants me to be and play along with his fucked-up game?

I pace the small townhouse, checking locks on windows and doors. Not that it seems to make any difference. Skull—or Landon?—has no trouble breaking in. How the hell is he doing it?

Recalling the noise I heard earlier, which seemed to be coming from the attic, I go to the hallway and look up at the dangling string. God, is he coming from a window up there? He'd have to climb the roof. I've never been in the attic, and I can't imagine climbing a step ladder through that stupid, small pull-door and facing off dust, rats, and poisonous spiders before crawling through filth to check the lock on a little window. He's a big man. No, he can't be coming from up there. But then, how else is he getting in?

I pace the house, checking every window, trying to answer that question.

I text Mom, telling her I'm fine. She lives outside town, and her yard is flooded, but it should be better by tomorrow. When the phone rings, I'm not expecting it to be Dad. I haven't spoken to him in months.

I hesitate a moment before answering.

"Hey, Dad."

"Hey, Beth. How's it going? You aren't underwater, are you?"

"Nope. Not too bad. Water levels seem to be going down quickly."

"Good. I saw what happened on the news."

My stomach sinks. "Oh, yeah, *that*."

"Pretty crazy stuff. Think they'll catch the killer?"

"Hope so." *Why did I answer the phone?*

"It's been all over the news."

"I know, Dad. So, anyway. How have you been?"

"Oh, fine. Working, mostly."

"How is it? You're still at the casino?"

"Yep. A few weeks ago, I was promoted from pit supervisor to shift supervisor. It's better pay and better stock options."

"Congrats."

"Thanks. I'm only one step away from being head manager. That's the goal."

"You'll get there, Dad."

"Sooner than later. Listen. If you and your girlfriends

want to stay a weekend, play games, have fun, and hit the indoor pool, I'll discount you a two-room suite."

"Cool, thanks. I'll talk to the girls and maybe plan something soon."

"Alright, then. Well, I'd better get back to it. Be careful, Beth."

"Always. Bye, Dad. Love you."

"Love ya."

I hang up with a sigh. Dad has always been a workaholic and an alcoholic. I wonder if he ever runs into the Greylinns. Greylinn Casino employs many people in the region, including Dad. I still have trouble wrapping my mind around the idea of Skull being Landon. I need to see his picture again!

But first, coffee. On second thought, I should have something more calming. I make myself a cup of chamomile tea before settling into the sofa with a blanket and my laptop. I open the tab with Landon's picture in the article. This was a few years ago when he was eighteen years old. I momentarily stare into his grey eyes, imagining them ringed with a mask. I copy and save the photo before opening it in my photo app.

Then I crop it to make his eyes bigger before applying a vignette around his face, darkening it until all I can see are his eyes framed in black shadow. Just by the eyes alone, it could be him.

I start over, focusing on his chin, mouth, and subtle smirk. When I zoom in, goosebumps break out over my entire body. It's the square of the jaw and the divot in the chin that gets me. God, it looks identical to the man who was just in my bed—the man who tied me up—twice now —the man who thinks I'm *his*.

Landon. Fucking. Greylinn. The billionaire next door.

If not him, then who? I shake my head, sighing. What will I do to keep myself from going insane with all this while stuck at home? I can't open the shop back up until tomorrow. The streets are still too flooded, and my car has small tires. At least the cops probably won't come asking questions yet.

I turn off the light and head to my room, locking my bedroom door before climbing into bed with the horror novel he gave me. Reading this feels like a game wrapped in a game. This dark madness…is becoming my life.

* * *

I think it must be the come-down from the crazy adrenaline rush of Skull's intrusion—in my house and body—that makes me so tired after he leaves. I fall asleep while reading the horror book. When I wake up, it's three p.m. I sip water, consume some crackers from the drawer in my nightstand, and then resume reading.

It's a full-length novel and not a fast read, written in a contemporary literary style. But the horror vibe sneaks up on you. What makes it creepier for me is that this is personal. It matters to him, so it must matter to me. Somehow, this book symbolizes what's happening in real time, and the red ink scrolled inside its front pages was written for my eyes only.

Skull breaks all the rules while demanding that I follow them. Or at least follow his. How can I describe him as anything other than criminal? He has insider knowledge of these murders, and he just broke into my house. Through the attic? Back to that again. What to do…

Maybe I can hire an exterminator to go up there and check the window while he's at it? I don't know.

For a moment, I relive the intensity of him in my bed, the thickness and urgency of his cock and his dominant thrusting, the way he gripped my thighs like handles, riding me like he owned me, filling me up so completely as his groans strangled my moans. I hate how right now, blood rushes downward, and my pussy throbs, ready for more, like my body doesn't understand the difference between right and wrong. Or is it so wrong that it's right? I'm a confused mess.

I put down the book and climb out of bed, heading to the living room window to check the water levels. I tap my mouth. Not too bad. Maybe a few inches in the yard and on the road. A board is hanging from the side of the window. I'll have to tell the manager. People are out of their houses, looking around. One guy plucks a floating lawn chair from the roadside.

The good news is that I can open the shop in the morning and surround myself with books—my happy place. The bad news is that the threat of talking to the cops still looms. And what am I going to do about Skull? Landon. I'm pretty sure he's Landon Greylinn. But it's hard to wrap my mind around.

With a ragged sigh, I head to the kitchen. When I get there, I'm startled to see the picnic basket in the middle of the table. A classic wicker basket with a lid and tan leather handle has never looked so menacing. He said there's more for me in the basket. So far, he's pulled out black duct tape and zip ties. So what the hell else is in there? I don't want to know.

A large leather shoulder strap drapes down, and there are round straps on the side where the expensive French wine bottle must have been. Those dark glasses he brought are still in my kitchen, as are the black candles—proof that he was here.

My heartbeat picks up as I open the top flap, pressing it backward. Remnants of checkered red fabric are torn along the edges, indicating that the liner was removed. I squint my eyes. The cavern is empty except for...a photograph. I reach in and pick up a small stack of Polaroids. It's a man sitting backward in a wooden chair. His chest is pressed to the back of it, and his ankles seem to be attached to the legs. He has brown hair and wears a white dress shirt, dress slacks, and dark shoes.

I flip to the following picture, and my breathing sharply hitches. It's the same man, but taken from behind the chair. He has black tape over his mouth, and he's looking right at the camera—wait, no. It *can't* be. I turn on the kitchen light and intently study the face resembling my father. My heart sinks into my stomach, and my throat turns lumpy with shock. It looks...just like him. Holy shit, I swear it is.

My entire body flushes hot, making me dizzy. What the *hell* is going on?

I flip the photo over, and red writing jumps at me from the white background. It's the same font as before, the same shade of blood red. Its message cuts me deep, hooking inside me like a curved blade.

I'm your Daddy now, Beth.

No. I just talked to Dad earlier. When was this photo taken? I rush through the house and find my phone, my heart thudding like a bass drum in my ears as I call him. No answer. I text him. Waiting. I call again, leaving a message.

"Dad. Call me back."

I bring my hand to my head. What else can I do but call 911?

My phone rings. It's Dad!

"Who were you going to call next, Beth?" comes a low, deep voice I recognize perfectly: *Skull.*

"What the...why do you have my dad's phone? Is he—"

"Relax. He's at work. He and I had a little chat before he was promoted. He's been dirty dealing for quite some time. But he's seeing things my way now."

"What the *hell* is going on?"

"You didn't pull everything out of the basket."

"Huh? *How*...can you know that?"

"You're a smart girl. Take a wild guess."

I turn my eyes around the room. "Is there...a...camera?"

He snickers.

"*What?*" I gasp, my eyes trailing the walls as I slowly spin in a circle. "You've been spying on me? Are you fucking crazy?"

He puffs out air. "I have to say. That's a stupid question. I have an appointment to get to, Beth. But I wanted to make sure you got your gift."

With tears in my eyes, I shake my head. "I don't want any more of your sick and twisted gifts."

"Oh, come on. I promise that you'll like this one."

"I should call the police."

"But you're a good girl, Beth. So, you won't. Please don't keep me waiting longer."

I blink my eyes.

"*Basket,* Beth," he orders, and I jump before moving toward the table, tears streaming down my cheeks. I peek inside the wicker frame, studying the seemingly empty cavern. At the bottom is a red cloth perfectly folded into a triangle.

"Pull it out," he says with a teasing tone.

I do as instructed with a drawn-out sigh, dread coiling in my gut. The napkin is wrapped around something, and my heart races as I place the cloth on the table before slowly opening it into a square. A rectangular, flat, black velvet case is at the center.

"Open it, Beth."

I pick it up, clutching the edges and flipping the lid open. A necklace on a silver chain is fastened inside, holding a sparkling black heart gemstone.

My mouth gapes at the sight of it. Afraid to touch it, I visually study the half-broken silver skull encasing a curve of the heart, and on the other side, a skeleton hand wraps around, holding a silver rose.

"I had it made just for you." His voice is low, husky, and almost heartfelt, drawing me in.

"It is made with a flawless black diamond. Rare like you."

The lull of his voice dances like particles on the glint of light, illuminating the gemstone's dark sparkle.

"Wear it for protection," he says.

"Protection?" I mutter.

"Yes. I would have preferred to put it on you myself," he sighs. "But duty called. What are you waiting for, Beth? Do you not like it?"

He sounds genuinely concerned, baffling me further.

"It's not that... I mean, this whole thing is—"

"It's a game—just a wicked little game. But that necklace will keep you safe, and I expect you to wear it at the party."

"Huh? What party?"

"Check your mail. I hear everybody in town has received an invitation. I'll be looking for you. Wear the necklace."

He hangs up, and I stand dazed in the center of the kitchen. Is this what Alice felt like when she slipped through that dark, black, and tangled hole in the ground?

Like, what the fuck has happened to my life, and how did everything get so twisted?

He's been watching me. Not just outside but inside.

I wish I could make the yellow kitchen lighting brighter so I can spot the cameras easily. Are they all over my house or just here? I need to find and remove them promptly.

But first. Dad. I need answers. I'll talk to him outside, away from hidden cameras. I head to the small living room foyer and pull on my rainboots before trudging a few steps into the swampy front yard.

I call Dad, but get his voicemail. I text him, telling him I want to talk.

I stare at the mailbox. I have to know what the hell Skull was talking about. What party? Usually, I check the mail after getting home from the shop, but I was too rushed today due to the storm.

I slosh my way to the edge of my soggy yard. A partially smashed blow-up jack-o-lantern is floating in the oversized puddle surrounding the base of my mailbox. I tap it with the tip of my boot before leaving it there. Somebody will be looking for it. How many more blow-ups are floating around town? One more week until Halloween is officially over.

When I open the box, atop the stack of mail is an oversized black envelope addressed to me in gold ink with no return address. Butterflies swarm my stomach. Is this from *him*?

Plucking it, I head back. I enter through the doorway before I open the envelope, pulling out a large, thick, black velvet card. Skull faces occupy the corners of the card, surrounded by embossed vine, and between, an ornate, red font is scrolled:

TEN

bethany

I SPENT HALF the night searching for cameras that seemed not to exist. Where the hell did he put them? Was he lying? But then, how did he know I would make another call if he was? It was impossible without seeing me.

I spent the other half of the night restless in bed, wondering if each toss and turn was being counted like sheep through a spying lens.

How much longer can I live like this?

A paper flyer blowing in the wind hits me in the face as I struggle to open the front door to *Bethany's Books*. So much for the calm weather that's supposed to follow a storm.

This time of year is always weird, with October being the peak hurricane season.

After heading in, I flip the open sign on the front window with a yawn. I need more coffee.

I turn on the lights and head to the other side of the counter, where I pour cold coffee from the pot, reheat it in the mini microwave, and add creamer. I nearly spit out my first sip when Dad calls, and the image of him tied to a chair with duct tape over his mouth flashes into my mind.

My stomach churns at his voice on the other side of the phone. He sounds shockingly nonchalant. If it weren't for Skull leaving me that picture, I would not be able to tell that Dad was in trouble by his tone.

"I got your message, Beth."

"Yeah, I wanted to see if you were okay."

"Sure. Why do you ask?"

"I just…with everything going on…um…"

"You okay, Beth?"

My heart races as I muster the nerve to tell him what I know.

"So…somebody left me a picture…um, of you, Dad. You were…tied up. Tape over your mouth."

He puffs out air. "Holy *hell*. What? No, not me. Who gave you this?"

"Just somebody."

"Did you-uh…see his face?"

"No. Why?"

"Just wondering."

"Odd question to ask, Dad."

"There is nothing odd about it. I want to know if you saw whoever gave you this. I mean, how could you not have seen him?"

"He wore a mask."

He goes quiet.

"Dad?"

"Are you being harassed, Beth?" His voice is low and measured.

"Maybe, I don't know."

"What…did he say to you?"

"Nothing."

I can hear the stress building in his sigh. "Listen. Whatever you do. Do *not* go to the police."

His words slam into me, chills breaking out over my entire body. Did he really say that?

"So, it was you in the picture, then," I say.

"I didn't say that."

"Then why the hell are you telling me not to go to the police? If you're not involved, that's a completely abnormal response."

"Involved in *what*?"

"Are you kidding me right now? This is bullshit. Just admit that it was you."

The door rattles open, and I look up from my phone. My stomach drops at the sight of the police officer. It's the new, younger cop, the skinny one. I've seen him around town. I can't remember his name, but he was a sophomore when I was a senior in high school. So, he must be around twenty-one years old. Barely old enough to buy alcohol.

"Gotta go," I say before hanging up and clicking silent mode.

"Morning," he dips his head politely.

"Good morning."

"Officer Gibson," he smiles.

That's right, John Gibson. Or was it James?

"Nice to meet you. I'm Beth," I say, and he nods knowingly, then glances out the window.

"Winds pickin' up again," he says.

"Yep."

God, get to the point, please. I know why you're here.

He casually picks up a random book off a table and looks at its cover. I placed that book there last week—a pink-colored ballet memoir about a teenage girl. Unless he has a daughter or niece he's shopping for, it's probably not his type of book.

"Just doin' the rounds," he says.

"Rounds?"

He looks up on cue, then strolls to the counter with the pink book still in his hand. With a pleasant smile pasted on my face, I take a calming breath through my nose.

"Yep, just trying to gather all the different stories floating around out there."

"You mean about the party?" I ask, cutting to the chase.

He raises a brow. "Are you referring to the Halloween party at the Hollow Inn?"

"Isn't that why you're here? Because I was in attendance?"

"Well, now that you mention it."

Seriously?

"What would you like to know, officer?"

He tucks his lower lip and taps his fingertips on the pink book.

"Oh, just anything you have to say. Anything you would like to tell me that stood out about that night?"

I pretend to think about it.

"Hm. Not really. It all happened so fast."

He nods, tapping his fingers again.

"I hope you didn't get hurt fleeing like some."

I shake my head. "Nope. Luckily not."

His brows pinch slightly. "That's good."

"Yeah," I smile.

"You got out pretty quickly, hm?"

The suspicion in his tone puts me on edge. "Mm-hm," I nod, cheeks flushing. Dang, this is awkward.

The door rattles, and a customer walks in. It's Grace. Sweet elderly lady. She usually comes in early once a month to look for new arrivals in the garden section.

Officer John or James Gibson sighs at me. Have I disappointed him? What is he expecting me to say?

"Well, alright, Bethany. Feel free to come into the station if you think of anything else you'd like to share."

"Okay, thank you. I will," I smile.

Before leaving, he puts the book on the wrong table, and I come around the counter to put it back where it belongs. Then, after helping Grace find something new to buy, I get a very disturbing text message from Dad.

If you see him again, Beth. Take my advice. Do what he says.

ELEVEN
bethany

SOMETHING ALARMING HAS SWITCHED over inside me. I think I am seeing this for what it is now.

It's like the book I'm reading. At first, I wasn't even convinced it was a horror. It felt like a suspenseful game. Something I can handle. Not even real. Darkly intriguing, it sucks you right in from the get-go. But then, a few chapters in, the slowly building creepy vibe transcends into something genuinely nightmarish. Suddenly, you realize you were wrong.

This has become my life. It is not just a thrill ride. And it is very real.

The last few days have been such a crazy whirlwind that I don't think my survival instinct quite kicked into gear. My baffled mind needed time to process what was happening. But now, with the shock of Dad telling me to do whatever the masked man says--wow. Let that sink in!

How bad must it be when your father tells you to avoid the police and to put yourself at the complete mercy of the mystery villain who tied him up like a hostage?

I'm your Daddy now.

Skull's words, scrolled in blood red ink, are loud and clear, and my dad has given his dark blessing, anointing this twisted, dark romance. Skull is in charge. Be a good girl and do what he says.

I'm thinking about this as I reshelve books and straighten display tables, and I feel like a zombie each time a customer walks in. I force the muscles in my face to rise into a fake smile that doesn't quite reach my eyes. I look away, busying myself before they notice something is wrong with me.

The sound of the cash register as I ring up books is background noise to my racing thoughts. What the hell am I supposed to make of this party invitation?

When April calls this time, I answer my phone. I've been avoiding her, but now I have a couple of questions. But first, I must answer hers. Yes, I've spoken with the police. No, I didn't have much to say. What rumors?

"Oh, you know, you went upstairs with um…a guy—not saying it's true! It's just something I heard."

"Why would that be anybody's business? What would that have to do with the murders? Nothing!"

I sound defensive. I need to calm down.

"You're right. Nothing at all. It's just…"

"What, April?"

"Well, they thought they saw you go up after. Not before."

"After what?" I play dumb.

"You know, after the attack. Someone said they saw you go upstairs when people were running away."

"Not true. But even if it were, why would it matter?"

"I honestly don't know for sure."

"Well," I sigh. "I think people were panicking, and it all

happened so fast. But I was scared and left, just like everybody else."

"Of course. I'm sure."

"Yeah, so. Anyway, I have a question for you. Did you happen to get an invitation—"

"Oh, to the Greylinn party?!"

My stomach jumps. "Yeah."

"Who hasn't? This news is almost as big as the murders. There hasn't been a party at the Greylinn estate for years. They used to have an annual ball way back when. What changed, I wonder."

"Hm. The kids grew up. Parents moved away. The traditions stopped, I guess."

"Yeah, they closed the lower grounds to the public. Such a bummer, right? We used to go there when I was little."

"Me, too. Sorry, I've got customers coming in. But please do me a favor and help me with those dumb rumors being spread."

"Of course, hon! Talk to you later."

Two tall guys in dark clothing walk in, letting the door slam shut. One is wearing a grey, bat-like gargoyle mask with a blonde goatee sticking out from the bottom; the other has dark curly hair and the upper half of his face shrouded by a horned, devilish-red mask. It's Halloween, so nothing odd here. But then, the Devil looks at me in a way that instantly gets under my skin, making me uncomfortable.

"How's it going, Bethany?" the Bat says with a tone of familiarity. I don't think I know these guys, but it's hard to tell with their faces half-covered.

I straighten my posture.

"How may I help you?"

They look at each other briefly.

"That remains to be seen," says the Bat.

My eyebrows raise. "Excuse me?"

Devil smirks at me. "Could you please direct us to your true crime section?"

"Sure. Middle aisle, toward the back," I point.

They nod, disappearing. I don't think I like these guys. I pick up my phone and check the time. It's getting late—two hours until closing. I sigh, thinking of the party again. I don't know what to make of it. Am I going? Is anybody and everybody going to be there? What would I wear? Most importantly, will people die?

My stomach churns as my name rises gratingly from the back of the store. "Oh, *Beth-any*. We can't find the book. Come *here*, please."

Every fiber of my being says not to go back there. But these are customers. Shit. What do I do? Maybe I'm just being overly cautious. So, these guys are jerks; that doesn't mean they are here to hurt me.

"Be right there," I call out.

Thinking quickly, I put on my denim jacket and slide my phone into one pocket and my pepper spray into the other before heading back. A girl can't be too careful these days. What if--god, what if these are the slashers?

That word—slashers—echoes darkly in my mind as I meet them in the narrow space between the rows of books.

"Which one are you looking for?" I ask, voice slightly shaky. I clear my throat. "Excuse me," I say with more confidence.

"American Predator," hums the Bat.

"Hm. Let me see," I shuffle along as I read the titles, then slow my steps to a stop when I reach the guys. Suddenly, the Bat disappears around the corner. I continue reading titles when he reappears at the other end of the aisle. He glances at the shelf while running his fingers over the spines as he steps in my direction. When I turn back, the Devil is closer to me than before. So close I can smell the alcohol on his breath. Beer. My heartbeat speeds as I realize I'm cornered between them.

"I don't have the book, sorry," I say, attempting to push past Devil when he grabs my arm.

"Hey, let go!" I snap.

"I just wanted to ask you a question, Bethany."

"Let go of my arm!"

He drops it, stepping closer. "There's a rumor going around about you. Some people think you might be involved in the murder spree."

"What? Who are you? Just move aside, please."

I attempt to push past him again, and this time, he grabs both of my arms, pushing me hard against the bookshelf.

"What the hell! *Stop!*" I yell, and the Bat puts his big finger in my face.

"Keep your voice down," he hisses.

"Makes you seem like a bad girl, though," continues Devil. "What will you say to the cops if they confront you about this rumor?"

I shake my head. "Nothing. It's a lie. Now let go!" I tug my wrists, and he tightens his clutch.

"You telling me you don't know anything? You don't know anybody else involved in this? Nobody at all?"

"No, I don't know shit, okay!"

The front door opens, and he briefly turns his head.

"One more thing, Bethany. If the rumors are true, you'll be in so much trouble. It'll make you unpopular with those who believe in law and order."

"It's probably best for you to keep quiet," adds the Bat before the Devil releases me. They both storm off, slamming the door on their way out.

"I'll be right there," I call out to whoever entered, then rush to the bathroom. My knees nearly buckle as I reach the sink, splashing my face with cool water.

Dammit! I should have pulled out the pepper spray before he got hold of me. It happened so fast. But my instincts were spot on.

I look in the mirror, pressing my hair back with angered resolve. One thing is sure. I will *not* doubt my instincts again.

TWELVE
skull

STANDING in the middle of the hotel suite I own and use as a condo, I rub my chin while staring at the dismembered hand on the coffee table. The wrist is cut at an uneven diagonal, and strips of dried, red, and charred-looking black flesh stick out from the swollen hand. The otherwise pale skin is mottled with splotches of red, and the curled fingertips are bluish.

    I crack my neck in both directions with a scowl. The problem here is the body was buried without the fucking hand! Sometimes, I want to wring the necks of my idiot cohorts.

    With an angered huff, I go to the kitchenette and grab the plastic bag from the icebox. Then, I collect bags from the trash cans. I use one as a glove to pick up the hand before pulling the bag inside out, the same as you do with dog shit. I place that into another bag, then another, before tying it off and dropping it inside the complimentary paper snack bag under the candy bars and chips.

    After cleaning the coffee table with bleach wipes, I exit

my hotel suite with the snack bag. I'd rather not dispose of body parts in my trash can; it's not a good habit. I raise my phone to my ear, and my heartbeat speeds up when I hear her voice.

She doesn't know it's me. All she can hear is my breathing as I take the fire steps down to the parking garage. After saying hello several times, her anxious voice rises in pitch before she hangs up. I call her back, and she sighs.

"Who the hell is this?"

"Save this number, baby."

The catch in her breath is sexy.

"Skull," she whispers, and I smile.

"Have you been a good girl?"

I can hear her choosing her words. She's debating between what she wants to say and what she thinks I want to hear. This makes me smile a little as I get inside my car, parked near the stairs--always the Mercedes when I stay in town. I never use a valet.

"Yeah, sure," she finally says.

"What are you not telling me?"

She hesitates.

I start the car and exit the garage before heading down Main toward the Old Highway.

"Don't be shy, I encourage.

"Fine, then. *Where* are the cameras?"

I light a cigar with a smirk.

"Hidden," I say.

"I've looked everywhere!"

"I use the latest and best technology. My cameras are undetectable by the human eye. What are you wearing to the party on Friday?"

"Huh?"

"What are you wearing?"

"Seriously? I-uh...not sure I'm even going."

"You're going. I will arrange a ride for you."

"I can drive my—"

"*No*. It would be best if you didn't drive yourself while wearing a ball gown. Be ready by six-thirty."

She goes quiet.

"Don't pout, Bethany."

"I'm not pouting!"

I exhale smoke, exiting the highway. "Tell me what you're thinking. I want to know."

"Okay. Did you send some guys to *scare* me?"

My smile fades, jaw clenching.

"No. I did not. What happened?"

"Two guys in masks came into my bookshop. Threatened me."

"Describe them."

"Tall. One had a blonde beard and wore a devil mask. The other one had curly dark hair and—"

"What did they do to you?!"

"They cornered me...held me...until I promised to keep quiet about the murders at the Hollow Inn."

My knuckles turn white as my grip on the steering wheel tightens.

"I will be looking into this. If you *ever* get any more threats, call me *immediately*."

"Counting you?"

I laugh. "I'm not threatening you, Bethany."

"Isn't that what this twisted game is? One big, threatening mind-fuck?"

"Oh, there's much more to it than that. You'll learn. I'll see you at the party."

"You'll be the man in the skull mask?"

"You won't find me until I find you. I am looking forward to it. Six-thirty, Bethany. Don't be late."

THIRTEEN
bethany

"SORRY," says Stella, opening the boutique door to let me in. "I've been keeping it locked. Can't be too careful these days. Welcome back!"

She smiles, and I'm unsure if she remembers me or is just being polite.

"Thank you."

She looks the same, a bit older. Petite and wearing a white silk blouse, light grey dress slacks, and nude heels, she has short grey hair with angular bangs and black cat-eye glasses.

The boutique smells like vanilla and wilting roses. I haven't been to Stella's since I was a senior in high school, and it's just like I remember it. Formal gowns line the walls around a white catwalk with a large floor-to-ceiling mirror behind it and red and purple roses painted along its edges. Velvet, mauve benches are arranged in pairs on either side of the stage, with additional rows of gowns running behind them.

She gently clasps her hands together. "Do you have

wedding plans, or are you here for the Greylinn Masquerade?"

"The Masquerade," I nod.

"Of course!" she gleams.

If only I shared her excitement. This party is the talk of the town. It's one of those rare events that nobody would dare miss. It's isolating to think I am the only one with a reason to be petrified.

"Unfortunately, we are out of red ball gowns. But I have some red formal gowns that we could add a bustle skirt, too."

I blink my eyes, confused.

"So…people have been getting red dresses for the party?"

"Oh, yes. I've rented out fifty-two and sold eight. I could only get a limited amount of new inventory on such short notice. I brought some in from my seasonal storage. You are the first to request a white gown. I haven't sold one since the Debutante ball in June, but I was informed that other colors would be needed, so I brought in a few extra white gowns. What dress size are you, dear?"

"Size eight-ish."

"Perfect! I have seven through ten in white. Follow me, please. Do you want strapless?"

"I'm…not sure."

I follow Stella between rows of gowns until we arrive at the back wall, crammed with several poofy, white, floor-length dresses. Stella pulls a couple out and places them on an empty rack near a small bench. It occurs to me that there is little difference between a white ball gown and a wedding dress. I've never worn either.

"See what you think of these, and I will look for more in your size."

I gravitate to the simpler, less fussy of the two. It looks like something out of a fairy tale. It's strapless, with a silk, brocade corset-style top and a flowy chiffon skirt that is flowy and pleated but not overly poofy. I'm not sure if I can squeeze into that corset, though.

"I have a similar one you can try, as well," Stella smiles, taking it from me. I follow her to the dressing room, where she unfastens the top half of the corset and unzips the other gown's back before leaving. I will have nobody to zip my back tomorrow, so it'll have to be the corset gown, which I can do if it fits.

"What shoe size are you, dear?"

"Eight."

I strip down to my undies and carefully step into the gown, pulling it up before fumbling with the little metal button loops.

"Need help?" she asks, but I'm determined to do this myself. I don't know if it's supposed to be this tight or if I'm too big for it, but my torso feels entirely encased, and my breathing is constricted.

Stella slides a pair of cream-colored heels under the door. Bending to take my socks off is impossible, so I stuff my socked feet into the heels before exiting the dressing room, where Stella guides me up the side steps to the catwalk. I turn to face the mirror, and my cheeks blush at the sight of my breasts spilling hardcore from the top of the corset--nobody will be looking at my face when I talk! At least I'll be wearing a mask--oh, shit, the mask.

I'd planned to stop by the costume store before it closed for the day, but I had some late customers at the bookstore. Tomorrow, I'm leaving work early to go home and prepare for the 6:30 p.m. deadline enforced on me by Skull.

"Do you happen to have any Halloween masks, Stella?" I ask. It's worth a shot.

She taps her chin. "Hm. I have a seasonal bin in a closet with a few items I planned to give to consignment. Be right back. Careful on the catwalk, dear."

Slowly, I walk to the end of the stage before turning around and watching myself in the mirror on the way back. I look ridiculous. This looks like a wedding dress, and my boobs are out of control. Also... Why are so many others wearing red? How many got invitations saying to wear white like me? I'm the kind of person who likes to blend in and go unnoticed. The only saving grace here is going to be the mask! Thank God for the mask.

"I should have a couple of things in here," chimes Stella, climbing the steps with a box in her hand. She digs around before pulling out fuzzy brown reindeer antlers with a Santa hat. "Wrong Holiday. Hold on..." She digs some more and pulls out a rubber, grey monster mask with giant teeth, followed by a black and white furry cat mask. "Ooh, this matches!" she says, handing it to me.

I pull it over my head and look at my pointy-eared reflection, my green eyes peering through the open slits. The white and black fur stops above my mouth, and big whiskers shoot out from a black button nose.

"Not exactly spooky," I say.

"So, add a little blood," shrugs Stella. "You could put some red makeup around the mouth or add red teardrops below the eyes."

"I have red lipstick," I say.

"That works. I think the dress is perfect. What do you think?"

"I'll get the dress and shoes. Thank you for the mask."

"Free of charge," she winks.

She helps me down, and after changing back into my standard leggings, a long tee, and tennis shoes, Stella sweeps in and takes the dress and shoes to the counter. She rings me up while rattling on about the Greylinn estate. How grand it was, and oh, the ballroom! But she hasn't been there since that girl died.

This catches my attention.

"What, girl?"

"Oh, the cousin. Amy, I think her name was. A terrible thing. I'm sure that's why Charles and Blythe moved away. They were tired of the scandal. I went to school with them. Had a crush on Charles, but so did every girl. He was out of my league."

"How did the girl die?"

She looks at me and blinks, seeming surprised, like I should know this. "Drowning, of course. It was in all the papers. Underage drinking. She was only sixteen. She fought with her boyfriend—the Blackmosh oil heir! These old-money families were still into oil then. It's about real estate and casinos nowadays. Anyway, when they accused the Greylinn boy of killing the sole Blackmosh heir, that's when the scandal blew up beyond control. They managed to suppress the newspapers, but that didn't stop people from choosing sides."

"Landon Greylinn," I mutter, stunned.

She nods, bringing the bagged gown around to me. She hands me a small bag with the shoe box in it.

"I'll help you to your car. Landon was never convicted; there was no proof beyond a love triangle. Who knows what happened?"

I open the backseat of my car, and she hangs the dress

bag on the garment hook. "Regardless, I think this party symbolizes a new chapter!" she adds cheerfully.

But all I'm thinking is that a new chapter in a horror story isn't something to look forward to. The closer you get to the climax, the greater the blood spill and the higher the body count.

FOURTEEN
bethany

THE CORDS around my wrists become apparent when I attempt to lower my hands from above my pillow. I open my eyes in the darkness, feeling blatantly not alone, and my heartbeat quickens with alarm inside my chest. There is foreign energy in my bedroom, and a spicy, masculine scent permeates the air.

Candlelight flickers as a shadow moves forward at the base of the bed.

"I needed to taste you," the low, deep voice rasps. *Skull.*

I sigh, only partially relieved. Glad it's not somebody else, somebody worse. But still.

"You have no right," I say, attempting to lift my knees.

His white mask floats high on his shadowed frame until he crouches over the base of the bed. I tug my bound ankles as he crawls between my legs. Chills spread over my body as the shadowed slits in his skull mask peer up at me menacingly.

"I disagree," he hisses, his tone biting. His anger is palpable, confusing me.

"Thought you said it was just a game," I whine without meaning to.

"A dangerous game, Bethany. I may have waited longer, but you covered my cameras. How did you find them?"

"Research..on the web. Covered the pinholes in the outlets with tape," I say defiantly.

"Naughty girls get punished." When he flashes a devious smile, I realize he's wearing an altered or different mask with an open mouth.

He grabs my legs beneath the knees, one in each hand. I jerk my legs, but it's useless. He has me right where he wants me.

"I'll scream! The neighbors will hear me."

"Mm. You know I like it when you scream."

He sticks his tongue out and licks his upper lip as he scoots on his knees between my thighs.

I suck in air, and with all my might, I empty my lungs with as much sound as I can manage while lying on my back. This seems to excite him, and with parted lips, his head knocks back slightly as if he's listening to a symphony while his hand drifts down the middle of his torso, clutching himself.

I scream again, and he unfastens his pants, releasing his pale, hard erection. He firmly grabs his cock in hand. "You want this demon inside you, don't you, naughty girl?"

I shake my head, saying nothing as my mouth waters at the sight of him, and the cotton panties I've got on under my tee-shirt dampen. If I could control my rogue bodily fluids, I would. But I only get wetter as he strokes his big cock before me.

I scream when he tears my panties from me, then drops down on all fours like an animal between my thighs. He taps his tongue against my clit teasingly before slowly sucking—*mm, shit*. My eyelids and mouth drop in unison, squirming in anticipation as he relentlessly teases my pussy, slowing his rhythm and pausing just as I reach the edge. When his tongue touches down again, he laps my pussy before thrusting hard inside me. A moan escapes my lips... *Oh...god, yeah.*

I can't resist grinding my hips into his face, my body flushing hot with need as I finally fall over the edge.

"That's right. Come all over my tongue, baby."

Gladly, I do as he says, moaning shamelessly. Catching my breath as he pulls away, I blink at the skull mask in the flickering light. He widens his stance, kneeling on each side of my arms and scooting higher before lowering over my chest.

He yanks my shirt up over my breasts, and when the tip of his cock slaps against my lips, I open my mouth. When I choke, he doesn't stop, swelling and thrusting in my mouth as his cock repeatedly grazes the tips of gaping teeth.

His meaty head slides deep, cutting off air as my throat fills with hot, spurting liquid.

When he pulls out, I gasp as he lowers his body over me, and for the first time, I feel his mouth on mine as his still-erect cock penetrates my pussy. He bites my lower lip, sucking as his shadowed eyes peer down at me through the mask while fucking me. My mind shuts down; my body gets lost in the absolute pleasure of his rhythmic aggression, slamming my clit, and deepening inside me as I fall over the edge with a scream.

He groans as he pulls out, grabbing his shaft in his hand and coming over my stomach.

"I can't...get enough of you," he rasps. "Too bad I have to go."

He steps from the bed and pulls something from his pocket. When I see the shiny metal, I know what it is.

My heartbeat thuds in fear that he's going to cut into my other foot, giving me a matching X-shaped scar.

"I shouldn't have let you orgasm," he rasps, still catching his breath. "But I couldn't resist hearing you scream again."

He cuts the cords binding me to the bed one by one, except the one around my left wrist.

"Don't worry. You'll figure it out," he says before leaving me in the dark purple light of early dawn.

* * *

I put the phone on speaker while I curl my hair, disbelieving my ears.

"You're seriously going?"

"Why wouldn't I?"

"You don't like to dance, Mom."

"But I do love architecture. The Greylinn mansion is something else."

"But what will you wear?"

"Invitation said red. My Yule gown is red."

"Mine said white. God, am I the only one?"

She laughs. "Guess you're special. Are you sure you don't want to carpool? I can be your designated driver."

"Tempting, but...I'm supposed to go early."

"Oh, yeah?"

I can tell she wants me to elaborate, but I'm at a loss for words. How can I possibly explain one iota of my situation to my mother without causing more problems for myself than I already have? In addition to messing up her peace of mind, she'll expect me to go to the police. When I say I can't, she'll insist. She may even tell them I'm in trouble, thinking she's helping. But then, what happens to Dad? What happens to me if word gets back to Skull that I've tattled? He knows who my father is. Does he also know my mother?

Though Dad admitted that Skull has power over him, I have no proof that Skull is Landon Greylinn, only a strong hunch. I know he is somehow connected to the recent murders, but that's where my knowledge ends. April mentioned copycats. I don't even know if what happened at the Halloween party is connected to the other murders.

"Well, let me know if you change your mind," she sighs as I yank the curling iron from the outlet.

"I'll see you there," I murmur, dabbing charcoal liner around my eyes in the mirror.

"Is something wrong, Beth?"

Followed by mascara. "Why?"

"I don't know. You sound...weary."

Then, rose-tinted lip gloss. "I didn't sleep well."

She puffs out air. "Yeah, lots of folks have been losing sleep since the murder spree. Maybe it's done, and we can all return to our lives."

"Or maybe it's just getting started."

"That's a morbid thought, Beth."

"Sorry. Blame the horror novel I'm reading."

I check the time--6:20--*shit*. "Gotta go, Mom."

"See you later. Oh, by the way, I'll be in a green witch mask. You?"

"A cat. Bye!"

After attempting and failing to stuff my pouring cleavage further down into the corset for a more modest look, I rush to find my phone and wallet, placing them into the only dress purse I own, black with sequins and a chain strap.

I turn on the foyer and porch lights before exiting. The black town car waiting in my driveway is a sobering reality, making my stomach lurch. This is happening.

Fucking happening.

My heart races when the friendly elderly driver gets out, opening my door with a smile as if he isn't delivering me to a similar fate as the girl whose body was found floating face down in water atop Skull Hill.

A love triangle.

The three sides of the phrase form a mountain in my mind, and I'm mentally scaling it as I look out the window, watching passing scenery while sitting stiffly upright in a ballgown--white like a wedding dress that I'm giving myself away in, with the sinking feeling that there is no turning back now.

I run my silk-gloved fingertips along the cold silver chain around my neck, studying the pendant in my compact mirror. It was custom-made for me by a man I barely know beyond the physical. He chose this for me: a cracked silver skull encasing a black heart, a dead head with a shiny black diamond soul shining through its one eye, its skeletal hand reaching around, offering a silver rose —a token of romance from a fractured, rare and twistedly beautiful thing—just like the man who gave it to me, and it clings to my neck like a collar of ownership.

Feeling overwhelmed, I snap shut the compact with a sigh, swapping it for red lipstick in my purse before pulling the cat mask down from atop my head, which hangs just below my nose.

Where shall I put the "blood marks" to make this mask spooky, as the invitation called for?

Stella suggested under the eyes or around the mouth. An image of a drugged-up glam-grunge New York socialite named Cat comes to mind. Her image was in the paper, donning a white silk dress on the red carpet, and her red lipstick was smeared haphazardly along the edge of her mouth. She smiled like a pretty zombie with dark rings around her eyes.

I'm thinking of this when I cover my lips in crimson red before smudging it along the corners. Tonight, I will hide behind this mask. I'll be Cat, Kitty, or Kitty-Cat, recklessly pretty and collared by an undead master, come to do his bidding like a good little kitten.

"Just up this way, Ma'am," says the driver, glancing at my furry face in the mirror.

"Thank you," I smile behind streaks of red.

As the vehicle reaches the edge of town, nearing the base of Skull Hill, covered in orange and red fall foliage, I remember the last time I was here. The big iron gate is open, just like it was back then.

My parents were still married, and Dad pretended not to be drunk. We parked where everyone else parked, in the gravel near the edge of the lower grounds. I recall studying the large, ornately carved headstones. Chills ran down my shoulders, and I wondered how the cousin, Amy Greylinn, might be buried there now.

I looked her up online, confirming her name and the suspected love triangle between her, Alex Blackmosh, and Landon Greylinn. There were rumors about Alex having a violent temper and that maybe, in a crime of passion, he was capable of killing Amy. But he was never charged.

Also, there are rumors about other cover-ups within the Blackmosh family. A long-time housekeeper died falling down the stairs after a disagreement with Alex's father,

Charles. Her family was paid off, and the case was closed. Then, there was the teenage boy who was bludgeoned to death outside the Blackmosh grounds. He was friends with Alex and his male cousin, who was rumored to be gay. Supposedly, Alex disapproved of the rumored affair between them.

When the car reaches the top of the cemetery, the Halloween décor stops me cold. The bodies hanging from the tree look shockingly *not* fake.

"Please, stop a minute," I tell the driver as we pass. He slows and pulls up close as I fix my sights on the liquid dripping down into a red puddle beneath the battered bodies hanging from the neck: four discolored men with gaping mouths. One has a bulged eye and a face tattoo. Another has his fingernails painted black, chipped along the edges, with an overly long pinky nail—such detail.

"They look...*real*," I whisper in horror.

"Yes," says the driver. "Special effects these days," he muses.

I've never seen anything this realistic in a Halloween store before, but I'm not in the habit of visiting the home of a billionaire, either. For all I know, the Greylinns could have bought these from a Hollywood movie special effects pro for thousands of dollars.

"Would you like to continue, Ma'am?"

"Yes, thank you."

The trees clustered around the graveyard push back as we climb the hill, making way for the expansive, manicured grounds. Nothing macabre hangs around the koi pond I used to love peering into. The little bridge over it remains, and the white gazebo on the other side is covered in brown, sleeping vines.

Two limos are parked in the stone porte-cochere, with space for many more to come and go.

As we near the massive, sprawling stone mansion, my gut furiously swarms with butterflies. I check my phone. Six forty-two. The party is at seven, so it won't get going until eight. Why did Skull arrange for me to come early? What does he have planned?

When the driver pulls past the other limos, I crane my neck to see who is inside—unfortunately, nobody I recognize. If the invite hadn't been on such short notice, I could have arranged for my girls to come up from New York. But then again, maybe they should stay clear of Sleepy Hollow for now.

This sleepy town is wide awake amidst an ongoing murder spree, and tonight, we're gathering at a mansion that might be at the center of it all.

That jolt you get before entering a notoriously scary haunted house, one that is guaranteed to make you scream and cry—that's how I feel right now. Enter at your own risk, Kitty-Cat, and watch your back at every turn.

I've only once been behind the large, black, framed double doors with ornate wrought iron between the glass. But as the doorman leads me inside after checking my name off the list, the memory jumps out at me from the shadows.

I was eleven, and Mom had signed us up for the Christmas Tour of Homes, where local, often stately historical houses served to satiate the local appetites for a chance to see inside. All the homes on the tour were beautifully decorated for the holidays, adding to the novelty of being invited in, where the hosts would lead small groups, pointing and giving insight into the history and architecture. These homes were living museums.

"Right this way, Ma'am," the unmasked man wearing a black-and-white tuxedo interrupts my thoughts.

I follow, my heels clicking across the dark wood flooring stretching the large foyer, eyes on the classic, gold-framed paintings alongside modern, black-and-white photographs. Old World meets New World—just as I remember it.

The Greylinn matriarch, Blythe, gave us the tour, and she said the oddest thing that stuck with me. We were passing a large glass curio cabinet full of dolls collected worldwide. The adults had moved on to more serious art while I remained fixated on the porcelain dolls locked safely behind glass. Mrs. Greylinn leaned down to me and said in my ear, "We have a lot of nice things, but most of them don't mean anything."

She smiled politely, and I stared at her, bemused and speechless. Later, I decided she was trying to make me feel more comfortable in her extravagant home by downplaying its value. But when I think of it now, her comment seems like a riddle that begs to take on new meaning.

"Please, make yourself comfortable, Ma'am," says the man, after leading me inside a lavish sitting room with a high, coffered, carved wood ceiling and large tapestries hanging from the walls, where only two other people—a man and a woman—stand near a large marble mantle behind a set of leather chairs. I might know the couple, but there is no way to tell. The man wears a grim, long-nosed black plague mask, and the woman in the red ball gown has her face painted severely like the undead version of the Queen of Hearts.

They are too busy leaning into each other and whispering to notice me standing awkwardly in my busty, blaring white gown.

With a sigh, I return to the edge of the room, peeking into the hall before standing there. Why did I have to come early? What is he planning?

I reach my gloved hand to the necklace around my neck when a man appears from an archway of another room down the sconce-lit hall.

He's tall, broad-shouldered, in a black and white tuxedo, wearing a mask that partially covers his face, starting just above his brow line and ending at his mouth. The mask looks like it's made of metal. Or maybe it's resin, painted the color of wrought iron, with elegant vines climbing the sides of a regal-looking skeletal face as if cast from the remains of a dead prince. High cheekbones slant toward sharply arching, angry brows over dark blue eyes pinning me with a weighted expression.

Oh, dear, God, it must be him.

The doorman appears beside me in my peripheral vision, but I can't keep my gaze from the masked man.

His eyes grow more intense as he approaches, hinting at a smirk behind the mask as the doorman introduces us.

"Sir, this is Miss Bethany Peters. Miss Bethany, this is Mr. Landon Greylinn."

"Pleased to make your acquaintance," says Landon with such perfectly annunciated formality that I hardly recognize him. His voice is not graveled whatsoever. His eyes are less grey and brooding, bluer, with a measured expression.

Have I had it wrong? Is Skull someone else?

But what about his scent? I would know it. His firm touch and spicy masculine scent fill my senses when I sleep, wrapping tightly around me, making me hot and bothered.

Landon's cologne wafts, masking anything recognizable as he motions me down the hall. He offers me a glass of wine from a decanter at a bar in a smaller yet just as swanky room as the last one. Instead of tapestries, a jungle mural wraps the walls, and potted palms fill the corners. The bay window overlooks a view of the koi pond.

"Have you been here before, Bethany? Or shall I call you Kitty?" he chuckles, handing me a beveled crystal glass of port wine.

"Once. F-for the tour," I stutter, feeling bewildered. Is he, or isn't he? I think I've had it with masks, yet this is the beginning of an evening filled with them.

"Do you mean...the Yule Tour?" he asks.

"Yes. When I was eleven, Mrs. Greylinn was very nice."

He nods. "Everybody was still nice back then."

He sniffs his wine, and I gaze at the perfect metallic teeth. Goosebumps hit my spine as I fixate on the shadows outlining the masculine cleft in his squared jaw. The divot doesn't lie; it's a damn-close match.

"Salute," he says, raising his glass at me.

"Cheers," I attempt to smile politely with red smudged lips and a furry cat face.

"What do you mean by that?" I ask, playing dumb as I do the math. The tour was before the incident where his cousin died, and what followed.

He shrugs. "Come, and I'll show you something."

I hesitate, my breath catching as the measured look in his deep blue eyes wavers like a hint of something unhinged. A warning alarm goes off inside me. This man is hiding something.

"Sure," I say politely, against my better judgment, my curiosity reigning supreme as I follow him deeper into the mansion with a racing heart.

He slows as I catch up in heels I'm not used to wearing. Though I would go out often enough in New York, there have not been many opportunities to dress up since returning to Sleepy Hollow to run a new bookstore single-handedly.

Blue eyes glance at me behind the metal as my ankle wobbles. He offers me his arm, and I take it.

"I'm going to show you a room that few have seen, Bethany."

"I'm intrigued," I say, suppressing the butterflies in my gut as I marvel at the ornately carved paneling and crown moldings that cover the walls.

Reaching a big, arched door, he presses his thumb to a keypad, and my brows shoot upward as he leads me inside a rectangular, cathedral-like room. That same dark paneling covers the left and right walls, with added dark pillars extending to buttresses arching into a soaring glass ceiling.

"Wow," I whisper, lowering my gaze to the towering plants lining both sides of the space. At the back are steps leading into a room with glass walls.

When we reach the top of the steps, I wobble, clinging to the solid strength of his arm as I catch my balance.

"Careful," he says with a hint of gravel in his tone, which causes me to pause.

"Can you guess what this room is?" he asks.

I trail my eyes around. The stone walls have handles on them and carvings of words. A row of benches lines the lower half of the walls—no, not benches. They look like... caskets.

I raise my free hand to my mouth before he gently tugs me toward a black leather chair and parks me in front of it.

"Rest your feet a moment."

Leaving me there, he goes to a table that resembles an altar. Gargoyle-like statues and dark candles sit atop black cloth. With his back to me, he removes his mask, and a jolt of adrenaline courses through me as I wait with bated breath for him to turn around. I already know what Landon Greylinn looks like from pictures, but I've never seen him in person. More than that, it might be the first time I've seen the man behind the monster known as Skull.

He lights a candle, and I stifle a gasp as he glances back at me with all those handsome bones in his face.

"Well? Can you guess?" he asks, lighting another candle.

"A...memorial room?"

"Of sorts."

When he turns around and moves to the side of the table, the candlelight silhouettes his face, and his dark blue eyes turn grey beneath dark brows. A shade of grey that sends chills down my spine.

"How do you think Skull Hill got its name?" he asks.

"Um," I clear my throat, trying to regain composure. "From...the rock at the base of the hill."

He shakes his head, reaching his hand to one of the handles on the wall and fiddling with it. "No. It's because the peak is inhabited by the dead."

He releases the handle and sits in a chair near the table, half cast in shadow. "See...a long time ago...a local land dispute among settlers turned into a blood bath. Those who died on the hill were buried on it. The wealthiest among them—my ancestors--were put to rest inside a mausoleum built for them. When certain others threatened to destroy it, my great-great grandparents built their house around it. Then, they built a gate around the house. The rest is history."

I can hardly believe my ears.

"The stone in the walls, those are—"

"Caskets inside," he finishes.

"Wow. I'm...at a loss for words."

"I've rarely brought anybody in here. But now, you've had the full tour. Mrs. Greylinn didn't tell you the old secret, the sacred tradition of Skull Hill, where the victors sit atop the bodies of their enemies."

His voice drops deeply on that last word, graveled as hell, and every hair on my body lifts as the blood leaves my face in recognition that the monster and the man are the same.

"What about..." I trail off, feeling stunned.

"Yes, Bethany?"

His voice has returned to the polished formality expected of Landon Greylinn.

"Were there not tombstones for the dead?"

"Yes. All removed."

"But not the bodies."

He shakes his head. "The gravestones were relocated to the lower grounds, which were opened to the public in an attempt to keep the peace."

"But nothing under them," I mutter.

"Oh, there are bodies buried there. It has functioned as a cemetery ever since."

The rumors I grew up with of ghosts roaming Skull Hill take on a new meaning.

He stands, bringing his phone to his ear before putting on his mask.

"The ballroom is filling up," he says.

I feel dazed as he reaches me and offers me his arm. He locks the mausoleum before leading me back toward a procession of men and women in black and red. The men wear red bows, and the women wear red gowns.

"Why don't I match the others, Mr. Greylinn?"

He stops where the hall intersects with the grand entry,

dark blue eyes framed by fierce silver brows upon me. It occurs to me that he doesn't match, either. His black tux is paired with a white bow.

"Good point," he says, lifting his hand to my neck and bringing the pendant between his fingers. His touch makes me stiffen, and my cheeks flush, spreading down my neck and chest. Voices hush as people stop and stare, filling my periphery. My stomach jolts as I imagine the image of us posed like a wedding cake topping.

"Seems you were destined to be my date for the night, Bethany. Consider yourself lucky. Only I can protect you from the poltergeists that haunt these halls."

As we follow a woman in a black gown wielding a walkie-talkie, Landon takes my white-gloved hand. The woman tells us when it is time to descend the wide, arching wooden staircase to the basement ballroom, where party-goers pour from an elevator across the room as we near the bottom.

White columns wrap the sprawling space, filled with the swish and shuffle of red gowns and pressed suits. Macabre masks perch above elegant necklines like mismatched paper doll cut-outs.

The space is dimly lit with candelabras placed on tables. A projector screen covers the back wall, and a movie depicts an orchestra rehearsing while actors in medieval garb take their places on a stage.

As we reach the bottom landing, heads turn toward us with a collective hush. The cat mask conceals how red-faced I feel with so many eyes on me—me, of all people, here as Landon Greylinn's date. Not that anybody knows it's little ol' me under the mask—at least, not yet.

I clutch his arm, controlling my wobble-prone left ankle as he leads me to the center of the dance floor.

"We must kick off with the first dance," he says, wrapping his hand around my waist and lifting my hand into the air as he spins me around. I hold my breath, carefully focusing my steps to keep up with his pace.

His lips part, cracking into a smile beneath the skull mask. His blue-grey eyes twinkle. "I haven't done this since…prom. Too bad we weren't on speaking terms back then."

"I was a freshman when you were a senior. I knew you and your family, like everybody."

"And I knew of you, Bethany."

"Me? You're just being polite."

He spins me again, and when he slows his steps, the big screen rises behind Landon's towering frame, cutting from the stage to a dressing room where a man lies on the ground in a puddle of blood. The scream of the woman who finds him is drowned out by the orchestra we are dancing to.

"What…is this playing?"

"Murder at the Opera. No, I wasn't being polite."

He spins me just enough that the screen is out of sight, and just as his storm-colored eyes lock with mine, another real-sounding scream rises from behind. My shoulders tense, and goosebumps break out over my body. I try to turn around, but Landon stops me, pulling me into his chest.

"Don't worry," he whispers in my ear. "It's all just part of the show."

When he loosens his grip, I turn my head to see a tall guy in a red mask with white fangs dramatically extending a curved blade as he chases another guy from the ballroom. A woman trails behind. She screams from the stairway before disappearing.

Amidst a gasping crowd, Landon raises his hands into the air. "The night is young!" he yells, clapping above his head. The crowd breaks into applause before resuming chattering. A woman at the bar rings a bell, and a stream of people flows in that direction.

"Would you like a glass of champagne?" Landon asks casually.

I blink my eyes, unsure about what I just witnessed.

"Yes, please," I say, seizing the opportunity to have a moment to collect my thoughts. Landon leaves me, and I find the first available chair at one of the round tables near the edge of the dance floor. All I can think is how much the devil with the knife resembled the one who accosted me in my store. Same black curls sticking out from a red mask, too. "All part of the show," Landon said. That would mean that the devil is an associate of his.

The skyrocketing pitch of the opera singer on the big screen commands the room's attention before the picture cuts to a woman tied up, her mouth covered with tape, and what looks like needles taped to her eyes, pointing upward toward her wide-open lids.

I turn my head in disgust, scanning the crowd.

When a green witch in red beelines in my direction, it takes me a minute to realize it must be Mom. She lifts her mask, briefly flashing her face at me as confirmation before sitting beside me. Relieved to see a familiar face, I do the same for her. A man appears beside her with a ghost face on.

"This is my neighbor, Todd. Todd, this is Bethany."

Todd lifts his mask. "Nice to finally meet you," he says with a smile before resuming his ghost face.

"That live show caught me by surprise," says Mom. "It seemed so real."

"That woman was a good actor," adds Todd. "She looked terrified!"

My eyes trail to the broad stairway, where she fled after the two men. The light cast down from a chandelier is gone, and the narrowing steps are now steeped in shadow, where something hangs. Or is it just my imagination?

When Landon appears and hands me the promised glass of champagne, I thank him before taking a hefty gulp to calm my nerves.

A round of introductions is made, and Mom rattles off a few questions about his parents. He answers with charmed formality, saying what is expected. Yes, both of his parents are doing fine, and yes, they visit Sleepy Hollow from time to time. And yes, they like California. When it isn't burning or sinking, he adds with a chuckle.

The conversation turns to the recent hurricane, and I quietly fixate on the dark outline in the stacked shadows at the upper corner of the room. The oblong shape flattens at the bottom, jutting out. Is it swaying, or am I just staring too hard?

When I lower my eyes, the image of the man standing at the base of the stairs raises the hair on the back of my neck. It's him. The devil is back.

*** * ***

The memory slowly creeps into focus like a dark, ballooning spider floating down, making my skin crawl.

It was...this time of year. I was in sixth grade, thirteen years old. We came to see the decorations. Everybody knew it wasn't the Greylinns who decorated the formerly public lower grounds adjacent to the old cemetery. It was the townsfolk.

Fabric ghosts hung from the oak trees between the holly hedges and the dirt path behind the last row of gravestones. Near an oversized jack-o-lantern, a row of unmarked graves stood in the back corner.

This seems ironic, considering what Landon said: many of the tombstones were moved to the lower grounds "to keep the peace," but the bodies remained buried atop Skull Hill.

We didn't know this at the time. We only knew that amongst the many rows of headstones stood rectangular blank spots of grass where nameless bodies were supposedly buried. Or maybe these were empty underground like all the others. I don't know.

My heartbeat quickens as I realize the importance of this memory: the gate. Beyond the blank spot where the hedges were overgrown, they formed an archway over the big, locked iron gate where gargoyles perched, three sets of stone eyes downcast over the cemetery. Each statue was different. One looked like a horned devil with fangs, the other was bat-like with wings, and then there was the skeleton. The skeleton was the creepiest, as it seemed to slither from around the edge, its skeletal hand arched in a climbing gesture above the bulging-eyed skull, trailed by a coiled, reptilian body.

This time, the gate was unlocked to foot traffic, allowing an exploration of the middle grounds. But passing under the stone monsters felt like an act of courage. Even though, on the other side, we were rewarded with a mineral spring drinking fountain offered by a stone mermaid, I couldn't help but feel like we weren't supposed to be there. Then, something hit me in the head: a pebble or acorn. I looked up and saw him. The Greylinn boy reclined on a tree branch, peering down at me.

"What say you, Bethany?"

"Hm?"

Mom touches my arm.

"Would you like a slice?"

I look up at the platter extended in my direction, plucking a small plate holding cheesecake.

"I'll be back," says Landon, leaving us, and Mom pinches my arm. "You match!" she gleams, witchy and green.

"Yeah."

"So that's why your invitation was different!" she adds as if the solved mystery needs further explaining.

I eat my cake, mulling. Those statues. A devil. A bat. And a skull. Gargoyles lording over the tombstones of the defeated while keeping the gateway for the victors on the hill.

She stares at me. "Well?"

"Well, what?" I shrug.

"You didn't tell me that you two were a thing."

"I...didn't know we were."

"But you've been talking, right?"

"Sort of."

More like madly fucking at odd hours when I'm least expecting it, but obviously, I can't get into that.

"Well, that's great, Beth. Wow, I wouldn't have expected..." she trails off.

"Yeah, I know." But it stings a little to hear it. Nobody would expect it, not even me. I'm basically a commoner, and Landon is crème-de-la-crop in this neck of the woods. Oh, but he's so much fucking more! Surely, I must be one of the few who has Landon figured out. The man behind the mask is the monster behind the man.

"Why haven't you told me?" she pries.

"It's complicated," I shrug, my tone tense with angst.

"That's okay," she smiles encouragingly. I can tell she's giddy over the idea of Landon and me together. Ever the architecture buff, she'd love to have free range to this manor.

"Can we change the subject, Mom?"

"Sure. Did you know the mayor is here tonight? He's wearing a wolf mask."

We look up at the screaming woman on the big screen. A man wearing a suit with his head shrouded in black fabric stabs a woman repeatedly with a dagger. The scream gets louder. Closer. We turn our heads away from the screen toward a commotion.

I stand, watching the crowd shift in the direction of the elevator, where a knife-wielding man in a bat-faced mask drags a woman inside, closing the doors. Gasps turn to applause and excited chatter as every inch of my skin breaks out in goosebumps.

"What the fuck!" yells some guy, and people laugh as he pushes the elevator button repeatedly. The room gawks at him until he disappears behind the doors. First, the fanged devil. Now, the bat. The same guys that threatened me at the bookstore?

It's all part of the show.

All part of the game.

Before a packed room full of suits and gowns, the opera resumes amidst the bloody backstage slashings. Screams are drowned out by the male and female singers in period costumes, belting to each other with pained expressions as if in a lover's quarrel. The screen cuts to the masked man ripping the black fabric from his head and revealing a handsome, young blonde guy with blood trickling down his face from his head. This is no scar-faced phantom. This serial killer has the countenance of a fucking angel.

This time, a platter appears holding empty champagne glasses. The man sets them on the table where we're seated, our chairs angled toward the screen. A woman appears with an oversized champagne bottle. She places it on the table with a smile, corking it. Both wear white Phantom of the Opera masks.

"Enjoy," she smiles curtly before they disappear into the crowd toward the bar. The other tables have no bottles. Did Landon send this over? I crane my neck, scanning the crowd for his statuesque frame and silver mask, but I don't see him.

Me, Mom, and Todd spend the next thirty minutes or so drinking bottomless champagne glasses while watching the murder spree play out on the big screen. Most of the crowd is either watching while dancing or has quit dancing altogether. The graphic energy of the music and accompanying gore dominate the space, and the tension of the violin rises in fevered pitch as the lead female opera singer unwittingly enters the danger zone: backstage. She must go for a costume change. She doesn't know what awaits, but we do.

Suspense builds with each layer of hastily removed costume pieces until, finally, the shadow of a dagger rises on the wall behind her. It strikes down continuously until her white slip saturates utterly red from the bottom up.

The ballroom goes dead quiet. The room is darker. Only one of the three candelabras is still lit, and the slowly swishing cluster of red gowns takes on a sinister vibe, like walking-dead. Then there is conspicuous me—the singular lady in white, the Lord's date, the mistress of the "show," sticking out like a sore thumb. Doomed to be slayed.

FIFTEEN

"SCREAMING WON'T SAVE YOU," I warn the man tied to a black pillar topped with a gold-etched Corinthian capital. His eyes widen, goggling comically at the sight of his predecessor.

"You know the guy?" I ask, stepping into sight from the shadows, but he only stares dumbly at the motionless body slumped in a chair, head tilted forward, gaping mouth trickling with black blood.

"Ah, fuck, man," the new guy gags.

I crack my neck from side to side. "Yep, livor mortis is nasty business. But if you puke on this floor, you die. Got it?"

"Y-yeah, man. W-what is this about?"

"You tell me. This is your chance to make a better decision than *that* bastard. He didn't take my associate seriously. But you *will*. Right, Lexington?"

"H-how do you know me?"

"I know everybody."

"Who the fuck are you, man?"

When I sigh, the heat of my breath fills the inside of my

white mask. I should have worn the cloth one; it was more breathable.

"Knowing who I am won't make a difference in the outcome, Lex. Nobody lives unless I want them to. So, tell me. How long have you been fucking the mayor's wife? I might let you live if you got some good intel from the deal."

"What?"

I approach, clutching the knife handle peeking from its sheath on my belt. The soft friction of pulling the curved blade from the leather whispers darkly in the confined space.

"You heard me, Lex."

"*Fuck.* Okay. I-I'll tell you anything you want!"

"How long have you been fucking her?"

"Uh...about...a few months.

"Tell me what you know about Blackmosh Pharma?"

"Oh...*shit*. That-that's what this is about? I...don't know much, man. Can you just untie one hand? My skin...I'm... fucking itchy," he whines.

"Sounds like a personal problem."

His breath hitches as I lunge forward, grazing the thin skin over his Adam's apple with the blade's edge. Lifting the knife, I present it at his eye level. His pupils are suspiciously tiny, pin-hole-sized. And he's got itchy skin. A personal problem, alright.

"That's *your* blood, Lex."

"Okay, okay! Look, I-I was only fucking her because I was hired...to cozy up to the bitch...to find out her supplier. I'm just a lawyer, man."

"We talkin' about fentanyl, Lex? How long have you been using, and who hired you?"

"I don't take fentanyl. A client hired me."

"Do NOT lie to me! *Name* him," I shake the blade.

"Mitchell Fauling," he whimpers.

"A competitor to the Blackmoshes, hm? Is he into drugs and casinos?"

"Just drugs. Far as I know."

I look at the time on my watch. Only two hours until midnight.

"Time to die, Lex."

"W-what? But I have information! I've...got names. Let's strike a deal, man."

I shake my skull. "The Blackmosh supplier is public knowledge. FDA-fucking approved. So, unless you have another name, I'm done with you."

"Goes by Dr. Rx, lowercase x. Black-market supplier."

"For all I know, that's your shady connection. I'll look into it."

I walk around the back of the column and slice the cords binding his wrists.

"I know where you live, Lexington."

His knees smack the ground when he falls. "You're letting me go?"

I barely stomach the relief in his sickly tone, wanting to be rid of him.

"Get up! I'll let you live for now; I'll learn by watching you. Go about your regular business. Don't change a fucking thing. Don't say a fucking word to anybody about this. Got it?"

"Yes, yes. I'll do that. Thank y-y—"

"Shut the fuck up."

I unlock the back door, shoving him out of the building and onto the grass, where a very realistic but fake dead body hangs from a tree. I swipe at the liquid dripping down, touching my finger to my tongue. The corn syrup is a nice touch. Lex screams like a girl at the sight of the body while scratching his arms furiously with both hands. I laugh in disgust, shutting and locking the door. I send a text message to a cohort to keep an eye on him.

Now, it's time to scrub my hands and go downstairs. I want to see that girl of mine. Sweet, sweet Bethany. God, she looks fucking glorious in white. Like a pure offering to a tainted devil like me, she begs to be sullied.

SIXTEEN
bethany

THAT'S a lot of damn blood. How many more will die before the show ends? I've lost count.

"Care to dance?" the phantom asks, hand extended before the green witch.

"Great idea!"

I envy the relief in her voice. She relishes taking a break from the movie violence. Real life is so much better, right? Or so we pretend. These days, this shit hits too close to home for comfort.

With my would-be dance partner still nowhere in sight, my gaze flicks back to the big screen.

Due to her status as deader-than-a-doorknob, the blood-drenched Prima donna doesn't take her cue on stage. She's quickly replaced by another soprano singer who finally gets her chance to shine. This blonde gal is smaller-framed, with a less powerful voice to match. Regardless, the tenor belts at her in pleading retaliation, angrily emotive. He intensely broods, pinning her with brown eyes replete with absolute intent, framed by fiercely knitted brows. He might not deserve her, but that serves as no deterrent. He knows her little secret. Deep down, she wants to be convinced. She has a weakness for an undeserving bad boy. And so, the lovers' quarrel continues, backdropped by the question: Who will die next?

Only a single candle is lit on the candelabra now. Rogue cell phones strobe in the darkness, violating the strict "Keep them concealed, and no photos" policy.

Suddenly, my gloved hand involuntarily lifts, and the gasp that was coming gets stuck in my throat as I look up at him. His eyes couldn't be more grey, troubled, and dangerously desirous.

"Skull" floats high-pitched from my parted lips.

His grasp tightens as he lifts me to my heels. It's Landon, Bethany. Calm the fuck down. Same guy. Different mask.

"I've waited too long," he rasps huskily, pulling me tightly to his chest. I yelp, and his smirk is evident beneath the half-faced mask, ending just below his upper lip. I stare at his chin dimple as a reminder that I've figured him out.

He holds me tight, swaying to the overlap of music and death rising and falling from the speakers in the background.

"Let's go somewhere private," he whispers in my ear before biting and sucking my lobe. Mm. Shit.

It's not that I'm surprised by my body's heated reaction, the frantic rush of blood down low, but my lack of control only adds to my deep-seated frustration.

I want a release. Need it.

From the miseries of this evening, the embarrassment of standing out, the pain of this corset, the strange and disturbing actors, the murder, and the mayhem.

Landon got me here. Skull will get me out. He can give me a darkly delicious escape, and I know he delivers.

I look up into the bone-colored sockets, shadowing his eyes into an imminent storm. Right or wrong, I will take his violence and reap the rewards.

The edge of my mouth lifts, and that's all the confirmation he needs.

"Stay close to me, Bethany," he warns, sending a chill down my spine as he leads me through the black and crimson crowd.

Skull opens a door beneath the stairs, and the moment my heels touch the wood flooring on the other side, screams break out from behind. I jerk my head back only to be yanked forward, biting my tongue. I bring my hand to my mouth, muffling a groan.

He releases me long enough to slam the door shut. The click of the lock falls flat in the cramped space behind the screams. The underlight of his phone cuts upward in the darkness, accentuating the Hollows in his silvery skull.

"What is happening?" I whisper without meaning as if I'm part of a secret plot. Maybe I am.

His hand finds my jaw, gripping it like I'm a naughty child who asked a dumb question.

"What *they* expect, silly. Entertainment."

I raise my hand to him, pulling to loosen his clutch.

"*Careful*, Beth," he warns, the familiar gravel in his voice sending me a heat shock. His phone's light switches off. My hand is too dangerously close to his head for comfort, and he doesn't trust that I won't try to reveal the man beneath the mask.

"I wasn't going to--"

"Shh," he says, releasing my jaw and snatching my hand. He raises my hand to his lips, slowly kissing and sucking my fingers like hors d'oeuvres to be savored. I close my eyes in pitch black, feeling like I'm drifting. It's disorienting not to know what's around me. His arm finds my waist, pulling me into his hard chest and steadying my head with the weight of his mouth pressing into mine. The wet and breathy sound of our melting mouths rings villainous amidst the chaotic cries on the other side of the door. Why are they still yelling? Is it merely entertainment, or...

"What's going--"

He cuts off my speech by sucking my tongue, then reaches his hand down as if trying in vain to find the bottom of my dress.

"Pull it up," he demands, and my heartbeat quickens in anticipation as my fists fill with satin, lifting high as his hands find my ass, one hand slipping between my thighs. His fingertips silkily dance circles around clit, teasing me before cupping and caressing my mound until I'm so wet his fingers glide inside me with a thrust. He kisses me heavily, intoxicatingly, and the arousal in our shared breathing fills my ears. I know he's fucking me with his fingers like he wants to fuck me with his cock: aggressively shameless. God, yes.

"Paramedic!" a man's shout interrupts from behind, just outside the door. *Shit.*

"Did you hear th--"

"Shh. Come on me, baby," he demands, undeterred as the palm of his hand hits my clit, his fingers thrusting hard inside me. Flushed hot and reaching climax, the back of my mind senses guiltily that this is a repeat of the night of the murders. Are people dying again while I'm getting off?

Just as I fall over the edge, moaning in sweet release, something or somebody slams into the door.

Skull grabs my wrist. "Let's go." He leads me in a narrow, straight line by the light of his phone. A door slides open, and we get inside, followed by the wooshing feeling of downward movement.

"Where are we going?"

"*Deeper.* I want to show you something beneath the house," says the underlit skull, unworldly as he looks down at me, broad-shouldered, with shadowed eye sockets and a smirking mouth beneath a skeletal nose.

"Deeper?" I repeat, alarm surfacing in my reasoning mind. "That guy shouting at the door--like, somebody is hurt."

"I'm not letting you get off that easy, Bethany."

"I need to check on my mom."

"I told you. Everything's fine."

"But, is it? Do you even care who gets hurt? Or is it all just..." Just a game. Panic rises in my throat, turning my mouth dry. I've got to think of something to convince him.

"I...need to see *Landon*. He'll be looking for me."

"Will he now?" he snickers.

The mocking humor in his voice needles under my skin. I'm tired of the charade! I already know more about Skull than I'm supposed to, and he hasn't killed me yet. He's trusted me with his dark riddles. So, what difference does it make if I know his true identity? I'm tired of pretending.

"*Who* is Landon to you? I want to know!"

He stares at me a moment, head slightly cocked.

"That's complicated."

"Is he...your alter ego?"

He shakes his head. "You've got it wrong. But after tonight, it won't matter," he shrugs.

"*Why*, what's happening tonight?"

"I am righting old wrongs."

When the elevator stops, the phone light goes out as he pulls me into his arms. The cool air wraps around us, smelling of earth and damp stone. I protest, twisting and kicking, as he lifts me, taking several steps before setting me down on a surface. He grabs my wrists, and the cold sensation wrapping them ends with a resounding click. I look down at the handcuffs. *Fuck.*

He steps away, and I visually search the pitch black, feeling helpless. Why am I so damn stupid? How did I get so sucked into all this?

I smell the flame before I see it, offering a small glimpse into this brick-walled, dirt-floored space. I squint my eyes in the flickering light.

Skull shuffles forward, a towering silhouette that smells like sex and danger. Good God, this monster of a man has the power to make me feel like heaven while putting me through hell.

"Welcome to the crypt, my girl. Down here, you can scream as loudly as you need. Nobody will ever hear you."

SEVENTEEN
skull

"TAKE OFF THE MASK, Bethany. I want to see your face."

I glance back every few minutes, watching her eyes widen with each newly lit candle on the tall, gold stands circling the tomb. The room grows exponentially as dark corners expand, illuminating wide archways into tunnels.

"What the...?" she trails off, looking pretty, perched on a mahogany coffin in her bridal gown. She squeaks when a heel slips from her dangling foot, falling quietly on the dirt floor. She doesn't even know she's on a casket holding the bones of my father. There is something poetic about Bethany, my bright future, sitting atop my dark past.

"Catacombs. Hundreds of bodies buried in chambers," I explain, lighting the three altar candles. She turns her head, watching me with a slack mouth.

"The dead from the war are buried on top of the dead," I continue. "Where do you think the locked iron gate built into the hillside leads? It's a regular fucking dead-man sandwich under Skull Hill."

When I laugh, the shadows dancing over her face seem to twist with her expression.

I pick up her heel from the ground, holding it like a piece of lost treasure.

"You know about the war, right, Beth?"

She nods. "Yeah," she mutters, "Landon...I mean..."

"Landon told you?" I smirk beneath the mask. She's still unsure about my identity. Funny how she thought she had me all figured out.

"The war was always about the dead, Beth. No cemetery laws stopped the Greylinns' ancestors from building over an old cemetery. Certain folks took issue with a grand estate taking over the hillside, disrespecting the dead. Those willing to fight over it only buried themselves. Ironic, yes?"

The flickering light on her face seems to accentuate the confusion shaping the delicate bones.

"You speak of the Greylinns as if—"

"As if they're not my relations? Only on paper. I never fucking knew them."

"You mean because they were...emotionally distant?"

"No. Because there were several hundred miles between us, I'm not from the lap of luxury like you think I am, baby."

"What? What the hell do you mean?"

Her words are breathless, as if her heart is racing with confused panic. I reach down and take her naked foot in my hand, and she flinches as I run my fingertip up the middle of her foot, feeling for the scar I gave her.

"Stop!" She pulls her foot from my grip. "Tell me the truth, dammit!"

"Okay." I reach out and grab both of her ankles in my hands. She resists, slipping from the casket until I catch her in my arms. With bound hands, she fights like a netted mermaid as I hold her tightly.

"You want the truth, Beth? I'm not the man you want me to be. But I can be...if you marry me."

"You're crazy!" she struggles.

"Marry me, and people will stop dying."

Her wiggling slows to a stop.

"Are you serious?"

By the exasperation in her tone, it's like she isn't just confirming what I said but what it *means*. I'm not just on the sidelines of the murder sprees. I'm an integral player.

I lower her to the ground, my arms wrapped around her as I reach for her mask. "You can put this back on now. You've heard of a masquerade wedding? Two people will enter that door in about five minutes to officiate our nuptials. See, the terms of the inheritance state that the beneficiary must be fully employed, of age, and *married*-- that's where you come in, Beth. With you by my side, I'll take my rightful place on the hill."

"Nothing makes sense," she whines, tears running down her cheek. I pluck a tear, sucking her liquid salt from my finger.

"Mm, sweet Beth," I sigh. "I'll be frank with you now. Landon 1.0 has been dead in the ground for years. I'm Landon Greylinn 2.0."

"What? *Who* are you?"

"The one they gave away. The heir's identical nobody."

"His...*twin?*" she gasps as the elevator door opens.

I lower my mouth to her ear, whispering, "I'll take off the cuff if you promise to behave. Marry me, and we will greet our guests as husband and wife. That's the big surprise, the grand finale. Don't worry; I'll tie you up again for our honeymoon. I'll even wear the mask."

She presses her lips together in a pained expression. "Nobody...nobody died up there?" she cries.

"Shh," I say, gently kissing her salty mouth. I know I need to tell her what she wants to hear. "Murder isn't the main event tonight. *We* are. Marry me, and the game stops, Bethany. Help me make this right."

EIGHTEEN
bethany

HE ONLY UNCUFFS one side before linking my right wrist to his, just as the woman in the slinky red dress with the walkie-talkie appears in the doorway, carrying a flashlight. The tall man in black beside her stops my heart cold. It's him again. The asshole who threatened me at the bookstore, the knife-wielding bat-faced creep who moments ago dragged a woman inside an elevator upstairs. Just part of the show. Part of the fucking show.

I don't know what is real.

The woman's red lipstick grin gleams white beneath an evil-clown mask in the flickering light. Her short, red hair sticks out from the edges.

Skull motions at her. "Bethany, this is Jada."

"Pleasure, Bethany. Oh, you've done a costume change, Landon. Well, it's positively hopping up there," she purrs. "You should have seen their faces! Went over well. Applause. Brilliant."

Should I be relieved, or is she *in on it?* Part of the game.

I don't know what to think.

"It is nearing midnight," warms Skull with a polished

veneer, masking the crude-edged gravel but not the dark and brooding, at least not to me. I realize now that there has been this underlying misery in him all along. Something sad and angry in his tone, even when he's getting his way. Even when he's fucking me. Even now, on the eve of his wedding night, he is blackmailing his chosen bride into marriage so he can collect his brother's inheritance.

Twins. Holy shit.

"Yes, sir. We'd better start," chirps the clown. She's either oblivious or totally lacking a conscience. If only I knew. She could help me. Or we could both die. More people could die. Mom is upstairs. Her life is on the line. Dad's life is on the line. His words cut through me like a foreboding mantra: "Take my advice and do what he says." Only a desperate man would tell his daughter such a thing. This isn't a little game. The scale of this is larger than I know. I'm in a corner. My choices are null. God, that fucking rhymed. This whole goddamn thing rhymes like a sick joke.

Clown-lady walks to the raised wooden altar at the back center of the room and clasps her hands with a widening grin. Skull pulls at my cuffed hand, motioning me forward, but my legs are bolted in place from shock. I imagine myself dying here and becoming a ghost that haunts the catacombs. Little Bookstore Bethany forever lost and wandering the dead-man sandwich.

The clown snickers. "So quiet, you *two*. How are we doing? Nervous? Don't be." She must be ignorant. She can't be truly evil.

"Naturally," hums Skull, his voice slightly cracking as he squeezes my hand.

Bat-face approaches me menacingly from behind, fear

activating my lead legs forward to the jolt of my quickening heartbeat.

I feel outside myself, with no time to process any plan other than attempting to run. I won't get far attached to Skull. If his grand scheme is ruined, more people could die. I need a better plan.

The clown looks directly at me, the cat. "Isn't this romantic?"

I nod like an automaton because I don't know what else to fucking do.

This isn't reality—I've no skills for this shit. No lesson in life or books can prepare you for a moment like this. It's too surreal.

The clown inhales, mouth ajar. "We are gathered here today..."

Oh, God.

The candlelight no longer flickers but swirls, taking me with it.

"Do you, Landon Greylinn...take Bethany Clarkson..."

Skull turns, steadying my wavering body by holding both of my hands.

"Yes-s, I do." His words fall flat in the dirt beneath my heeled feet. But then they resonate, rising like winged phantoms in the shadows between candlelight. The swirling shadows sway, rocking the room like a sunken ship. This is a graveyard wedding—dead from the start.

"And do you, Bethany Clarkson..."

No. I will...sort this out...survive. I will--

"...lawfully wedded husband...until death do you part?"

A meaty bat hand tightens over my shoulder from behind. My mouth opens in protest, but nothing comes out. The arm around my waist jerks upward in a swatting motion until the hand on my shoulder releases its grip. A yelp escapes my lips.

"Wonderful!" chimes the clown, high-pitched. "Now, the rings."

What? But I didn't say—

A rose-gold band with black and white diamonds slides onto the index finger of my free left hand. It fits. He's already wearing a matching one. How long has he planned this? Is this why he tied up Dad? Showed me the pictures. Was it always about this marriage plot? He knew I'd be at the Halloween party that night? He knew where I lived— his chosen one.

"...husband and wife!"

"But, did I even say...?" I mutter dizzily, totally outside myself, and the clown bitch laughs at me, the silly cat. Yeah. In on it. Has to be.

A champagne bottle pops open on a table as Skull turns me around. Glasses are poured. No, not a table. A...casket. Shiny. Modern. Whose? I was sitting on a--

"Congratulations!" is delivered with a glass in my face, followed by the finality of tapping. My immediate future is set within the confines of a burial chamber.

I must snap to it. I must force my voice to surface. If I'm going to concoct a successful escape plan, I need to learn things.

"How long..." I clear my throat, gathering strength and sanity from the dizzy haze. "How long have you been...an ordained minister, Jada?" *Is the bitch even qualified?*

She smacks her lips from the edge of her glass. "Oh, going on three years now. There's a market for unusual and themed weddings. That's my specialty."

So, she's legit. But still, I married under duress. Terms for an annulment. That's the easy part.

"Why the walkie-talkie?" I ask.

"Event planner. My other specialty."

"The *time*," reminds Skull, impatient. Glasses are quickly refilled and downed before Bat-face leads us to the elevator.

"That was strong champagne," I say, drunk and attempting to play along casually. Not just for appearances but to calm myself and regain composure.

"Cava DO," says Landon 2.0. "13.5% alcohol."

"Yowzers. High content for champagne," laughs Jada heartily, putting her hand on Bat-face's big arm. He puts his hand over hers, making me cringe. Are they a thing? Yuck.

I watch the elevator door. There are no button lights, so I have no idea how many levels there are between the tombs and the basement of the house where the ballroom is. When the elevator stops and the doors slide open, followed by the next door, I'm not expecting to see people dancing—no dead bodies on the ground, no blood splatter, no police or paramedics. The screen only shows a night sky, and the candles are relit. A few people are huddled near the bar, looking glossy-eyed and into deep gossip. I search the room for Mom or Todd, but don't see them. A large clock on the wall shows the top of the hour.

"It's midnight. Now what, Landon?" I say resentfully as his hostage. He turns me so we're facing each other, wraps his free hand around my waist, and lifts our cuffed hands, his palm closing around mine.

"Now, *Mrs. Greylinn*. We dance."

My captor leads me through the motions of another glass of champagne and another Waltz—1—2—3. My body feels made of stuffing, numb, and doll-like, and with each rise and fall, my pliable limbs lifted by the strings of my puppeteer. His grip on my waist holds my legs up, dangling heels tracing the shape of an L on polished wood. Floating. What's wrong with me? Was there something extra in that drink?

It's hard to think, my brain blunted by the cocktail of shock and alcohol and whatever else.

It's hard to imagine beyond this point. Only this moment exists on repeat.

This fucking corset has permanently dissolved my ribs.

Passing faces are glittered with starlight from the big screen. They all stare, smiling stupidly. "Congratulations" and "Congrats."

How do they know? The wedding attire paired with handcuffs? Is that a thing? Do the rings on our fingers glint in the low light?

I look up at the skull head from behind my cat's mask.

"Did you tell them, Landon?"

Landon Two Point O...and nobody will ever know.

The grey eyes in the sockets gleam from a nearby candelabra.

He turns me to face the screen. "It's written in the stars," he says coolly, and I squint my eyes, studying the message scrolled in white at the center, like streaks from a crazed shooting star: Mr. and Mrs. Greylinn: Just Married!

My mind jumps to Mom. What will she think? I know the answer.

How could I have kept this from her? Wow, but it's so exciting. All that old, ornate architecture and décor at her fingertips, and I can afford to expand my bookstore now. Oh, and soon, there will be grandchildren! What is not to love about this arrangement? My dark secret is forgiven instantly before I've even said a word.

"How long...have you planned this?" I slur.

"Long enough. It's time to go upstairs."

"Why? Was something in my drink?" My words seem to run together.

"You'll see."

The ball joints in my doll body lock upright as he leads me into the elevator. I lean dizzily into Landon for support.

"Why am I so drunk?"

"You didn't eat enough. Strong champagne."

"It's just fucking champagne," I slur.

"Gets you drunk faster than wine. It's the bubbles."

"Fuck the bubbles. I'm…in shock. This whole thing is… so twisted."

He chuckles, strong arms holding me as I lean into his hard chest. The tuxedo villain smells scandalously delicious. God, I'm so messed up in every way. I should be sleeping in prep for a day at the bookstore checking inventory. Not in this mansion, married to a skull-faced killer.

He caresses my cheek with the back of his hand.

"You'll get used to this arrangement, Bethany."

When he lifts my chin and kisses me, the tears flooding my tongue remind me that I'm real. Real enough to wish this was love and not made on a deathbed.

"You might not believe me," he says. "But I want…to make you happy."

The elevator opens, and a group of blue-clad men and women gather around a stretcher. Men's dress shoes stick out from under the white cloth covering his body.

"Thank you for coming so quickly," says Landon from beside me, our cuffed hands down at our sides.

A woman stands beside the stretcher with her mask atop her head and smudged mascara around her red eyes.

"He wouldn't kill himself," she cries.

I recognize her from somewhere. When I trail my eyes to the wolf mask she holds in her hand, goosebumps break out over my body. I recall that Mom had said the mayor was wearing a wolf mask.

Scanning the foyer full of gawking partygoers, I feel a knot form in my stomach when I don't see Mom or Todd. Where have they gone?

Jada appears. "I'll handle it from here, Mr. Greylinn," she assures as a train of guests exits behind the paramedics.

"I want to find my mom, Landon."

"That's easy," he shrugs.

He clasps hands with me, and we walk side by side down the marble hall until we reach an enclave with a small sitting area before a set of double doors.

"I've given your mother and her guest this suite for the night. Probably best not to interrupt them."

I stare at the doors, wishing I had my dress purse so I could use my phone to text her and confirm that she's okay.

"I want my purse back," I demand.

"Of course. It's in our room. I'll show you the way."

He leads me back into the hallway.

"Our room? But I have a life. An apartment. A bookstore to run!"

"You can run your bookstore while living here, Bethany. I will hire movers for your belongings."

"Why is that necessary? You've gotten what you wanted. Collect your inheritance, and let me go free."

"Ah, but that's where you are wrong," he says firmly as we reach another set of double doors. A gothic-style painting of Blythe and Charles is ornately framed in gold upon the wall. Landon Skull Greylinn raises my free hand to his mouth, running his lips over my skin. "Letting you go…was never part of the plan, Bethany."

I jerk my head away from him.

"Leave me alone,"

"Why?" he smirks, and I want to slap the fucking madman hard across the face. If only my hands weren't bound.

He walks around the back of the chair and puts his hands on my shoulders, soothingly rubbing at the tension.

"Stop," I say, resisting the urge to relax into his touch. It's just a manipulation, part of the game. I won't fall for it.

I jerk forward, rising from the chair with a stumble. I dart my eyes to the door. I could slam into it and scream. But then I remember what he said about more people dying.

Don't be selfish, Bethany. This is bigger than you. Bide your time and plot a strategic escape.

"Yes, I'd like a bath," I say. "*Alone*, please."

"That can be arranged," he says in a low voice that gets to me somehow. There was no mocking in his tone, but that same old brooding that's always tucked under the surface of his *act*.

Who is the real man hiding behind the monster? What name did he grow up with? Was he always searching for an identity? It must have been torture learning about the life that he was robbed of. How long in the making is this grand scheme he's dragged me into?

I have so many questions, but he doesn't want to discuss the past. He's obsessed with the stolen goods comprising his future.

He walks ahead of me. "Watch your step, babe."

His tone is dead flat.

One minute, he acts like he's on top of the world, a dark god playing us all. Next, he seems so low, like he's coming down from chasing an unnatural high.

I follow him quietly across the room. He flicks the light

in the luxe bathroom, motions me inside, and then turns the water on above the golden claw-foot tub.

"Turn around. I'll remove the cuffs."

But he's interrupted by his phone.

I step back from the sound of pouring water, listening as he slips into the bedroom.

"Police," he says. "No. I'll come...be down in five."

He appears in the bathroom, and I pivot, sticking my wrists out from behind my back. My hands jerk defensively as he releases them.

"I'll be back. Be good," he says before leaving me.

I turn off the water and race to the front door, turning the knob. To my surprise, the door opens. He didn't bother locking me in. He's either confident I won't dare run, or he's being hasty.

Police are here.

I could seize the opportunity to speak with law enforcement, attempting to explain the tangled web I'm caught in, beginning with the night I had sex with Landon 2.0 while people were scrambling for their lives. This isn't the real Landon! His identical twin is an impostor. I didn't mean to marry him. I was forced.

It's so outlandish. Would they believe me or think I'm totally insane?

My stomach sinks when I think of Mom, tucked away in a room with her date. Now I know why Landon settled her in. She is leverage over me. The fucker is plotting a deadly game of chess, and I'm caught right in the middle.

I can't run, and I can't snitch. Mom's, Dad's, and others' lives are on the line, too.

That is why Skull didn't bother locking me in. He knows I'm smarter than that. Despite the seeming chaos that the murder spree has brought, he has set the pieces perfectly into place to his advantage.

I stand in the little foyer, listening to strange echoes through the marble halls, my mind racing with possibilities I can't pursue.

Not yet.

Biding my time.

Must be smart about this.

My shoulders drop as I fall back against the wall, defeated. I run my hand over the black diamonds, wrapping my finger. For now, this is my reality.

I am the new wife at the top of Skull Hill, presiding over a mountain of corpses, and my husband is Landon Greylinn.

The billionaire next door.

NINETEEN
skull

"A HEART ATTACK?" I feign surprise at old Officer Raymond.

He nods solemnly, tucking his thumbs into the black belt looped into his jeans. Clouded moonlight backdrops him in the sprinkling rain, and coyotes yip in the near-distant woods.

I step forward, crossing my arms with my fingers just beneath my chin.

"Well, it's exceptionally unfortunate," I add.

He tucks his lips, nodding. "Sure is. Until the coroner declares the exact cause of death, we'll conduct a standard investigation."

"Of course. If there is anything my estate manager, Jada, hasn't already informed you about, I'm glad to help in any way I can. I wasn't present at the time of his passing, as I was in a marriage ceremony in a different wing of the house."

"So, I've heard. Congratulations, by the way. Who, may I ask, is the lucky lady?"

"Bethany Clarkson."

He cocks his head, thinking.

"Oh. Tim Clarkson's daughter? Runs the bookstore?"

Bookstore Bethany.

I nod. "That would be the one."

"*Hm.* Well, I'll be darned. Congrats again."

"Thank You."

"If I do say so myself, it's been a long time since a family lived at the Greylinn estate. I think most folks are pretty glad about it. A fair number of local family traditions in visiting here over the years."

I crack a grin. "Most, but not all, are glad about it."

He laughs. "Well, we can't win everybody, Mr. Greylann."

"Please, call me Landon."

"Will do. It might be nice to see some little Greylinns running around again. You may not remember, but I did regular security patrols when the gates were still open to the public. You were a scabby-kneed kid then," he chuckles.

"I did have a habit of collecting scars."

"As do we all."

"Yep."

We nod at each other.

"Well, then. I'll let you get back to your wife. Sorry that a tragedy happened on such an important night."

"Me too. I will send my condolences to Mrs. Grenshaw."

"Life is unpredictable," he sighs.

"Sure is."

"We'll be in touch, Landon."

"Yes, sir." I'm about to shut the door when he turns around at the bottom of the wide steps, his foot slipping slightly on the wet stone.

"Will-uh...you be heading out of town for a honeymoon, Landon?"

"Not quite yet. I must finish my *work* before disappearing to a secret island with my bride.

He nods approvingly, and I match his smile before closing and locking the big double doors to Greylinn Manor.

Home. Sweet-Revenge. Home.

TWENTY
bethany

THIS TIME, the memory doesn't just flash into my mind; it takes me over. Like I'm there at the scene of the crime all over again.

With clammy hands, I slide to the ground in my wedding dress, not caring about the sound of ripping silk as the vision of blood—so much blood—pours over concrete from the man with the knife in his throat.

The man in the white skull mask looks up at me as I flee.

I desperately listen for his steps as I run, but I only hear the thud of my heart. When I look back, I don't see him.

He isn't worried that I saw him. His face was covered. I'm safe.

But I'm still running, panicked, with the wind at my back as I turn down the sidewalk toward my place.

The murder happened in the alleyway behind Sunshine Laundry, just around the corner from where I sleep at night, pretending the neighborhood outside my door is peaceful. Just a sleepy little town called Sleepy Hollow. All that murder and mayhem is for New York City, not here.

But I was wrong. We were all wrong.

Was it him? Was it *my* Skull that day?

He killed that man in broad daylight.

Did he follow me without me knowing it? Stalking me for an entire year? Bugging my place. Did he watch me sleep?

I had consoled myself by believing I was lucky compared to the one who was murdered.

I was the girl who got away.

But no. He got me in the end, didn't he? I'm the one he chose to marry.

Until now, I did such a good job of forgetting the murder I saw. Too good. I blacked it out of my mind, compartmentalizing it like a silly nightmare from too many scary movies. It didn't happen. To the point that when a new murder occurred, it didn't connect. Just another random injustice. It's illogical to think that all killings are linked. Conspiratorial. Paranoid.

But how many in a twenty-mile radius that has occurred in the last two years have been random, and how many have been part of the sick game?

When did Skull kill his twin, and how long has he been at this?

Goddamn. This can't be my life.

I've got my head in my hands when his socked feet appear between my legs, buried under white satin. He lifts my chin with his fingers until my teary eyes meet his blue greys. There is no happiness in those eyes, only a s Hollow satisfaction that must continuously be filled. He'll never be pleased.

He holds out his hand, and I take it, letting him lift me from the floor.

I break from him the moment I'm standing, taking

myself into the bedroom.

"You're supposed to be in the bath," he says from behind as I hurry across the room. I slam the bathroom door behind me before locking it.

He rattles the knob.

"I could *easily* break this door in, Bethany."

"I'd rather you not," I say firmly but calmly.

He's quiet for a beat.

"Enjoy your bath."

With a sigh, I turn the hot water on, steam rising as I try with all my might to get the damn corset undone so I can finally pull off this miserable gown. But it's no use. I need help.

Begrudgingly, I unlock the door, peeking out.

The room is dark, and when his towering frame suddenly appears, I jump, startled.

"Shit! I-uh...need help undoing this, please."

"No problem," he mutters, his tone dropping.

"You sound...depressed," I say, baiting him. I want to pick his brain. Figure him out.

"How would you know how I sound when depressed? "

"Well, you don't sound happy for a guy who's getting his way."

"Awe," he mocks. "Does *Be-ffany* want me to be happy?"

"Shut up."

He spins me around, letting the gown fall from my body as he grabs my arms in his hands.

"That can be arranged," he warns wickedly.

"Let go!" I demand, and he smirks at me.

One thing is for sure. He's not as nice now that I'm his wife. He's no longer pretending.

"Don't take out your self-loathing on me, Skull, or Landon, or whatever the hell your real name is!"

Anger flashes in his eyes, and he squeezes my arms tightly before releasing me. I stumble, catching myself.

"Was it *you* that day?" I mutter, wincing at my choice of words. Why did I have to ask?

"What day?" he shrugs.

"In the alley. A year ago. Rob Miller."

"Oh," he says flatly, sighing as if bored.

My heart thuds as I watch him, looking for clues in his eyes as he shifts toward a chair with his hand in his hair. He sits down, dropping back. The room is full of shadows around him, the color in his eyes receding like clouds at sundown.

"Go take your bath," he orders.

"Are you going to sit here and babysit me? I'm not going to run."

"Maybe I have plans for you on our wedding night."

His words jolt me, my heart speeding.

"Maybe?" I repeat, my voice cracking.

He puts his head back, closing his eyes. He exhales through his nose. "I might not be in the mood," he says.

"Okay. But, are you going to answer my question?"

He shrugs, saying nothing.

Frustrated, I leave him. At least I can take solace in the hot water, reminding myself that for all his sins, he hasn't shown me real violence. He can't. I'm part of his plan. That is, unless...

My head emerges from under the water as it dawns on me that he might not need me now that he's fulfilled the terms of his will. Once he gets his money, he can kill me off, be rid of me.

What if that's his plan?

Factor that into your escape scheme, Bethany. Getting on his bad side is not strategic. You'd better find a smart way to play along.

I realize now that I was never the girl who got away. I saw too much from the get-go. He's kept me close. I am nothing but a liability. No way does he plan to keep me alive.

So, stay on his good side for now.

He doesn't like questions; I'll stop asking. He wants to be alone in his misery; his pain is too deep to share. Nobody could ever understand his hell. Especially not somebody like me.

After all, I'm just Bookstore Bethany. An ordinary woman sucked into an extraordinary, hellish scheme.

* * *

When I finally emerge from the bathroom, wrapped in a towel, Landon is gone. I sigh, relieved, as I look around the room, wondering what time it is.

I cannot find a clock, but I'm guessing it's around 3 a.m. I'm lost without my phone.

Though I'm afraid to fall asleep, not knowing what the madman has planned for me, I'm too tired to keep my heavy eyelids open.

With no clothes to change into, I climb into the bed naked, taking comfort in the silky sheets and the thick, cushy blanket. Knowing that Mom is a few doors down makes me feel less isolated. We are in this prison together.

I don't know what tomorrow will bring, and it's too terrifying to try to sort out while so overcome with exhaustion.

My mind swirls as I sink into the pillow, quickly losing consciousness.

When I finally wake, I see the mask I was dreaming

about. White with black sockets and ending just above the skeletal nose. Except now, I'm awake, and it's still there, head cocked aside, watching me from the shadows.

A hand reaches out to me.

"Take it," he demands, his voice deep and gravelly as he drops something in my lap.

"What...?" I sit up, trying to focus my tired eyes on the strange object. I pluck the cold, long, slender metal thing with my fingers, raising it to my face. It's...a key—an antique, brown skeleton key, like the one he used that night at the Hollow Inn.

I look up at him, confused.

"What's this?"

"A wedding gift."

"I...don't understand."

"It's one of many. The keys to the old city."

I stare at him, trying to make sense of it. I recall the article about how many buildings in town are owned by the Greylinns. Sleepy Hollow is full of beautiful historical buildings used for modern purposes. The Greylinns own over half of them, leasing portions of them out. They rarely sell.

"What is this for?" I ask.

"Don't you want to expand your shop?"

My jaw slowly drops as I process his meaning. The ground-level space I rent is a tiny portion of a towering Victorian townhome, separated by locked doors.

"This key...grants me access to more space?"

He subtly nods, and I stare at him, baffled. This doesn't seem like something he would do if he planned to kill me off. Or is this meant as leverage to keep me quiet while he finishes his scheme? Maybe he isn't quite done with me yet.

He tosses another object in my lap.

"You won't be needing this anymore."

I pick it up and yelp, startled as I drop it from my hands. "How did you...?" Pink and curvy, it looks like my vibrator, which I keep tucked away in my dresser drawer.

He swipes it from the bed, brings it between both hands, and makes a breaking motion before slamming it on the floor. The symbolism is not lost on me. It's a reminder that he's fucking crazy and that his possession of me comes with rules.

"Be a good girl and ask me to fuck you when you need to get off."

I hate how his words are felt deep between my thighs, activating my pussy without my permission on command.

"Understood?" he says, and I nod.

"Why are you...wearing the mask?" I ask, stalling what I know is coming. If I can hear the change in my voice, laced with arousal, I'm sure he can.

"I like to be the *real* me when I fuck you."

He climbs onto the bed, making me jump when he yanks the blankets from my body.

"Spread your legs wide, Bethany. I'm craving the taste of your sweet pussy."

Slowly, I slide my legs outward until his hands clamp around my naked thighs. I feel his hot breath on my clit before it tingles with the tip of his tongue, making my pussy instantly wet.

He laps at me, making me squirm. He tightens his grip on my thighs, holding me in place as he glides hungrily over my slit, penetrating me in one thrusting motion. I moan in pleasure as he deepens his thrusts, hitting my G-spot while he fucks me.

I claw at the sheets, clutching at the silk while rocking my hips against his hungry mouth.

"Mm," he groans, rising to his knees just as I'm at the edge of climax.

The length and girth of his erection springs forth from his hand as he towers over me. My pussy throbs with need as he strokes his cock above me.

Finally, he lowers between my thighs, forcing himself inside me with one deep thrust of the hips. When I reach my hands to him, he grabs my wrists, pinning them to the bed while he fucks me.

"*Fuck.* You're so fucking tight, baby," he groans, pounding his pelvis against my clit as his cock hits my cervix. *Mm...oh, hell yes.*

I don't last long before I'm coming all over his big fat cock. His urgency increases to the sound of my desperate moaning as I fall over the edge of a powerfully delicious orgasm.

When he pulls out, he climbs forward on his knees and shoves his tumescent manhood past my lips, fucking my mouth without warning. He grabs my hair in his fist as he releases himself down my throat.

I gasp for the air I was deprived of when he pulls himself from me.

"Good girl," he rasps, catching his breath before standing.

"You're...free to go to work, *but.* You will return here at night. No later than 10 p.m. Understand?"

"What happens if I don't?"

"Bad things, Bethany. Very bad things."

"How long...do we go on like this?"

"As long as it takes," he shrugs.

He turns to go, and words seem to spill from me.

"I don't think it's the real you."

His back to me, he stops briefly inside the doorway

before shutting it. I probably shouldn't have said that.

TWENTY-ONE
bethany

A WOMAN WITH SHORT, red hair appears at my door with a suitcase full of my clothes. She's wearing impossibly high heels with skinny jeans and a silk blouse. This must be Jada sans clown costume: same build, same voice, same fake gleam in her brown eyes. There is something forced and calculating about her. She watches me like she's keeping tabs while hiding behind a fake smile.

Weirdly, she seems to have fulfilled many positions around here—minister, party hostess, and estate manager. I'm guessing she's in her mid to late forties and twice Skull's age. How does he know her?

She waits for me as I dress in jeans, a tee, and a grey cardigan. I slip my feet into brown suede slipper loafers with warm fur lining inside. I feel more like myself again, wearing my clothes and no longer stuffed into that stupid wedding gown. Transport me to my bookstore, and all will be well with the world again. If only it were that simple.

Admittedly, I'm dying to use the key that Skull gave me. But first, I must play nice and pretend to be a happy newlywed in front of Mom. What would it be like if Dad were here, too? Not that we've all sat at a table together since I was a kid, but how would he behave if he were here? How much does he know? Maybe he has no idea that Skull and Landon Greylinn have merged into one monster of a man.

"How long have you and Landon known each other?" I ask as she leads me down the marble hall.

"Hm. For a few years."

"You're from Sleepy Hollow?"

"Mm-hm."

"I've never seen you before."

"I can say the same," she answers quickly, almost defensively.

When we reach the large dining nook overlooking the gardens, Mom stands, holding out her hands.

I rush to her, giving her a tight hug. I nearly lose it, holding back tears.

"Well, congratulations!" she laughs.

I wipe my eyes, trying to find an excuse for how clingy and emotional I feel. "It happened so fast, right?"

She shakes her head, eyes watering.

"Biggest surprise of my life, Beth. I'm ecstatic. But did you have to elope? I would have loved to be part of your wedding. Come on, let's sit."

I sit in a chair across from the booth. Todd smiles, sipping coffee while Mom stares at me with bated breath. This is the part where I'm supposed to spill the beans. How long have I been planning this behind her back? Why didn't I tell her that I was dating Landon? Why the secret wedding?

Jada stands at the nearby window, making me nervous. She's obviously been tasked with managing us.

"It's been a whirlwind," I offer, but that's not enough. Mom's eyebrows raise higher, expecting me to go on.

"I was so busy with work, and…our relationship moved quickly. He thought it'd be romantic to elope."

I swallow the lie thickly like a bug in my throat, chasing it with a full glass of water before buttering a slice of bread. The table is covered in eggs, bacon, and bread, and my hungry stomach grumbles in anticipation. This strange feeling washes over me—a mix of relief and trepidation, like I've survived one crazy night, with many more to come.

Mom and Todd watch me eat, and my cheeks flush with embarrassment over what they must be thinking. That last night, I had so much post-wedding sex that I'm ravenous with hunger. They aren't totally wrong; they don't understand the dark details. And they won't have to if I succeed at my goal here. To somehow come out on the other side without me or my loved ones being hurt. Or anyone else, for that matter. But that may be asking too much. How blood has already been spilled?

"Jada has offered to give us a tour. Will you come?" smiles Mom, with eager eyes. Her mind is an open book. Finally, she gets to explore this grand, old mansion fully, as if she were a member of the family. I couldn't have married better. How did we get so lucky? Blah, blah. I envy her ignorance.

God, I wish it were Monday, and I could go to work.

"Of course," I agree, with a sigh. I might as well take the opportunity to get more intel about this place and Jada.

We all stand, following the click of stilettos. Like a new museum docent, Jada speaks as if she memorized a pamphlet, telling us factoids about art and architecture. But I've heard all this before. That's not the part I'm interested in. I want to know the hidden secrets about this family and why they cast one of their own to the wolves. I'm sure they didn't see it that way at the time. But how did they decide which twin to give away, and why?

It dawns on me that, eventually, Skull will have to face his parents. Will this be for the first time? I don't know how long he's been at this game. But, surely, they will see the change in him, if they haven't already, and wonder what happened to the son they raised.

My stomach pits at the thought of it. What Skull has pulled off here is a shock to my system, especially considering I'm one of the few who know his dark secret.

We eventually arrive in a narrow hallway near a big, arched doorway, which I recognize. This is where Skull brought me. The mausoleum hiding behind those big doors is another historical reminder of how the victors sit atop the bones of the defeated—the twisted legacy of Skull Hill.

But Jada has no interest in showing us that section of the hallway. This is where the tour ends. She only wanted to show us her favorite room. She opens a doorway to a multi-level sprawling suite much larger than Skull has put me in. It makes me wonder where he usually sleeps. I want to see his private lair, where the head of his true self hits the pillow at night. Does the real him even exist?

She pauses in front of a family painting in the foyer. The perfect family of four has a new meaning, considering one sibling is missing. I can feel Skull's ghostly absence in the painting.

"Agreed," I smile, and her eyes narrow briefly before her face settles into its standard pasted smile. Her brown eyes gleam cold, sending unexpected chills down my spine.

Dread coils in my gut when I think Jada may see me as a competition. Depending on how deep her ambition runs, I might be the thing in her way.

How far is she willing to go to get what she wants?

The dread sinks deeper, knotting. Jada isn't going anywhere anytime soon, and I am stuck in such a tangled web that I doubt I will make it out alive.

But I hate how deep down I want to know the real Skull. Part of me wants to get on his good side, not just for survival but because I'm fascinated. He's the tornado that came into my life, stripping me bare and sucking me into his violent vortex. I'm at his mercy, and the only time I like how that feels is when his body is all over mine and I witness that flicker of humanity hiding in his deep, grey, troubled eyes.

The only saving grace I have to cling to in my current situation is that Skull gave me a key to expand my bookstore. That alone is what I'll look forward to until I dig my way out of this.

Jada looks at her phone with a frown. The space between her brows doesn't wrinkle when her perfectly shaped red brows narrow, just like there are zero lines on her face when she flashes me that fake smile. I'm guessing Botox? It's not that I care or would usually judge a person based on their beauty choices; it's just that her face is too perfect. It makes me feel like she is hiding behind a mask, like her employer, Mr. Greylinn.

"Well," she sighs, glancing at her phone again. "Everything you need is in this part of the home. The kitchens, the library, the gardens."

I have a sneaking suspicion that Jada only gave us this tour to satiate our wanderlust and keep us on a tight leash. As she said, there is no need to go beyond our little section of the house.

"I'll be in my office in my quarters," she adds before leaving us, her phone immediately to her ear.

I decline the offer to go for a walk outside with Mom and Todd. My mission today is simple: figure out where Skull sleeps. He didn't stay even half the night in my room with me, so where did he go? There has to be a place in this mansion where he keeps his things, where I can get more intel on him. My guess? It's near the mausoleum in that back corner that Jada avoided. She said there was nothing down that way, but is that true? That's what I want to find out.

I scan the halls for a clock as I walk along. I'm not used to being without my phone and not knowing what time it is. I'll need Skull to return that before I go to work tomorrow. That he still has my phone makes me doubt that he's letting me resume my regular life, as promised. Was he telling me what I wanted to hear? But then, he did give me this key.

I reach into my pocket, feeling for it. The old metal under my fingertips is comforting. I never knew how much I could value something as simple as a key. But this one is weighted with value; it represents a promise that I will survive and be given freedom. But it's more than that. This means I can expand my store, opening doors previously closed.

But I don't want to get my hopes up and assume that this is Skull's genuinely thoughtful gesture, like a wedding gift. I'm sure it's to pacify me until he finishes his plans. But if there ever were a perfect wedding gift a wealthy heir could give to a bookish gal like me, showing support for my bookstore is pretty high up there.

But I can't let myself believe this gift comes from the heart. I don't even know if the man has a heart or if the scar tissue from a lifetime of getting and giving pain has formed a black hole in his chest that can never be filled.

I peek inside the library at the grandfather clock, confirming that it's one-thirty in the afternoon. I don't know what difference it makes today. But I feel better knowing.

When I finally reach the big doors of the mausoleum room, I put my ear to the door. After listening to silence for a few seconds, I continue into a dark corner of the hallway that abruptly ends at two doors. One is locked. One isn't.

I open the door to darkness, feeling along the wall on both sides until I finally find the light switch. The musty-smelling room is full of storage. Stacked chairs, white, cloth-covered sofas, and shelves full of lampshades beside a set of armoire cabinets. Some paintings are on the ground, leaning against the wall beside a large mirror.

As I step closer, studying the defaced faces with criss-crossing slashes exposing white canvas, something crunches beneath my shoes. It looks like somebody took a sharp knife to the paintings. These aren't the only damaged goods. A large mirror with an ornate gold frame is cracked from corner to corner, spanning from a hole caving in the middle. Glass shards are scattered over the wood floor and pieces of wood. Broken chairs are piled in the corner: mahogany, distressed grey, and black lacquered pieces stacked like expensive firewood. Just add fire.

I walk along the covered sofas until I reach a row of open storage bins. The lids are tossed on the ground and bashed like someone took a baseball bat to them, and their contents are strewn across the floor. Mostly knick-knacks—decorative spoons, crocheted animals, lacquered vases, a small doll with a missing arm, and tiny, doll-sized objects scattered around a three-story, light-blue Victorian doll-house. I squat down, picking up a miniature China Doll, reminding me of the ones I gawked over years ago during the Christmas tour. Smaller than a Barbie, maybe eight inches, this one is a little boy. Blonde hair and grey eyes, he's dressed in a plaid sweater vest and corduroy pants, and he's holding a carved jack-o-lantern pumpkin in his hands with a big smile on his face.

Carefully stepping over the strewn objects, I place him inside the dollhouse, among a few others—a man, woman, boy, and girl—sitting around a dusty, oval dining table. At the center of the table is a miniature silver platter with a pig head on it. I plug the little plastic pig head between my fingers, studying the object in its open mouth. Not an apple, but...a hand. I pull on it, and a sucking sound follows the release of an entire arm. Gross.

When I put the pig head back on the platter, I notice a shadow lurking underneath the doll stairs to the third floor. I swipe at it, finding another doll. This one is headless, dressed in dark pants and a dark grey sweatshirt, and wielding a long knife in its right hand.

Was Skull playing house in here? The thought of it creeps me the hell out. Especially when I notice the long-haired girl doll isolated in the attic, sitting in a chair. Is she being kept there for safety while the headless knife-man does the rounds?

Or is he saving her for last?

Standing and backing away, I feel a strange mix of sympathy and dread as I imagine Skull creating this scene, thrashing the room before arranging the dolls. The man is so fucked up, and he's absorbed me into his demented vision of reality. I get the feeling he's been planning this game his whole life and has no intentions of stopping anytime soon.

Hearing a noise from behind, I jump, startled, before hurrying out of the back room. I don't know if I'll return to snoop more in the other bins. This place of broken glass, defaced portraits, and twisted dolls is too unsettling and creepy. When I shut the door, I turn with a gasp to the shuffle of footsteps from behind. Strong hands clutch the back of my arms, yanking me into a hard chest. Hot breath hits my ear, teeth grazing. "Nosy girls are naughty girls," rasps a familiar voice.

My body goes rigid as heat floods downward. "Skull."

"Mm," he growls, biting my earlobe before firmly sucking. He runs his hands down my arms, keeping his grip.

"You know what I do with naughty girls?"

"What?"

He clutches my wrists tightly in one hand while his other hand smacks my ass hard, making me yelp.

"Stop!" I squirm.

Ignoring me, he grinds his apparent erection against my ass. Both of his hands have my wrists now, and in the fleeting moment I let myself get lost in his grinding motion, he's tied my wrists with something. I jerk backward, trying to twist from his control. His hands lift from me, letting me turn, but that only causes pain. He yanks the rope binding me so hard that my wrists burn as I fall forward. He steps back, letting me drop to my knees.

Looking up at him, I'm met with a grey skull mask with black sockets framing cold grey eyes.

"I'm sorry," I say, and the skeletal face looks at me blankly. I don't know if he's smirking or sneering underneath, but his dark eyes seem unmoved.

He tugs the black rope, forcing me to slide forward on my knees.

"I was just...getting to know my new home," I offer, hating how small my voice sounds.

"But this isn't your wing," he says in a low, deep voice that chills me.

"I didn't know. *Please*, untie me."

"Only if you beg for it."

"Isn't that what I just did?"

"No. I want you to beg for *this*," he says, unzipping his pants.

I don't mean to gasp when his massive cock springs forth, but I can't help it.

He tugs the rope, and I slide forward until I'm looking up at the underside of his big, thick shaft.

"I'm waiting," he demands.

"I--"

"*May I,*" he orders.

"Fine. May I please...give you--"

"*Suck*," he demands.

"May I *suck*...your cock?"

He shakes his skull. "You didn't say, sir."

"Okay," I sigh. "*Sir.*"

"Say the whole fucking sentence, Bethany."

My cheeks blush red hot with humiliation. *This* is my punishment. To make me feel like his slave.

"May I please suck your cock, sir," I rattle off.

He tugs the rope. "Say it like you fucking mean it!"

My eyes water as I prepare myself to beg truly, and when I say it this time, my voice whines, adding to the effect. "*Please,* may I suck your cock, sir?"

"You may," he says, backing and sitting in a chair tucked into a shadowed corner, the rope trailing a few feet between us.

"Crawl to me, Bethany."

On bound hands and knees, I awkwardly lumber until I

reach the space between his parted legs. With no free hand to hold onto his manhood, I feel like I'm bobbing for apples as I try to aim my gaping mouth. When my lips close around the head of his cock, he grabs my hair, forcing me deeper. He thrusts every inch of his manhood to the back of my mouth until the tip of his head taps my throat. My air supply is cut off as he thrusts, clutching my hair tightly with a groan. Relentlessly, he fucks my mouth until hot liquid fills my throat, making me drown with a gargle just before he finally, slowly pulls out.

Coughing, I gasp for air as he lifts me from the ground. He unbuttons my jeans, shoving them down with my panties until all the fabric is pooled at my ankles—his hand slides between my thighs.

"As suspected," he declares with a wicked chuckle. Yes, my secret is out. I'm drenched.

With flushed cheeks, I step out from the fabric at my feet, and I'm about to climb into his lap before he puts his hand up.

"Where are your manners, Beth?"

I clear my throat. "May I *please*...ride your cock, sir?"

"Good girl," he hums, his voice low and less edgy.

I slide one knee up, resting my bound wrists against his chest as I pull up my other leg. Just as I lift to my knees on his thighs, he shoves me back down, his erection stretching my pussy as he fills me up inside with a forceful push.

"*Mm-fuck*. You're so tight," he groans, clutching my thighs as he thrusts deeper, making me moan. His hands slide to my ass, squeezing. "Fuck me, Beth," he rasps, his hands all over my ass as I grind my hips into him; over and over, my clit hits the base of his shaft as I ride his steely cock. He shoves my shirt and bra up, lifting my bound wrists over his head, his tongue relentlessly sucking and biting my nipples into hard candies, our bodies knocking together like tectonic plates ready to burst.

Skull's deep, guttural growl fills my ears as my thighs clench tight around him, my pussy spasming hard in a wave of delicious ecstasy.

"Oh...mm...*fuck-k*," he groans. Then, with sudden urgency, he lifts me from his cock. My legs give out, and he catches me, lowering me into the chair as he zips his pants.

"That was...an accident," he mutters, and it takes me a moment to catch my breath before I understand his meaning. He didn't pull out in time; he came in me; I could get pregnant. *Oh, shit.*

He tears off the mask, dropping it to the ground.

"What are you doing here?" he says, confusing me. But then I realize that we are not alone. Somebody is in the hall, and my hands are bound, so I can't put my clothes on.

"Help," I whisper, and Skull cocks his head.

"Sorry, boss," I hear Jada say. "I was looking for your *wife*." Her tone isn't pleasant when she says that.

"No need," he says.

There is a moment of silence before she responds. "Understood, boss." Her heels click away over marble.

God, we were so loud and into each other that we didn't hear her approach.

Skull returns to me, and I study his handsome face as he unties the ropes. He is the spitting image of a young man who grew up utterly privileged. The scar along the side of his face, and what it represents, is the deep gulf separating him from his dead twin.

"This is my quarters, Bethany. I don't like uninvited company."

"Including Jada?" I ask as I dress.

His grey eyes lock with mine, and I don't know why, but it pangs me. He looks even more tortured than usual. He holds out his hand, helping me from the chair.

"Why does it matter?"

"I was just wondering," I shrug.

"She's only my assistant," he says.

"I didn't mean--"

"Yes, you did," he smirks, grey eyes twinkling.

"Not like it matters," I frown.

"Is that what you want, Beth? For it to *matter?*"

He leads me up the hallway, and we walk in silence until reaching the library.

"I won't see you again tonight," he says, squeezing my hand before releasing it.

"How will I get to work tomorrow?"

"The driver will be here at seven-thirty to take you and your family to town. Here's his card. Call when you're done with work."

"Where's my car?"

"It's being delivered. I've gotta go."

"To answer your question," I say to his back as he pivots back around with a raised brow.

"You asked if I need...*us* to matter," I remind him.

He looks away, sighing like he doesn't want an answer.

"I know it's just a game, Landon," I mutter.

He presses his lips with a nod, a quizzical look flashing in his stormy eyes.

"If I'm to go about my normal routine, I'll need my phone back," I say, switching to a less heavy subject.

He reaches into his pocket. "Glad you reminded me."

I've never been so happy to see that pink cell phone, a precious lifeline framed in durable plastic.

"Be a good girl," he says with a wink, his fingers brushing over mine like an electric charge.

He's given me two symbols of freedom now, proving that he trusts me to play along and be a good girl. I hate how part of me wants to please him while the other part of me wants to beat him at his own twisted game.

I'm feeling relieved and conflicted as I watch him walk away. The way he made me beg, humiliating me before rewarding me—what the hell was that? I can't say I didn't like it. God, what the hell is this man doing to me?

"There you *are*," calls Mom from behind, joined by Todd and our hostess. Jada offers me a tight-lipped smile, and there is a hint of disapproval in her brown eyes. I don't know what her expectations of me are. I don't even know how much she knows. I can't trust her.

"You will be joining us for an early dinner, *yes?*" she insists. It isn't a question. I'm supposed to agree to it.

"I know we all have a busy day tomorrow, so I figured early to bed, early to rise," she adds with a broad, plastic grin. I think she's in a hurry to get rid of us. Tired of being a sitter. What happens tomorrow night after I return to this mansion? What if Skull is gone, and it's just me and her? Will she be my constant shadow, this unknown threat?

Faking my way through a family dinner as a happy newlywed was more exhausting than anticipated. The minute I got back to my room, I went to bed. I just wanted to finish the day, and even though it was a fitful night of sleep, feeling certain that Skull was sitting in the dark in a chair watching me, I was in bed long enough to feel rested when dawn finally hit the horizon.

The driver was there waiting, as promised. He's a friendly, very normal local who has no idea what murderous plotting has been happening around him. Though I'm sure he's had his fill of backseat gossip.

Enjoying being alone and surrounded by the smell of books in my shop only lasts a few moments before April bangs on the door in her standard holiday ugly sweater. She has one for every season. This is a patchwork pattern of jack-o-lanterns, witch hats, bats, black cats, and...white skulls that now take on more meaning.

I push thoughts of *him* to the back of my mind as I unlock the door and let her in.

"You're here early."

"I'm sorry."

"It's okay; come in," I say, turning the open side of the sign forward in the window before leading April toward the counter, where I have a big box of deliveries to unpack.

"You hadn't returned my call, so I went by your place. Saw the moving truck."

"Oh. *Right.* I'm—"

"Moving into Greylinn Manor. Yes, I asked around."

I force a smile. If only I could get out of having this conversation. "Yeah. Sorry, I didn't return your call, April. I...lost my phone."

"Oh, no!"

"I found it. No worries."

"Good. Well, congratulations!"

"Thank you," I say, pulling out books from the box. I don't want her to study the look in my eyes too closely if I stand still.

"It's the talk of the town, Bethany! Well, besides the mayor's death. Sorry, not trying to rain on your parade. It's just...rumors going around."

I look up from my box. "Like?"

"Well, even though he died of a heart attack, it's just

weird that they found him with a rope around his neck like he'd tried to hang himself. I mean, he failed, but...still weird."

I recall his wife the night they took away his body. She said, "He wouldn't kill himself." This must have been before his cause of death had been announced.

"I mean, from what I hear, it was a crazy Halloween ball," April continues. "So maybe it was just a stunt gone wrong or something. *You* were there."

She looks at me with raised brows, waiting for me to divulge what I know.

"I was getting married at the time. In the..." I can't bring myself to say crypt. "In a different wing of the house."

She nods. "Did you see the mayor that night?"

"Not really," I shrug. "I mean, maybe. We didn't interact."

"Also, weird that one guy went missing."

"What guy?"

"Richard Santos. I don't know him. Nobody has seen him since."

"Hm. Weird."

"Yeah. His girlfriend won't talk to the police. Something is up."

I shake my head. "I don't know anything about that. Sorry."

"He got in a scuffle that night at the ball. With some guy in a red mask."

"Oh, yeah?"

I recall the devil wielding a curved blade while chasing a partygoer into an elevator, a woman screaming from behind.

April leans in, whispering as if we aren't alone. "Rumor is her boyfriend was beating her up, and he's in hiding for a drug deal gone bad. That's why she's afraid to talk. It's a wonder the likes of them would be invited to such a posh event."

I nod politely, saying nothing. It's not so odd if they were the Gargoyle Gang's next target. I've given this moniker to the dark trio because it's too uncanny how they resemble the three ugly statues guarding the gate between the old cemetery and the Greylinn grounds, separating the victors from the losers, the kings from the peasants.

Skull was on the outside all this time. But now he's got it all, and it's like he's devouring his would-be legacy from the inside out, hellbent on destruction. Suddenly, it occurs to me that he might be sick enough to sleep in the mausoleum. If his quarters aren't behind that locked door at the corner of the hall in his wing, the only other locked door there leads to the room of coffins. Maybe that's his lair where he sleeps and plots. The altar table, his place of dark worship.

I think of the horror novel he got me reading, in which dealings with the devil-demon make life a losing gamble. Just a game. A deadly, vengeful game.

"Crazy times," sighs April as I pull the box from the counter.

"Sure is," I frown.

She shakes her head. "Well, at least there hasn't been another massacre. But if the killer is going to strike again, all bets are on Halloween night. Lots of folks aren't letting their kids trick-or-treat around town."

"That's a shame," I say, studying the heaping stacks of new inventory, hoping she'll leave. I came to work to focus on work. I need a fucking mental break from death and mayhem.

A customer comes in, and April pushes off the counter

as the door slams shut. "Well, I'll leave you to it, hon. Have a good one."

"You, too."

Even though I should probably let her know that I have some new soft-boil mystery books in stock, I don't want to risk the chance of her hanging around more. I'm in no mood to chat, so I'll text her later.

As much as I feel determined not to think about anything but books, what she said about the dead and missing people from the masquerade ball follows me around the store like a haunted thing.

This ball seems to have served at least two purposes. To entrap me into marriage and to rid Skull of certain players. I suppose that the good news is that he wasn't crazy enough to slaughter every partygoer wholesale. This is more like a game of chess. He is targeting people for specific reasons. He's not even from this town, so how does he pick his victims? What are his criteria? It occurs to me that there might be a way to find out.

Jada.

She works for him regardless of what she knows and doesn't know. Surely, her en-suite office has notes, calendars, and bits of information that could give me a window into Skull's plans.

After shelving a few books, I straighten my posture with a sigh. I'm supposed to give my brain a break, but who am I kidding? I can't pretend that being inside my store means everything might be okay. I have no clue what tomorrow brings. Information could be my savior. Speaking of.

I reach into my pocket, feeling for the key. I'm dying to use it. At the end of the horror aisle, next to the bathroom, is a door that's been locked since I began leasing this place. Nobody has leased the upstairs portion of this old Victorian townhouse; I certainly couldn't afford to buy it. But this key is more than just the expansion of my shop. It's another window into the Layne dynasty. Another window into the world that Skull has stolen, and, in this small way, he is sharing with me his plunder.

It's almost...darkly romantic.

TWENTY-TWO
bethany

THE COLD IRON of the big, old skeleton key warms quickly between my fingers. Turning it, my heart jolts with anticipation. I have one hour to explore my new space while the shop is closed for a lunch break. I rarely use the "Be Back Soon!" sign, but today is unique.

The pine wood door creaks open, and I take a deep breath, calming my nerves. The back corner of my store will no longer be filled with storage but open to new aisles.

I can't let myself feel too excited about this, even if occupying the entire townhouse—two stories for the shop and one for my living quarters—has been a fantasy I didn't think would come true. I couldn't have predicted the strange and twisted way it has. But everything in my life currently feels too dangerously tenuous to be swayed by hopeful gestures on the part of my captor.

This key feels like a gift, but every gift I get from Skull is wrapped in a curse. The safe room at the B&B, the basket full of goodies, the necklace, the invitation, the marriage, and now...this key.

I don't know what I'm expecting on the other side. I

suppose cobweb-lined steps leading to narrow halls between empty, dusty rooms, some used as storage, with boxes and other odd-and-ends scattered about. What else should I expect from an unused historical building?

A musty, mothball smell wafts heavily in the air as I push open the door and lift the light of my phone, finding a hall switch. A light flickers at the top of the stairs before going out. I let my phone lead the way.

Thick cobwebs spanning narrow steps? Check. Narrow halls built with the same pine wood as downstairs? Check. But that's where my accurate predictions end. This is no warehouse but an abandoned home, ghostly and frozen in time with a faint scent of women's perfume.

The spacious landing's walls are covered in peach-patterned wallpaper, and gold mirrors flank a painting of a man and woman kissing inside a red 1900s wagon-style car. A round, pink marble table with gold legs is at the center of the room. I swipe my finger across the dust-covered vase atop the table, revealing the black and gold peacock feathers etched over it.

As I enter the first room off the landing, my jaw slowly slackens in awe. It is not empty and ready for aisles of books, but full of covered furniture perfectly placed around a table and a mahogany wood-mantled fireplace. Gold-framed paintings hang from picture rails over burgundy-colored walls. An antique, saloon-style piano and the remains of potted ferns fill a corner near the window, and opposite that, a dainty writing desk plucked from a Jane Austen novel. The anachronism is the gold, flower-shaped gramophone sitting on it, with a dusty record placed over the mahogany box. *Wow.*

All this time, this time capsule of a place was above my shop, and I hadn't a clue.

I circle the room, lifting the cloth covers to reveal a set of perfectly preserved green velvet chairs and a wing-back burgundy sofa.

Who lived here?

The question gives me chills. I'm half expecting to find a skeleton tucked into a bed.

As I continue through the upstairs, it's easier to imagine how the downstairs must have been, as its layout matches, like apartments stacked atop each other: foyer, sitting room, two bedrooms, bathroom, kitchen. Except downstairs, the sitting room is the open cashier's space sans a door, and the wall between the would-be bedrooms and kitchen is gone, with support beams remaining. The shop was used as an art store before I moved in.

My chills deepen as I step cautiously inside the bedroom with the four-poster bed, floral chair, and leather hat boxes. A black spider crosses a web before my eyes, and I jump back, startled.

I'm about to leave when the half-full pink and purple perfume bottles catch my eye: curvilinear and lined on a silver tray at a wooden vanity with three tall, paneled mirrors over several sets of drawers.

Pushing through the mesh of webbing, I take turns lifting each bottle, blowing the dust off the top, and plucking open the lids. Expensive, floral perfume dances flirtatiously in the air like a flapper to a decadent jazz tune. The scents range in muskiness, and I imagine which is for day, night, and special occasions.

My heart speeds when I pryingly open the top drawer. Envelopes are stacked beside a leather bag and a silver-framed hairbrush. The leather bag is full of faded receipts. The top envelope has a letter inside it. The cursive is insanely elegant and addressed to "My love."

Signed by "Charles." As in Charles Greylinn, I assume. This letter must be to Blythe! So, this was her townhouse back in the day?

Dying to know more, I attempt to decipher the ornate cursive. It's not often that I've read something longer than a phrase in cursive. It's a lost art. My generation didn't even study it in school. But here goes...

My love,

I know it has been too long since we have seen each other outside closed doors, and you have grown impatient with our arrangement. Though I have enjoyed those nights tucked away from the world, I understand the need to enjoy various leisure activities together.

Rest assured, all matters are in place as planned, and I will soon have some blessed free time.

As I have arranged, Blythe and the children are indeed leaving for Paris, but, of course, I have elected to stay home and attend to pressing business matters.

As planned, we will take a train to New York and attend the Opera. We will shop, dine, and have fun as you wish.

You only must be patient a little longer, my love.

Sincerely yours,

Charles

* * *

JASMINE P. DANE

In between customers congratulating me on my marriage and asking if I'll still run the bookstore--as if I've finally arrived in life and will stop doing what I love?--I read eagerly from the stack of letters that I swiped from vanity, reminding myself that though everything about that space, and even the stationary the letters are written on, feels pulled from the 1900s, these were only written twenty years ago.

The Greylinns are of very old-money stock and deeply rooted, so being in their private spaces feels like a time capsule. That's what makes their homes so enchanting for visitors: the lost art of Victoriana, for good or bad, is still living and breathing in these unusual families.

Once I have free time, I plan to explore upstairs more, even though it gives me the creeps up there. I didn't even go inside the other bedroom. I felt ghostly vibes standing outside the door, and I only peeked in, eyeing the shadowed, rose-colored curtains and matching floral chair beside a small bed. But after finding this treasure trove of information, I know I've got to be brave and see what else I can find. My life depends on learning everything I can about the Greylinns.

The weird thing about these letters is that they are a collection sent between Charles and his mistress and addressed not only to Sleepy Hollow but also to New York City. So somebody got a hold of all these and stashed them upstairs in her bedroom, and they did it long ago enough that a thick canopy of spider webbing formed blankets across all the walkways, and everything was covered in a foot of dust.

Hoping for answers, I carefully read the pages one by one. There are over a dozen letters, each dated about a month apart.

Four and five letters in, I get to something beyond the annoying lovey-dove stuff between Mr. Greylinn and the "other woman." Mariam used that phrase several times as they argued back and forth on the topic. She hated being second fiddle to his wife. Every other letter is a kiss-and-makeup "Sorry, my love." But that didn't mean she got her way entirely.

She wanted more from him than he was willing to give. He didn't want to remarry or have more kids, so she would have to settle for being his mistress. He was very firm on that, especially the *children* part—not just with Mariam but his wife, Blythe. "I don't like children," he flat-out said.

Mariam wasn't satisfied with his reasoning, and so he shockingly divulged his big secret to her, proving that it was a lost cause because he was truly a cold-hearted fucker.

First and foremost, he only wanted one child, a son and heir, "Strictly practical. To carry on the line." But Blythe wanted a little girl. So, they compromised. The billionaire man put a cap on the number of children he would financially support, and it was written into their marital contract that a maximum of two children would be produced between them. When they had the twin boys, it caused a big upset. Charles wasn't convinced that a "spare heir" was necessary, and Blythe was set on having a daughter. Three children would break the marital contract, and Charles wasn't having it. Neither wanted the mess of divorce.

Blythe was left with a choice.

Be content with two sons or give one away and take a chance on having a girl. It's hard to imagine her sacrificing one child for another. She didn't have to give one away, but she did. "It was her choice," he explained coolly to Mariam, resolving himself of the role he played.

When the second pregnancy came along, a girl, Charles and Blythe got their way, and all was settled.

"I am finished with children, Mari." Family wasn't what he wanted out of his affair with her. Finally, she understood the terms between them.

But I wonder what Mariam was honestly thinking at this point. Wasn't she appalled? She didn't let it show in her reply. She agreed to drop the subject for good. "We will focus on us and only us," she conceded.

After that, the letters are about schedules and antiques she wanted to buy from Sotheby's for the "New York apartment" he promised to purchase. Mariam, a grocery chain store heiress, had her own money but didn't like spending it. Charles had her covered, and that seemed to be their arrangement. She spent half of her time here in Sleepy Hollow and the other half in New York, where she could be herself and "not hide from the world." New York society didn't care that she was his mistress, but conservative Sleepy Hollow didn't like it. Nor did Blythe. So, Charles and Mariam had to be more discreet when in his hometown.

But then...things started to get tense again.

Ten letters in, Mariam tells Charles that she is seeking hypnotherapy and surgery and doesn't want to see him while she recovers in New York, that she "needs space." Doctor's orders. Charles lets her know that he disagrees with the doctor's orders.

A thought occurs to me when I pull out the envelope of receipts, looking through the various expenditures before discovering the doctor's bills. Seems she was charging Charles for the therapy sessions. *Did the affair drive her mad, or what?*

The irony. Here I am falling into a similarly twisted fate with Skull, the aftermath of his parents' choices. The thought pits in my stomach as I pull out a receipt with a note in red ink in the bottom corner that reads, "Pregnancy."

Oh...shit.

Goosebumps break out over my body, a feeling of doom settling in. Did Mariam have a baby?

If filthy rich, Victorian-minded Charles was willing to give away one of his children for financial reasons, what the hell would he do with a so-called bastard?

It's hard to imagine a happy ending.

I hesitate to answer the phone when Dad calls.

I don't even know where to start with him. But I need answers, and he's one of the few people who knows about my masked man problem. We share this in common.

"I'm...sorry, Beth," he slurs.

"You've been drinking," I frown, sitting behind the counter. "Sorry, for what?"

"I didn't expect you to marry him."

When sardonic laughter escapes my lips, I realize how angry I am. It's not his fault, but then again...

"You literally told me to do whatever he says!"

My eyes flick to the rain-splattered door. The rain makes it harder to hear the space around me. I think I'm alone, but there is always the chance of an unaccounted-for customer reading in an aisle.

"I don't know if I said those exact words," he says, and my face flushes with frustration.

"You did," I whisper sharply.

He sighs. "I was...coming from a place of fear."

"Fear of what?" Seems like an obvious question, but I still don't know what part he plays in this mess.

"Look. I was afraid of losing my job."

"What?"

So, this was all about saving his ass and not about dying or loved ones dying?

"I panicked, okay? He's...powerful. But I shouldn't... shouldn't have involved you."

"What are you talking about, Dad? *He* involved me. He threatened you and then showed me the proof. I saw the pictures of you tied up!"

"Yeah. But that's...not the whole story, Beth."

He sighs, long and heavy and full of guilt. Goosebumps spread over my scalp, and I pull my cardigan tighter over my chest as I brace for whatever bullshit he's about to divulge. I've always had mixed feelings about when he drinks. On the one hand, it's an unhealthy disease; on the other, it's one of the few times I can get some straight answers out of him. He's honest when he's drinking.

"What's the whole story, Dad?"

"It's...complicated. I don't want to involve you any more than I have."

"Are you kidding me right now? Too late for that. I'm married to—" I stop myself, feeling paranoid about the tilt of a curious ear from someone tucked inside a hidden nook. I'm pretty sure the store is empty, but still.

"Okay, Beth. I'll...tell you. Something changed. Greylinn...started taking more of an interest in the casinos. He wasn't leaving it up to leadership anymore. He started sniffing around. Didn't like what he saw. People were getting fired or disappearing. Some...showed up dead. When he came to me...I didn't want to be one of those people. You understand? I struck a deal."

"What kind of deal?"

"I...let him take pictures."

He stops and takes a chug of whatever he's drinking,

and my face goes numb as I process what it sounds like he's saying.

"You...let him tie you up?"

"Yes, Beth."

"Why would you do that?"

"To...show to you—I swear I didn't know that..."

"That I'd be forced to marry him!?"

"Yeah. I didn't know that, sweetie."

Angry tears stream down my face. "You told me to do whatever he said. You knew the photos were used as leverage against me. What the hell did you think he wanted me for?"

"He told me I could do a small favor for him. He needed a date for a formal occasion. I thought it was weird. A man like him shouldn't have to worry about a date. But he said this was going to be a twisted prank. His way of making me pay...for certain things. I felt relieved that's all he wanted out of me."

"All as in your *daughter?* You offered me up!"

"For a date, Beth! That is all."

"Right," I huff, wiping tears from my cheeks. "He wanted to make you pay for what?"

He takes another swig. "Some quasi-legal dealings, I had. Hell, I didn't make it this far on only a manager's salary, Beth. I dabble in stock and things."

"And things," I repeat.

"Yeah. Day trading, that sort of thing. Normal stuff. The kind of stuff any Greylinn would understand. I don't know. He got on some high horse and started shaking things up. Decided he was the good guy. The Batman billionaire. All I know is I'm truly sorry. Maybe...you can be happy with him?"

"And absolve you of guilt? Like you said, Dad. It's complicated."

With that, I hang up the phone.

I put my head down on the counter, expecting to cry. I feel the emotions welling inside me, but have nothing to show. I'm dry inside. It's like this haunted madness has crawled into my soul, sucking my life force and making me Hollow.

Dad's involvement only makes me feel more isolated. I already know not to trust him totally, but now I realize what he is capable of. When it came to bargaining, involving his daughter was a line he was willing to cross. In his twisted reasoning, he even felt relief over it. He rationalized it in his mind like he has a lot of things.

On the other hand, he has my sympathy. I know how persuasive and intimidating Skull can be. When Dad said he's powerful, he was referring to Landon 1.0. A powerful man, yes. But not unhinged. Not deranged. Not a killer. Skull is Landon's darker half. He's the one who was rejected, cast away like an extra game piece that came in a set. The game would go on without him, and all would be well at the top of the hill.

Or so it was thought.

Fueled by revenge, there is no stopping him now.

I lift my head, startled by the sound of the door slamming shut. But nobody has come in from the rain. God, did someone leave? Was I not alone this whole time and didn't know it?

Something catches the corner of my eye: a glint of light near the counter's edge. Goosebumps flash over my body as I focus on a familiar object draped over a piece of paper. A delicate silver chain trails the skull, rose, and black diamond—proof that he was here. That feeling in the back of my mind that I was not alone is now blatantly confirmed. Skull is keeping tabs on me. He brought this as a reminder: I am his.

I reach out and tug the piece of paper from beneath the necklace, reading the letter scrolled in red:

You forgot something. Be a good girl. Keep it on!

"For protection," I mutter with watery eyes. So I'm not dry inside, after all. I can still tear up for this man because he knows how to get to me. His every maddening calculation pulls me tighter in his grasp. I look down at the wedding ring on my finger. What would he have done if I hadn't worn it today? Would he notice or care as much? I only wear it for pretenses. The town expects to see it. I'm no longer simply Bookstore Bethany but a Greylinn, the new wife on the hill. This necklace isn't about that, though.

I pluck the cold chain, slowly pulling it into my hand until the gemstone rests at the center of my palm. This dark beauty is a blessing wrapped in a curse. He said it was for protection, but why did he truly give it to me? How does this factor into his master plan? The wedding ring makes sense, but this? This is something else. Something more... personal, somehow. He said he had this custom-made for me. Skull's twisted interpretation of something meaningful between two people? It feels like a declaration of ownership, not love. Maybe that's all he knows.

Will ever know.

When the door suddenly opens, a towering, broad-shouldered figure in a dark hoodie appears. He stands with his back to the rain, his face shrouded in shadow as he watches me.

"May I help you?"

He lets the door fall shut behind him before he locks it. "Quite the reverse," he says in a low, gravelly voice.

"What are you doing?!" I protest, reaching for my phone.

But it's futile. I can see enough of his face as he approaches to know it's him—his scent assaults my mind and body, flooding me with heated memories: skin to skin in the dark of night amidst screams. Not just my screams. He makes me feel so damn confused and naughty as blood rushes down, needling my core with angst.

"What do you want?" I ask, my voice tense.

He quickly comes around the counter, and I gasp when he takes my hand, tugging me behind the sorting table stacked with books. "Turn around," he orders, and my heartbeat speeds as I pivot to face the dark corner with the chair in it. "Am I in trouble?" I ask, half-joking.

My breathing hitches when he wraps his strong arms around my waist. His hands brush over mine, and he opens my closed fist, pulling the necklace from it.

"It occurred to me...you might need help," he whispers into my ear, sucking my lobe until my pussy tingles. "I don't need help," I pant as he reaches his other hand between my thighs, cupping my sex. "You do. Mm, your pussy is hot."

Teasingly, he releases his grip, bringing his hands to my neck before dropping the necklace down my collarbone. "It has a tiny clasp," he complains.

"I can do it," I say.

"No. I want to."

"Why do I have to wear it?"

"I told you."

"For protection?"

"Yes."

"From what?'

This time he slides his hand between my thighs from

behind, and I moan when he possessively grabs my pussy. He bites my earlobe. "Do you want me inside you?"

My mouth shoots open as he thrusts his hips forward, his hardening bulge smacking my ass. He slaps my thigh, making me yelp. "Answer me." His deep voice is low and full of urgency as the sound of his zipper slides down.

"Y—" As the first syllable leaves my lips, he palms my throat with his large hand from behind while shoving my leggings down. The steely length of his fat cock slaps between my thighs. "Fuck, you feel good," he rasps, sliding back and forth over my labia, making me dripping wet as he fucks my thighs. Each time his shaft hits my clit, an uncontrollable moan escapes my gaping mouth. His clutch on my throat slides upward to my chin, and I bite and suck his finger as he slides it between my teeth.

With his body weight, he pushes me toward the chair, and I climb into it on my knees. I grasp the back of the chair tightly as he slams his cock inside me, making me cry out.

"That's right, baby. *Scream* for me," he thrusts harder and harder.

He fucks me so hard that I almost forget where I am. I would never have imagined that I'd have sex at work. But right now... All I want is what he has to give. Maybe it's fucked up, but I don't care at the moment. I want to hear and feel him getting off inside me, and I want to come all over his monster cock.

His hard body gloves me fully from behind, his pelvis slamming against my ass. With each thrust, I widen my knees a little more until he's deep inside me. When he hits my cervix, I cry out again, and he grunts before slowing to a stop. I can tell that he's about to come and needs to pull out soon.

"Not yet," I beg, and he resumes, slowly, deeply, fucking me from behind.

Mm, god...ye-s-s.

I grab hold of his forearm, nails digging as my body flushes hot, nearing the edge. My body clenches around his manhood, and he suddenly pulls from my body, coming all over my ass with a groan. He pushes me back into the chair when I try to turn around. His fingers thrust inside me, replacing the rhythm of his cock as I grind my hips against his hand. I moan as I finally fall over the edge of sweet release. He slowly pulls his fingers from me before smacking me on the ass. "Good girl."

I hear his zipper as I catch my breath, and when I turn around this time, he doesn't stop me. He stares down at me, his face shadowed save for the shine of his grey eyes and where the low light catches the edge of his handsome jaw, chiseled into a square with that perfect divot at the center.

"Can you please hand me a towel from beneath the counter?" I ask.

He stares at me a moment longer before going to the counter. When he crouches down, I imagine this becoming a habit. Skull visiting at odd times and locking my store without notice. This is so unlike me. He's turned my life into something nearly unrecognizable. How many little dark secrets will Bookstore Bethany stack up due to this dangerously deranged, uber-sexy man?

I catch the towel he tosses, wiping myself before pulling my pants up.

I follow him as he walks around the counter toward the door. This is how he is. He comes and goes of his own accord without warning. He knows he can depend on me to be here waiting. Maybe not waiting consciously, but in the back of my mind, it's like I always am. Waiting for him like the good girl he knows I am.

He came crashing into my life; I'm the dependable sandy beach, taking the ebb and flow of his volatile tide. He makes me cry, he makes me come, and in his dark way, he keeps me alive.

"You didn't answer my question," I say to his back as he reaches the door.

He turns. "The necklace?" he asks.

"Yeah."

"I told you."

"To keep me safe from what?"

"From myself," he says, disappearing into the rain.

* * *

The feel of him all over my body lingers as I splash my face with cool water. I don't want to look flushed-faced when a customer walks in. I still can't believe I had sex at work. As I exit the restroom, a thought occurs to me. I bring my hand to the necklace around my neck, pondering a crucial question I forgot to ask Dad. Crucial to me anyway. When I reach the front of the store, I grab my phone from the counter and text him.

When was that photo of you taken?

At first, I didn't find it odd that Landon 2.0 would take the time to custom-make a piece of jewelry for an employee's daughter, whom he planned to trick into marriage—his way of wooing me. But I want to know how long he'd been planning this before closing in on me. When exactly did he have the cameras installed at my place? When my phone beeps, I'm already glued to the screen.

I forget—a while.

I'm talking about the blackmail photo, Dad.
Yeah. I figured—a year or so.

A year? I keep condensing the timeline to weeks or months since Skull stormed into town and stole his twin's identity. I didn't want to believe that this had gone on that long, that the crime I witnessed a year ago was him. I didn't want to believe the local conspiracy theorists that all the strange murders over the last year were connected.

But, now...

I pull out my laptop and sit in the chair, looking into the Sleepy Hollow murders. I know I saw a timeline in the local news at some point. Scrolling through search results, I finally find what I'm looking for, refreshing my memory over the list of "masked-man" victims and crime scene locations where their bodies were sliced up into a pool of blood, beginning in descending order with the massacre at the Sleepy Hollow Inn.

Before that, there was a murder in the casino parking lot and outside a warehouse. The list goes on. I pause when I get to the murder that occurred in an alleyway a year ago. My body breaks out in chills, recalling the slicing motion of the curved blade and the sudden turn of that skull mask in my direction, the grey eyes seeming to almost twinkle while pinning me in place, my knees wobbling before finally getting the nerve to run my ass off. This moment must have been a matter of seconds, but it felt longer, stretched into agonizing minutes as he chased me. With my deafening heartbeat in my ears, I sprinted, looking back until he was gone. Or was he? I was too afraid to do anything except hide and hope that he wouldn't find me. But he did. I didn't know it at the time.

I blocked out the trauma to the point that I wasn't one of the believers that the random-seeming murders every few months were connected. I guess I couldn't face it until it was facing me.

My stomach pits when I reach the bottom of the list. The first masked-man knifing incident in our area occurred at Rockefeller State Park over two years ago. Two fucking years ago! God, how long has the real Landon Greylinn been dead? How long has Skull haunted this town and my steps?

This time, when I send a text message, I send it to him.

You never answered my question.

I'm too afraid to text the words *Rob Miller* and make Skull think I'm setting him up or something. I want to know if it was him in the alley or one of his cronies that day. I want to know if he followed me home. It probably makes no difference. I'm stuck in this quagmire either way. But it nags at me.

I tap my nails nervously on the counter, awaiting his response amidst the sickening flap of black butterflies in my gut. We can't discuss this topic over the phone, so why bother? He's going to think I'm putting him on the spot again. I've never been good at confrontation. It makes me nervous, so I tend to avoid it. But my life has become a dark riddle that must be solved before it eats me inside out.

I jump when my phone rings, my heart racing.

"What question, Bethany?"

By the graveled brooding in his deep voice, I worry about what he's up to. He isn't in Landon Greylinn mode, that's for sure.

I clear my throat. "I...wasn't expecting you to call."

"I have a minute."

"Never mind."

"What is it?"

"I...just...want to know if that night at the party...was our first meeting."

He chuckles. "So that's what this is about?"

"I told you, just forget it."

"I think you already know the answer, Bethany."

"Do I? Fine, then."

"You don't sound satisfied. Do I need to pay another visit to your store?"

"No," my cheeks flush.

"Then what do you want, baby? Spit it out before I make you swallow."

Did he just say that?

"Alright. I want to know how long you've been... watching me. I mean, before we were..."

"Married? Long enough to learn."

"Learn what?"

"You. Your habits, quirks. What you ate...who you talked to...what you wore to bed. The way your nightie—mm—hugged your breasts and exposed your thick thighs when you crawled in to read, thinking nobody was watching. I...enjoyed getting to know my future wife. Is that enough answers for you, Beth?"

"And...what about the necklace? When did you have that made?"

"Not long after the first night I saw you."

"When?"

He sighs. "At your little shop. It was snowing. You had on those black reading glasses you wear sometimes. Grey sweater. Sitting in your chair with a book in your nose. I startled you when I asked you your name."

So it was winter. That would be over a year ago. I don't remember this.

"But you already knew my name," I say, referring to his scheme with Dad.

"No. I knew nothing of you. I wanted to change that."

"So that's what you set out to do?"

"Yes."

"Why did it take you so long?"

"To what? Propose? Put a ring on it?"

"To give me the necklace."

"Ah, back to the necklace again. I didn't realize it mattered so damn much to you."

"It matters to you, too."

"Yeah, and I already told you the reason."

"For protection."

"That's right. Do me a favor, and don't fucking forget it."

I sigh, frustrated. "But *why, Landon*?"

He goes quiet, like me calling him that has thrown him off. He's not in Landon mode right now. I said that to get to him.

"Because, *Bethany*. It reminds me...of why I chose you. When I'm angry, I might forget. Do something rash. Got it?"

The threat in his dark tone makes me shiver deep in my bones.

"You don't trust yourself," I whisper, finally understanding.

"I trust *nobody*," he grits. The anger of this man runs deeper than I could ever fathom.

He sounds so cold and distant that I get this tinge of desperation to warm him somehow, to find a way to lull him to sanity. And I hate how the idea of teaching this twisted man to trust me feels like a mission I half want to endure. I can't possibly make him whole. He's a broken soul. But, goddamn. Why does part of me want to try?

* * *

I should want to be here in this sacred place I worked so hard for, surrounded by books---my kind of heaven arranged in neat rows inside a brick-and-mortar, with my name on the signage above the front door. That was my dream from an early age, and I've made it happen. But now...everything is upside down.

Today, I ignored every phone call and text after the sickening exchange I had with Dad. Trying to put it out of my head, the feeling of being sold out. The irony is that everybody keeps congratulating me on the marriage that resulted from my own father's betrayal. A marriage that was never supposed to happen to a man who was never supposed to be. Not Landon Greylinn. Not even Skull. An empty shell.

But then I couldn't resist answering his call.

I can't see straight after hanging up, the dark timber of his voice reverberating inside me like a second pulse. His hold gets stronger by the day. The more I squirm inside, the deeper his darkness digs into my soul, eating away.

Why do I want to cling to the hope of being his savior?

How can I save him when he's killing me in the process? Slowly but surely, I feel like the old me is fading along with my old dream. Like I'll soon be too ruined to enjoy what I've built.

He acts like he wants to help, but is it all a sham, like everything he stands for? He gave me this key, but why? What's his plot this time?

Ergh...

I raise my hands over my eyes, pushing my hair from my face with a weary sigh.

I never thought I wouldn't want to be in my bookstore. I

would live here around the clock if I'd had the upper story when I opened this place. I'm the kind of person who needs no separation from work because books are my life.

But right now...

God, I'm overwhelmed with cabin fever. I hate the feeling, but I must get some fresh air before my workday ends, and I have no choice but to return to that awful mansion on the hill—*home* now. The limo will come for me soon.

I push from the chair behind the counter and head for the exit, flipping the sign closed and locking the door.

Pulling my cardigan tight over my chest in the cool mist, I hungrily inhale fresh air while walking. I need this: movement and some freedom. I could go on for miles.

The sidewalk is cast in grey, waning daylight, and that word--*home*--throbs my aching temples with each step.

Home is a concept.

Home is a dark riddle housing this phantom pulse inside me.

Home is where the heart is stolen, and the dead are buried—the losers of a forgotten war still raging inside one man.

Home is where the throne is taken: a death mask, the king's crown.

Home is an illusion, a cadaver, a black and empty skull.

Mist turns to rain as my steps quicken over concrete, determined to reach the bay. I refuse to turn around to the muffled sound of an engine trailing behind. It's been steadily following since I left the shop, but I'm pretending not to notice. Maybe the limo driver has strict orders to keep me in line from point A to point B. Work to home. Home to work. Or maybe it's just a tourist heading to see the waves at high-tide.

Home. What the hell does that even mean anymore?

My head is spinning, but it's not from running. I feel like I'm losing my sanity or identity--and maybe that's exactly what he fucking wants. For me to get so buried inside his maze of madness that my sense of self morphs into whatever he's decided for me.

"*Home*, home on the *hill*..." I sing, quickening to a jog until my shoes finally reach sand.

I can't hear the car anymore, but I still resist turning around. I don't want to know what might be following me.

Reaching the lower beach, I scan the white caps rushing forward under a churning, thunderous sky. Dangerous time to be near the water. The waves are huge, and there's an obvious riptide channeling from the shore. Lightening strikes through the darkening sky and the rain beats harder as I imagine letting myself succumb to the coming crash. The water is cold enough, I'll be too stunned to feel pain as the riptide gulps me, sucking me deeply down and far from shore.

As if called by a darkly sweet siren, I step forward into the cool froth. A new wall of water builds in the distance, quickly coming. It's strangely exhilarating to imagine letting it take me, having it's way.

The high crest of rolling water comes fast, my heart racing. Just when I think I might go ahead and die, a hand clamps my shoulder hard, pulling me back. Instantly, I'm in the air.

"What the hell were you doing?" his deep voice reprimands.

He jogs with me cradled in his arms, and only after he puts me in the front seat of his SUV do I realize how badly I'm shivering. He buckles me in and turns the heat up.

When he looks at me from the driver's seat with a

frown, his grey eyes look pained under a glistening sheen of raw anger.

"Stupid girl," he hisses, his grey hoodie drenched. He flips his wet hair back, turning his attention to the road. He looks different somehow. I don't know why.

"I was...just..." I say, breathless. God, was I really going to do that? Die? What the hell is wrong with me...

"You know what I wish?" he says sharply.

"What?" My voice shakes as I squeeze my arms together, trying to stop this violent shiver.

"I wish...I could fucking trust you."

"But you don't trust anybody. Right?"

He stares at me momentarily, the sheen in his eyes deepening, watering slightly. For the first time, the pain in his eyes almost overpowers the anger. He isn't Landon or Skull right now. I don't know this man. But I want to.

His lips part, and the memory of the taste of his mouth spreads over my tongue.

"Yeah," he nods, as if reminding himself.

"But maybe you can," I offer, trying to get what I can from the moment.

"What would that take?" he asks.

"Trust is a two-way street," I say.

His eyes flick my way suspiciously. "What do you want from me, Bethany?"

Wow, that's a hard question to answer. In the context of this forced arrangement, I want...to know his real name. Stupid, I know. What will that help? He'll think I just want intel to use against him. His real name won't help me to *understand* him.

"Maybe to...know the real you," I finally say, and he smirks.

"You want the impossible," he dismisses bitterly.

"Why?"

He shakes his head, and when his troubled eyes flash my way, my heart sinks. I have an idea what he's about to say.

"Can't help you there," he shrugs.

I think I know why. Because not even he knows the answer to that question.

He's just a lost soul.

TWENTY-THREE

SKULL

Under the increasing rev of the engine, her voice begs me to slow down.

But that only makes me go faster.

I hit cruise control at ninety-five miles per hour along a sleepy stretch of old highway where I've got the road to myself. I drift between lanes, and she screams.

But that only makes me go faster, slamming through the rain along endless farms and tree orchards.

"Skull, stop!"

I glance at her, clutching her oh-shit-handle white-knuckled. It's always interesting which name she chooses to call me at whatever given moment. When I'm more myself and misbehaving, she calls me Skull.

Including when I'm swollen between her thick thighs, fucking her sweet pussy.

"I meant what I said, Beth."

"What? Please slow down."

"I love it when you scream."

She shakes her head with tears in her eyes.

"Where are you taking me?"

Not having an answer, I shrug, eyes on the road. It's getting dark, and the rain is picking up. Just as I see the "sharp turn" sign, I switch out of cruise control, adeptly hugging the bend in the road.

But slowing down only makes her cry more.

"Don't be a baby, baby," I tease.

"Fuck you."

I smirk at her, tired of this game. Tired of running. But it makes no difference. I'm set on a one-way trajectory to hell, and I'm taking my sweet baby with me.

Her phone rings, but she doesn't answer it. It rings again.

"Your people are calling," I frown, tired of the noise.

"Not in the mood to keep up pretenses," she says.

"Do it anyway," I demand before the ringing stops.

"Please take me back," she pleads.

"Back where, Bethany? What's in Sleepy Hollow for us?"

"Us?"

She looks genuinely confused.

"Is there no us, Beth?"

"Stop messing with me! I've done what you wanted."

I pull off the road and turn the car lights off, catching a glimpse of her angry stare as the light fades from her pretty face.

"Quitting isn't an option, Beth."

I listen to her thoughtful breath like I'm listening to the ocean waves roll in. To think she contemplated suicide gets under my skin. Nobody is allowed to take her life but me, and me alone.

"What happens if I do quit?" she sighs raggedly. "If I stop pretending, what will you do to me? Kill me?"

Not an easy question. "I don't want to kill you."

"Then what do you want from me? How much longer do I have to go along with this?"

"As long as it takes."

"To get your money?"

"Money is just a means to an end."

"How does this end, Skull?"

She gasps when I reach over and squeeze her arm like a squeeze-toy in my palm, enjoying the supple feeling settling between my fingers. My cock hardens.

"Tell me. Tell me how it ends," she whispers.

"I can tell you how this moment is going to end. With you on my lap, your pussy slamming over my cock, hugging me like I was hugging that road, like I'm the fucking joy ride of your life. Because you know I am.

Your pussy is mine. I bet you're already wet for me. Admit it."

By the time she exhales, my pants are already unzipped, the seat pushed back, making room for her body over mine.

"Don't bring your panties with you," I tell her, listening to the sound of sniffles and the pull of fabric. Like a good girl, she quietly climbs over the console, naked from the waist down.

My hands instantly find her juicy thighs, palming the meat on her luscious bones as I pull her into my lap. Her wetness glides teasingly over the top of my shaft.

"Mm-fuck," I moan, guiding her back and forth over my erection until I'm rock-hard and dying to be deep inside her. But first...

I grab her by the hair, forcing her mouth to mine. I need to suck her tongue, I need to taste her essence while I fuck her.

The moan from her lips makes me violent with need

and I tighten my grip on her hair as I bite her lip, forcing my cock between her pussy lips--oh...fuck-yeah.

I release her hair, grabbing both thighs in my hands as I thrust hard inside her. The more she moans, the harder I slam her down, deeper inside her secret heaven.

But I need to taste her sweet tits on my tongue so I release my hold on her thighs, shoving her shirt up. She doesn't stop fucking me when my hands are no longer guiding her.

Like a pro, she grinds her hips into me, her needy clit smashing the base of my dick like she's just as desperate as I am. Just like I knew she would be.

"Yeah, baby. Fuck me hard," I mutter with a mouth full of nipple. My tongue swirls, sucks, and bites as her pussy pulses rhythmically over my swollen cock.

I'm damn near the edge when I retake control.

I slap her ass hard and she screams, making me lose it.

When I come inside her, violently thrusting her body into mine, she sounds as unhinged as I feel, moaning more loudly than I've heard her.

The beautiful abandon in her release is sweet music to my ears under the beat of the rain outside the vehicle. I want to hear that sound over and over again. But she tries to leave my lap before I'm done with her.

"Enough," she cries, and when I kiss her, I taste the salty tears on her tongue.

"Okay," I say, caressing her hair from her face.

"What are you doing to me?" she whispers, and I feel her words in my chest. It's a strange feeling.

She climbs from me into her seat, and we both dress to the sound of her ringing phone before I get back on the road. I had more plans for her than this tonight, but...

Funny how I don't like the sound of her tears as much as I do her scream.

"Shit," she mumbles, her phone at her face.

"What is it?"

"Nothing."

"Tell me."

She sighs. "Fine. It's my friends from New York. They're paying me a surprise visit."

I run my hand through my hair. I don't like the sound of that. I hate company, and I hate uninvited company even more.

"Friends? Didn't even attend your wedding," I snipe.

"They're going to be wondering the same thing," she says under her breath.

Yes, her life is a mess, and it's all my doing. But she has no idea how fucked up life could be for her.

"Rules. There will be rules," I say, already regretting it.

TWENTY-FOUR
bethany

HE PUTS ON SLEEP TOKEN, and we both go quiet, listening with eyes on the dark and winding road. Our sex in the air mixes with the rain scent when he cracks the window.

He wanted more of me. I felt overwhelmed, and he let me go. But I can still feel him lingering all over my body. His taste on my tongue and the sting of his teeth on my lips. The slap of his strong hands on my ass and the sore satisfaction between my thighs where he filled me up. My pussy throbbed for every bit he had to give, and god, I never wanted anything so bad before. Every inch of him beating inside me. The man is a delicious demon, and I'm the wayward sinner.

I didn't want to want him so bad.

It came on fast, just like before. Goddamn, how the hell does he have this effect on me? And he knows it. He fucking knows it.

When he lights a cigarette, I watch the smoke rise around his beautiful face, his pale eyes full of brooding beneath a troubled brow. Like the moon's dark side, he is even more unreachable than the former Greylinn heir sitting pretty up on that hill. His entitled position is no longer something to envy and aspire to. Those days are gone. The scarred remains of that legacy are scattered into the dark abyss, and I've been sucked into its cold embrace.

"What kind of rules?" I ask, trying to draw him out. But he's despondent, my voice a distant echo. Is he plotting his next move or regretting his last? Where do I fit into this equation when all is said and done?

Sometimes, it feels like we are both stuck in this together. But maybe he wants me to believe that. I don't know; even if we are in the same boat, he's driving it. The sharks circling answer to him. I am just a pawn, clinging to oxygen.

The hard part is when he makes me feel like he can give it to me. Those fleeting moments when he makes me high. Like slowly but surely, I'm becoming addicted to this shit. Surely, I'm getting more off track from reality with each passing day.

What will my friends think of me? God, I've never been a good liar.

Rather, I never knew I had it in me until my wedding night. Facing my mom with the biggest lie of my existence hanging over me like a death threat, I put on a stellar act. My mother believed the lie. In part because she wanted to. But maybe that is the case for everyone. They believe in what they want to, what is easy or convenient. But will my best friends be so easily fooled? Can I convince them this is the life I want, and all is well for the sake of survival? If I don't, they could be in danger—people who know too much end up dead.

So, I have no choice but to put on a smiley-faced show. My life is good. I married a billionaire and all that jazz.

Yes, it's been almost a year since I left them. I was supposed to stay in New York with my besties, but I drifted back to home base like a rogue. I wasn't cut out for the major city, but leaving wasn't as easy as I thought it would be. It came with pros and cons. I gained a bookstore but lost my friends. It's hard to make new friends in your small hometown where everything is set in place, and locals have already made up their minds about each other. We know too much dirt and rumors not to feel wary, and there is so much needless backstabbing. I call it the small-town mentality. Petty over the kinds of things the hustle and bustle of a big city doesn't allow time for. But regardless, this is home. The roads, beaches, and parks are the stuff of my memories, forever tied to my childhood. That and I was working hard to make a solid adult life for myself here. I had my bookstore. My excitement the catharsis found in books. I was good with that arrangement until Skull came along.

Life got fucking interesting, alright. Upended.

"Did you use the key?" his voice startles me from my thoughts.

He turns the music a tad lower. I've got his attention now.

"Yes."

"And?"

"And...I'm glad to have more space," I say, not wanting to get into what I found. I don't know what his reaction would be.

"Good," he says.

"Why did you give it to me?"

His brows pinch. "Why not?" he shrugs as if it's nothing.

"Have you...been up there before?"

"No need."
"But you have the keys to the city. Aren't you curious?"
"Could care less."
"What *do* you care about in this world besides--"
"Winning?"
"Is that what you call this?"

When his eyes cut my way, they are full of anger. "I'm not losing, Bethany," he hisses.

"Is it black and white? Maybe you're winning and losing at the same time. I know what that's like."

"What are you getting at?"

I shake my head, wishing I could think of the right words to convince him to—

"Don't worry, baby. This game will soon be over."

"How does it end?"

"It ends when it ends."

"Will more people...die?"

His ocean eyes are arctic cold when they flash my way.

"I can't tell you what you want to hear."

My eyes water. "*Why?* It doesn't have to be—"

"Oh, it does! I can promise you one thing. More. Blood. Will *spill*."

TWENTY-FIVE
bethany

THE STUDENT NEWSPAPER called us ABA—pronounced Abuh around school. Albi, Bethany, and Mary Anne sometimes went by her middle name because there were so many Marys at our Catholic school. The three of us have been together since we were five.

Reunited, I've never felt more distant from them than on this dark day.

"Let's see the koi pond!" chirps Albi, and I desperately let myself get sucked into her blissfully energetic ignorance, transporting me back to when we roamed these grounds as teens. We would get lost for hours, plotting our destinies in this place full of good fortune. Or so it was. Or so we believed. The rumors of ghosts only made it more charming and intriguing. Like a badge of honor, all old grand places have ghosts.

"Okay," I agree, lulled by the parallel between this surreal moment and happier memories. Albi looks nearly the same, just more mature and a little less skinny, in a good way. Same blonde bangs cutting just above her brow.

Same long, perfectly pressed hair swishing when she turns and leads the way over cobblestones.

"Remember, Big Bo?" laughs freckle-faced Mary, touching my arm, and I smile, remembering the giant among the orange fish. We used to point and giggle at the big fat sucker.

"Maybe he's buried in the pet cemetery," Albi winks over her shoulder.

We would always explore the different cemeteries. But we didn't know about the hidden ones or the ones underground. The tombs above tombs—the spoils of war.

"*Well,* Bethie," sighs Mary, tugging at her dark sidebraid as we pass under the shedding fall canopy.

"What?" I shrug, but I already know.

"I just…can't freakin' believe this is your home now."

She says that, like, she doesn't know the horrors under its roof. To her, this is still the place of dreams, the place to be, the highest and most decadent point in Sleepy Hollow.

Everyone lamented when the gates were finally closed to the public because we all had felt the magic roaming the grounds, inhaling the exalted air. It was almost religious how the beauty and grandeur of the old estate seemed to grace visitors, especially in the summer when the endlessly lush, expansive grounds were in full bloom. People left in a better mood than when they came. Britain has its palaces and castles, and we, in this little spot of New England, had Greylinn Manor.

"Fountain is off for winter," I say, staring into the dark water at the edge. I can feel Albi staring me down, wanting more answers than I can give.

"Would have loved to have attended your wedding, *that's all,*" she continues, starting where we left off inside.

"Agreed," frowns Mary, shaming me more.

"I told you," I sigh. "It wasn't a real wedding; we eloped."

Mary's brows pinch, perplexed.

"But you said you didn't leave town," she questions, begging for an explanation.

"I didn't."

Albi cocks her head slightly. "You eloped *here?*"

I nod. "Yeah. Right here. It was at a party. He…caught me by surprise."

They exchange a look.

"But we didn't even know you were dating," says Mary with a look that's meant to guilt.

"I know," I say, apologetic. " It moved fast."

They stare at me, perplexed and blinking. They are trying to process a lie that makes no sense. Their instincts tell them something is off, and they are not wrong. But lives depend upon the lie, and I must keep to it. Life is a game now. Or maybe it always was, and I was good at keeping on the sidelines. Now, times have changed. I'm fully embroiled in the worst of ways, and though there may be an end to it, I can't predict the outcome.

"I'm *sorry,*" I offer. "I know it's crazy," I swallow over the lump in my throat.

"Oh, it's okay, Beth." Mary opens her arms, beckoning me for a needed hug. I try not to cry when her arms touch down around me, but my eyes flood with tears. "Happy tears," I assure them both.

"Well, then. Congratulations, babe. If you're happy, I'm happy," concludes Albi.

"Thank you" is all I can sincerely muster because I don't have it in me to profess happiness. I'm sinking deeper into madness by the day.

"So, where is the *Mister* Greylinn?" Albi teases.

My face flushes hot with the mention of his name. The man they are referring to is dead, of course. But they won't know the difference when they see the dark-souled replacement inhabiting this mansion.

"He's around," I shrug as it starts to rain.

The rain picks up fast, so we hurry back, and a nauseating feeling hits me after the resounding click of the big black doors shutting behind us. It feels like a trap because it is. This isn't home; it's a living tomb, and I can't help but worry that I've sealed my friend's fate for the worst by closing them inside its haunted halls.

It will be okay, I console myself. I have to follow the rules.

His rules. "Don't forget, Bethany," he whispered, caressing my hair with a threatening look in his sky-grey eyes, his forehead wrinkled into troubled lines.

Rule number one. Don't go wandering the East Wing. It is forbidden. There are bloody, dark secrets there and fucked up memories. One of them is my own. Down on my knees. His cock in my mouth. His PA—that mean bitch—spying around the corner.

Rule number two. Don't go outside after dark. No idea why. But Skull was adamant. That's okay. I have no intention of doing so. There's a slasher on the loose—more than one.

Rule number three. Finish the dreaded horror novel. It started interesting, but it's creepy as hell. He wants me to keep reading until I'm done. *Why?*

Rule number four. Most importantly, keep lying. Lie my little heart out until I'm deep blue in my lying little face. That is my primary mission. To be a good girl and play along. Because good girls...

JASMINE P. DANE

Never.
Tell.

TWENTY-SIX
bethany

ALBI RUNS her hand along one of the large columns framing the foyer, and it occurs to me how the light, warm flecks of brown in the marble strangely match her eyes. She blows a wayward strand of blonde hair from her brow.

"I'm still processing that you live here, Bee."

I force a smile. "Yeah. Me too."

"*So*, when do we get to meet your husband? Officially, I mean," asks Mary.

"We know him, of course. But he doesn't know *us*," adds Albi.

Yes, everyone in town knows about the king on the hill. We grew up knowing and hearing the gossip. Like peasants, we would visit the grounds when the family was away on vacation or holed up inside, avoiding us, lowly tourists.

"Um, he's working," I say, hoping to drop the topic. "Doesn't want to be bothered."

Albi laughs. "Landon Greylinn working for a living?"

"*Al!*" shames Mary. "Don't be rude."

"It's okay, hon," I force a smile. "Believe it or not. Even trust-fund babies have work."

"Of course. I was only kidding," says Albi apologetically.

Mary hugs me for the third time in an hour; her soft black hair smells like jasmine. "I'm just glad you're happy. And *safe*. Man, I thought New York had crime problems. Sleepy Hollow's been in the news a lot, huh?"

My stomach drops. She doesn't know the half of it.

"Yeah, our little town is going mad." It's time to change the subject. "Are you guys hungry?"

"What does Landon think of all these murders?" asks Albi.

I roll my eyes. "How about what I think? Honestly, I'm worn out. It's all anyone's been talking about. Come on, I'll show you the fabulous gourmet kitchen."

"Food sounds good," says Mary.

"Wine sounds even better," chirps Al.

"Agreed." Drinking with my girls and forgetting my problems for a few hours sounds perfect.

I don't even mind answering a gazillion questions about the décor en route, most of which I don't have answers for.

"How's the master's suite? Remember how we always wanted to see it?"

"We're not in the same room as Mr. and Mrs. Greylinn—his parents. That would be weird."

"But, of course, this place has multiple suites."

"Yeah," I mutter, plotting how to avoid giving them the full tour they'll expect.

"Are you in the East Wing?"

The tone in Mary's voice says it all. Finally, the mysteries of this elite time capsule will be revealed. I am the key to the access they—*we*—always craved. If only it were so simple.

"No. The East Wing is…under renovation," I lie. That's to be my excuse for not taking them there.

When we enter the kitchen, I audibly gasp when I see Jada leaning against the bar and looking at her phone. I thought we'd been purposely avoiding each other. I don't want to know what she heard and saw the other night when I was down on my knees with a mouth full of—

"Well, well," she says, raising a skinny brow like we've entered *her* realm. She's always dressed like a New York fashion magazine executive. Tonight, she's wrapped in a skintight checkered dress, rows of pink and red gemstones winding tightly around her neck. Her glistening short red hair looks fresh from the salon, cutting a sharp, angular line at her jawbone.

Albi and Mary exchange a subtle glance. I know what they're thinking. It's not just the territorial look on Jada's face that makes this encounter awkward, but her outfit. We're clothed in jeans, leggings, and tees while she's dressed to the nines, reducing us to grunge. But, after all, she represents this grand estate, I suppose. Or maybe she's taking her job a little too seriously, just as she does herself.

"So, this is Jada, Landon's estate manager. Jada, this is Albi and Mary Anne."

"Pleasure," she smiles, eyeing my friends suspiciously.

My dislike of her deepens every time I see her. She doesn't want me here. That much is obvious. I'm a thorn in her side for *reasons*. I'm sure she has a thing for my so-called *hubby*. I don't believe her lies that she's from here. These two have a hidden history outside of Sleepy Hollow. As far as she's concerned, I'm the outsider. But I'll be damned if I let her bully me.

She pushes off the bar, and her shiny red stilettos tap on white marble. "I'm sure Mr. Greylinn has told you that—"

"The East Wing is closed. Yes, I know. Thanks, Jada. We'll be having dinner now."

The irritation in her face recovers quickly, followed by a curt smile. "Good to meet you, ladies. Have a nice evening, Mrs. Greylinn."

I smile at her, hoping Albi and Mary didn't pick up on the note of disdain at the end of her sentence. That would only lead to more questions I can't answer.

When she leaves, they look at me with raised brows.

"See, Sleepy Hollow has both crime and snobby fashionistas. Who needs New York?" I joke. They laugh, and Albi wastes no time investigating the wine rack, and I'm luckily out of dodge. Mary heads to the massive cabinet fridge, and I sit on a stool at the island, happy to have my old friends under one roof but nervous about how I will manage this without getting into trouble with the beast of the house.

When the door rings and rings again, I expect to see Jada or *Landon* appear when I head in that direction. But no.

It's me who ends up answering.

My mouth turns dry at the sight of him. His blonde beard is trimmed, short, and tidy. Same cold blue eyes. *Gargoyle.*

"Hi, Mrs. Greylinn. Can Landon come out and *play?*"

Never did the word "play" sound so sinister before. I stare at his smirking face. "Excuse me?"

He rubs the back of his head, the tattoos on his muscled arm visible through his thin, fitted white shirt.

"See, I've been trying to reach him. He isn't answering his phone."

"Well, I guess he's busy then." He looks over my shoulder, and I turn to see Albi and Mary donning glasses of red wine with curious eyes. "Friend of Landon's," I explain.

"He's buff," Albi whispers. I shake my head in disapproval, and when I turn back to Gargoyle, he's grinning crookedly before motioning at the car parked in the port cochere. The engine's hum stops, and a head of dark curls appears near the driver's side. Oh, shit. He brought the *Devil*.

"We aren't expecting company," I say, panicked. Skull's henchmen are not what I had in mind this evening.

He winks at me. "Oh, we just wanna have a word with the *man*. Then we'll be on our way."

I wish I could believe him.

Devil appears on the landing, nearly as tall and broad-shouldered as Gargoyle.

He steps forward. "How's it goin', ladies?"

Moving aside to let them in, I pull my phone from my pocket and dial Landon. When he doesn't answer, I leave a text. *Your friends are here looking for you.*

Where the heck is he? Maybe he's sleeping. He seemed out of sorts when we returned from the hellishly scary speed-ride he took me on after snatching me from the beach like a bandit. Only during sex in the driver's seat did I forget how much I hate him. Maybe hate isn't the right word. More of a deep-seated resentment, along with...other mixed emotions.

Before I can say a word, my friends have already introduced themselves. So, Gargoyle is named Ace, and Devil is named Jay, but everybody calls him Banks.

The most unfortunate part about this is that I can already tell who is into whom. Albi and Ace are already flirting, and Banks looks at Mary like she's on the dessert menu.

The red fabric bulging from his pant pocket catches my eye, and I swear I can see the tip of a horn. Is he carrying his mask with him? A chill runs down my spine as I recall the way he threatened me at my bookstore, and then there was the ball. At least one person died that night.

"Yeah, I'd love a glass," he smiles, keeping pace with her.

She only sees the man, not the monster.

God, this can't be happening.

We stop at the sitting room, and Albi is working the bar like a pro when Jada appears. For once, I'm relieved to see her. She can take these guys to find Landon, and I can lock my friends in a room until morning. I'm sure that will go over well.

"He's not here," she shrugs, and my stomach drops to the floor.

"Where is he?" I ask, but I seem to be the only one who cares. The flirtatious conversing in the background is coming on thick, and I'm losing control of my girls-only, psycho-free night.

"Business," she answers condescendingly. I cross my arms with a frown, wanting to slap some answers from her.

"Do you know when he'll return?"

She twists her lips, thinking. "Hard to tell."

"What *exactly* is he up to, Jada?"

She raises an amused brow. "Oh, he didn't tell you?"

I shake my head, cheeks flushing. Yes, Jada, there are things you know that I don't. But that goes both ways.

"I'm sorry. I'll leave that for him to explain," she yawns, looking at her wristwatch. "I've been up since three a.m.," she mutters. When she turns to leave, I grab her arm, and she looks at my hand like I've got the cooties.

"Listen, Jada. Sure, you don't want to take these guys off my hands?"

She glances over at the wine-clanking circle. Her eyes are getting heavier by the second, but I'm desperately hopeful that maybe she's used to dealing with these two;

perhaps she's into a kinky menage a trois, or something. I don't know. I don't care. Only to be rid of them.

I sigh in relief when she turns and goes to the bar and pours herself a glass of wine. That's the spirit, Jada! But without saying another word, she takes her glass of wine and exits. *No!* That won't do.

I follow her into the hall. "Jada, come back!"

I sound so pathetic, but I can't help it. If this is her turf, why is she suddenly not acting like it? She's the manager or the PA or whatever the hell she is. Isn't dealing with unwanted company in her job description?

"Jada, *please!*"

When she pivots around, she looks at me with a wicked twinkle in her soulless eyes.

"They're *your* problem."

"What? I barely know them. Can't you just—"

"Have fun with that," she says over her shoulder, leaving me.

My throat tightens with anger as I pull out my phone and try Landon again. This time, it goes straight to voicemail. *Dammit!* I'm unsure if not knowing where he is would be so unnerving if it weren't for his friends being here. But my gut is in a million knots. More than ever, I realize how dependent on him I've become. He's the center of this twisted game, the game master, and like a pawn on the board, I'm spinning out of control in his absence.

I'm about to text him when I jump, startled by screams. The hairs raise on my neck as I bolt down the hall, tennies smacking on marble. I can only follow the traveling noise—shouting, yelping, crying out. The lights shut off ahead, room by room, as the screams travel further away. It's as if the girls are chasing the light, and I'm running in the dark after them. After the ones hunting them.

Please, let this not be real--just some wild fun. No blood. No death. Nothing like that.

Just a silly game.

Note: before being released to retailers, the subsequent books in this series will continue exclusively as WIPs @ GothikaBooks.Com

volume two

HIS ONLY DESIRE

author's note

His Only Desire is a dark mafia romance.

Trigger warnings include stalking, dubious consent, bondage, captivity, graphic sexual content, gore, murder, gun and knife violence, and knife play.

playlist

Scan me

ONE

pirate

PINK TOOLS. Everything is labeled. There is a hint of vanilla scent in the air—no gas odor from the lawn mower that she never uses. A lawn maintenance crew comes twice per month. She isn't filthy rich, but she's doing pretty well for herself. Being a legal secretary for the mob pays well. She doesn't think of it that way. No, she's just a regular person working for a legitimate firm while finishing her law degree. Hard-working. Innocent. Squeaky clean. On the outside.

But I know a dirty little secret about Cherry Coleson, so I don't feel so bad about sullying her prissy, tidy shed. Its location is convenient. I needed to quickly get my latest target out of the trunk of my Aston Martin and into a private space.

It's a lucky coincidence that Cherry, who goes by Cher, is Dipshit's ex-girlfriend, and she happens to live near a popular body dumping ground. She is the next target on my list.

So I figure I can keep things efficient and interrogate or

kill Dipshit—probably both—while I'm waiting for her to get home from work.

"I don't fucking know anything!" he pleads, muffled through the fabric, as I pull a blackjack from my leather jacket. Mm, this one's a solid beauty. Vintage hand-stitched brown leather, leather strap, about eleven inches long, and densely filled with lead shot. Police don't use them anymore.

Tapping the heavy rod against my palm, I admire the weight of it--*damn*. "I call this the 'bone breaker.'"

He grimaces, shaking his head. "Look, *man*. I told you—

"I'm only going to ask once before I *strike*."

His panicked eyes flit around the room for an escape. He would much rather run than answer my question. The truth is painful to admit. But I've offered him the motivation of pain to outmeasure that. My cold blue eyes lock on him, and I speak in a low, firm tone.

"Where did you hide the money you stole?"

He hesitates, mouth twitching. I can tell he's racking his brain for a lie, a way out of this. But he's reached a dead end with me. I'm a one-way street to hell.

I raise the blackjack, and his small, dark eyes twirl. "I truly don't—"

"You *do*."

He's a liar by trade. It's my job to collect intel on targets. Often, that's done remotely. But sometimes, intel gathering gets physical. Deadly.

"I-I *swear* you've got the wrong guy, I'm—"

"A lying. Fucking. Shit! I snap, raising the blackjack before swiftly striking down against his ankle. The bone makes a slight cracking sound, and he wails like he's dying as I let the blackjack slip to the concrete. I was going easy. It's a minor break that will heal in six to eight weeks. I typically go for the ribs or fingers when interrogating, but I will need him to use his hands in a moment, and I want to keep him from running when I make him walk the cobblestone path leading inside Cher's trendy cottage with hardwood floors and painted brick. *Honey, I'm home.* The thought makes me smirk.

He cries like a baby, and it gets under my skin.

"You know what I hate about you, Dipshit? You're not just a skeezy liar. You're a pathetic fucking pervert."

Sometimes, after he leaves his law office, he likes to put on a hoodie and hang out at the arcade, hitting on underage girls and exchanging digits before meeting up at shady motels. Two of whom have gone missing. The HO doesn't care about that part, but I do. I'm going to find out where he hid them.

I step closer, bending down with my mouth to his ear. He reeks of alcohol and expensive cologne. "Last chance," I whisper, and a row of goosebumps forms along his skinny neck.

"B-bank, my fuckin' bank," he whines.

"Thought you'd say that."

I look up to the sound of a car pulling in. Going to the window, I recognize the white Volvo—*damn.* I've been watching her for weeks, enough to know she's home early tonight.

I untie his hands, not worried about him trying to fight or run since his leg is broken and his feet are bound. Pulling a laptop from my black bag, I unlock it before placing it into his lap.

"See that desktop note. That's the routing number where you will send the money you stole. Log in to your bank."

He nods, immediately getting to work as I look over his shoulder.

"Shit, I-uh...don't have my banking password memorized. I...can access it on my phone. In my pocket."

"Pull it out. Make one attempt at a call or text; I'll break your other leg."

He does as told, clicking on his banking app, logging in, and routing the money back to Sev Peters, the man he stole it from. Not just any man, but an associate of the H.O., aka Hellfire Organization. Named after the biker club the founder belonged to before his operation went corporate.

I fasten the cuffs around his wrists. "It's time to deal with your ex-girlfriend. Damn, your ankle is swelling like a balloon, son! If you leave here alive, you probably should have that looked at. Now *get up!*"

He hobbles to a standing position, and I grab him by the shoulder, hauling him out into the yard. We slip through the house's back door in less than a minute, and I lock the door behind us.

"This isn't my house," he whines, and I press him against the wall.

"Lower your voice, or she'll hear."

Confusion spreads over his pale face. He's getting paler by the minute. "How do you know...?" he trails off.

"It's her turn to talk, Dipshit," I explain. "If she plays nice, I might let her decide your fate once you confess where you put the missing girls. Now walk."

We pass through a mudroom, the kitchen, and the hallway. Cher's heels click over polished wood flooring from within the house as I push him down on a sofa in the sitting room.

"Call out her name," I order, standing out of sight. Her heels stop, and she gasps. "*Jason?* What the *hell*..."

I nod at him from behind a cabinet near the room's entry.

"Yes, it's me," his voice cracks.

Her hands shoot to her mouth upon seeing him bound on her sofa with a visibly swollen ankle.

Goddamn. Cher is even prettier up close. She has big, light brown eyes, an oval face, and wavy chestnut hair, and she's fucking curvy as hell. There is nothing skinny about this woman. No, she is deliciously thick in that floral dress that hits just above the knees. Even her ankles are sexy.

Before she knows what's hit her, I've got one arm around her waist and a hand around her mouth, tightening my grip over muffled screams. I force her across the room toward our reflections in the wall mirror. She tries to fight as I clutch tighter, my tattooed, muscled arm fully encompassing the curve of her waist, and pressing her white silk blouse tight over ample tits, hardened nipples visible. My cock smashes against her plump ass, my jeans getting tighter as my beast hardens at the ready. *Calm the fuck down, boy.*

I enjoy studying her flushed face in the mirror, the fear in her pretty brown eyes meeting my stern, ice-blue gaze. I want to believe she is innocent. But that's just my body talking. Hell, I wasn't expecting to be turned on by my next target while spending more time than is necessary stalking her. I could have been home or on the open road, enjoying my bike. But watching her through her windows at night became a new favorite hobby, and it took resistance not to turn that hobby into a sweat-inducing sport. I wanted to sneak inside. Take her in the pitch black on a moonless night. Muffle her screams while I fuck her.

It's not like she didn't know she was being watched. She'd made a bouquet in a vase on her dresser from the pink roses I left on her windowsill. She started opening her blinds more, glancing toward the window as she undressed by lamplight. She liked being watched, and it turned me on even more. Like a juicy plum fallen from the tree before me, I wanted to pluck her between my hands and sink my teeth in.

But I resisted.

She whimpers as I pull cuffs from my pocket, and the simple act of clasping her wrists only makes my dick harder. *Fuck.* This is going to be more difficult than I imagined.

Pushing her into the chair, I resolve to focus on what I'm here for. This is bigger than me. My job is to get answers and decide who gets to live before the HO gets impatient, sends in the kill squad, and burns the place down. I don't get paid as much when that happens.

I step closer, lifting her chin as I look down at her. "Hello, Cher," I say, my deep voice steady and laced with the satisfaction I get from looking at her. She responds by crying, her full lips quivering in a way that makes me want to bite and suck them.

She yanks her chin from my hand, brows pinching in defiance. "Don't touch me!"

"You don't mean that," I smirk. She has no idea who I am or what I'm here for. But she sure as hell is about to find out.

TWO
cher

"WHO THE *HELL* ARE YOU?" I snap, ignoring the way my body reacted when he was gloving me from behind like an animal. The man's body is made of muscle, and that hard bulge between his legs pressed against my ass sent shock waves crashing through me.

"They call me Pirate," says the statuesque man commanding my living room like a one-person SWAT team. He's nearly as tall as the seven-foot ceiling, and his shoulders are like cannonballs.

"I gave you what you want," pleads Jason from the sofa. Ah, so *he's* the reason for this! I glare at the bastard. No matter how hard I've tried to avoid his trouble, it still comes back to bite me.

"What'd you do this time?" I snipe.

Pirate smirks, his hard blue eyes twinkling. "I'll ask you the same question, Cher," he says, dumbfounding me.

I blink, momentarily tongue-tied under the pressure of Pirate's penetrating gaze. Since when do psychopaths have a gorgeous face like his? He looks like the militant version of a male runway model.

I clear my throat, getting the nerve to speak. "Why am I being dragged into this?"

He lifts a black leather duffel bag onto the coffee table, sorting through it. I crane my neck, trying to see what it's full of. Tools? Weapons? *Oh, shit. Is this happening?*

"Good question, Cher."

"Is it?" My voice cracks as desperation pits in my gut.

He nods. "You have a habit of working with shady lawyers."

I shake my head, confused. "What?"

"But you're only one bar exam away from becoming a lawyer yourself."

How does he...

"Do we...know each other? Pirate."

"So why screw that up, love?" he continues. "You've been studying your ass off every night."

My mouth drops, and my heart skips a beat. "How do you--"

He smirks, shaking his head like I'm a naughty child.

"*Yes.* I've been watching you. But you already knew that."

"What?" Utterly baffled, I watch silently as he pulls a strange tool or weapon from his bag.

"I'm *sorry*," cries Jason, but I can tell by his tone that he isn't apologizing to *me* for dragging me into this or for all the insane shit he put me through last year. No, he's begging for his life! Perhaps I should feel guilty for not having more sympathy for him. But this is the ultra-jealous man who "accidentally" ran my college guy friend off the road and killed him! It's hard to believe that it wasn't on purpose, given that Jason is so possessive. He didn't like it when I talked to the mailman or elderly neighbor, or wore a two-piece bikini to the pool. The irony, of course, is that Jason is a male-slut who cheated on me constantly.

"Why am I guilty by association here?" I ask the towering man with the foreign object in his big hand. "I mean, can't you just...take Jason elsewhere?"

The incredulous look on Jason's face! He can't believe I would throw him under the bus like that. But this whole thing is so shockingly crazy that his reaction almost makes me laugh. A mad sort of laughter fizzes inside me, but I suppress the feeling.

"*You* are part of this, Cher," Pirate says firmly as if reading my thoughts. His voice's low, deep register tingles the hairs on my spine. The recent memory of his cock pressed against my ass flashes through me like a red, hot warning, and my body betrays me, my panties dampening. *What the hell is wrong with me?*

My brows furrow in defiance. "I have nothing to do with him!"

"It's not just about him," he says, tapping a long black rod against his palm.

"What is that for?" I gulp, eyes darting to Jason. I can't stand to hold his angry gaze for long, and my eyes drift to his pale legs sticking out from hemmed shorts. His bloody sock is bunched around an expanding ankle—*ouch*. My stomach drops. Is Pirate about to beat the shit out of me, too? *Oh. God.*

"*Please*, don't!" I plead with my captor.

He looks at me quizzically, and the moment pauses as those fierce blue eyes penetrate me.

"You've been a naughty girl, Cher."

I shake my head. "No, I haven't."

His dark brow lifts into a disapproving line, making me feel like a sassy child. But I won't agree to lies!

"I've done nothing!" I spit out.

"Save your breath, love. You're going to need it," his smooth voice rumbles.

Tears flood my eyes as my mind races with thoughts of what this could be about. All the dirt I have on my current boss and my former boss. Same firm. Same bullshit. How I've kept all their secrets safe to keep my job. It was either that or—

"I'm just a legal secretary," I offer in defense. "I...can't control what my employers do. I'm—"

"Not so innocent," Pirate says sharply, annunciating his t's. My eyes widen in horror as he comes and stands between my legs with this thick, black, dildo-looking thing in his hands.

"Innocence didn't get you on a *hit list*, love. That's why I'm here."

"Oh. God. *No*. Please!" My face breaks into a horrified grimace as tears flood forth. Am I going to die? I'm going to...

Pirate grabs my chin, caressing it with his thumb. This only makes me cry harder. "Shh," he consoles.

He wants me quiet before he makes me scream. What a sick bastard. I should be begging for my life but all I can muster is, "Fuck you!"

"Gladly," he says without hesitation. "I'm willing to strike a deal."

"Huh?" I choke back tears, trying to get control of my emotions. I want to believe that there is a way out of this. I must keep calm and do what he says.

I shudder under his touch as he runs his finger along my jawline. He glances over at Jason, who is scooting toward the sofa's edge, attempting to stand. "Sit the fuck down!" shouts Pirate, and Jason falls back with a moan.

"You try to get up again, I'll break the other ankle. Got it?"

Pirate turns back toward me. "What did you ever see in a loser like him?" he scolds. I yelp when he grabs me by the hair.

"Did you help him get the girls? Were you part of that, too, Cher?"

I blink my eyes, genuinely confused.

"You pretend to be so innocent," he whispers, softening his clutch on my hair. "I want to believe that," he frowns.

"I don't understand," I say, and he peers into my eyes, studying me.

He releases my hair. "I could turn that rat over to the police, but that's no fun. My associates want me to kill him. But I'm thinking you help me decide the best form of torture for him if he doesn't tell me what I want to know."

"What…did he do this time?"

"He pissed off the wrong people," says Pirate. "But that's not the worst of it. It's his luring of middle-school girls to dirty motels that's earned him a special place in hell."

"No," I gasp, blinking my eyes as I process his words. Jason's a murderous scoundrel, but I never thought he could sink any lower. I glance over at him. "Is it…true?"

When he diverts his eyes from me, it makes my stomach sick. How could I not know? What kind of woman dates a pedophile?

"You don't still have a thing for him, do you, Cher?"

"Hell, no!" I snap back.

"Good. You help me follow this through, and I might let you off the hook."

"By helping you…torture him?"

"And get more answers in the process," he nods,

extending the object toward me. "You want to do the honors? I'll uncuff you."

Reflexively, I shake my head. As much as I hate Jason, I could never be part of hurting him physically. The only form of torture I could stomach would be... Making him so jealous that he'd want to explode. What would he do if, for once, he couldn't take out his anger on me or anybody else? What if he was forced to simmer until he was blue in the face?

I remember all the times he flipped out, embarrassing me and others in public. Looking at a man and talking to him was enough to send him over the edge. He murdered my friend and got away with it. If Jason had to watch me be with another man, that would be torture for him. But what am I thinking? I can't fuck a stranger in front of Jason! If only I could think of something else.

Pirate sighs, glancing at his sporty wristwatch impatiently.

"Well, Cher?"

I clear my throat. "And...um... *After* I help?"

"Then I will remove your name from the hit list."

THREE
pirate

"HITLIST?"

"That's right, Cher. 'Whom this concerns' would rather you be *dead*."

Her eyes widen another notch, making my insides tickle—how wide can she go? I want to test her limits. I can practically *feel* the chills popping up all over her sexy body right now. I want to feel her skin when it's like that, warming it with my hands until it's butter-smooth.

I try to ignore the part of me that wants to keep her alive purely for selfish reasons, the part that thinks killing her would be a waste of an intelligent, beautiful woman. Watching her for these last few weeks has come with the unexpected price of becoming infatuated, to the point that even after I got the intel I needed on her, I continued to watch her, learning her nightly rituals.

She has a habit of forgetting to shut the blinds completely when the house is lit from within at night, and some windows have no blinds or curtains, like the one in the mudroom or the small window in the kitchen where she stands at the sink. But then I left the first rose on her windowsill, and she started paying close attention to her bedroom window.

She started turning off her front porch light at night and cracking the bedroom blinds. Not enough for a neighbor to see inside, but enough for a nearby prowler who leaves a long-stemmed rose for a nightly show—a risky, dangerous game for her to play.

"What do you...want me to do?" she asks, fear in her eyes. I smile softly. She still hasn't figured it out.

Not just fear in her eyes. Curiosity. She glances at the blackjack in my hand as if it is... *Hm.* A thought occurs to me, and I go to my bag and pull a custom-made black leather Billy Club from a case. It's never been used; it's more of a vintage-style collector's item I planned to put on a shelf. This baby isn't heavy like the blackjack, but smoothly solid and tapered; it looks like the dildo I caught Cher using one night in her bedroom. Or did she want me to see that, too?

I hold it up, and Cher's eyes widen another notch.

"No fucking way, man," whines Dipshit from the sofa. Heh. He's worried I'm going to have her use this on him. But I wouldn't defile a fine antique like that.

"Shut the hell up before I break your other ankle!"

He shudders, no doubt remembering the sound of his bone cracking in the pretty pink shed.

I return my gaze to my latest obsession, sitting wide-eyed and sexy as hell in the chair. It feels like a rite of passage to finally be standing inside her house rather than on the outside looking in. As much as I enjoyed our little game, I've been fighting a deepening hunger to come in. To come inside her house. To come inside her.

She crosses and uncrosses her curvy legs nervously. I step closer, and her eyes widen even more. I lean down to her, and she quivers as my lips graze her ear lobe; her sweet and intoxicating scent wafts teasingly. Instantly my cocks twitches, and my jeans get tighter. Speaking of *torture*. Being this close to her and not ripping her clothes off is more difficult than I could have imagined.

She bites her lower lip, and it kills me a little inside. I want to be the one to bite her, suck her, make her cry and moan. I want her pussy wrapped tightly around my cock, clinging to me like her life depends on it. I want to fuck her all night and then throw her on the back of my bike and steal her away under the moonlight.

But, *damn*. I need to focus on my job here.

"So, what will it be, Cher?" I whisper, and she gasps, making me harder.

"I..." she hesitates.

"Yes?"

"I can think of..." she mutters, trailing off as her eyes dart to the couch cripple. I think she knows what she wants to do, but doesn't want to say it in front of him.

I bring my ear to my mouth, and her hot breath on my skin is nearly unbearable. "He's...very jealous," she whispers, and it takes me a second to realize what she is getting at. So, making him jealous is the idea of torture she's come up with?

"Is that so?" I ask, watching as her eyes dip to my mouth.

"Let's put your theory to the test, Cher," I say, and I'm about to smash my mouth into hers when I hear Dipshit fall forward and attempt hobble toward the hallway while bound.

Change of plans. I put down the billyclub and grab Cher by her cuffed wrists, following Dipshit as he clumsily hobbles into the hallway. He doesn't get far before he trips, slamming against the wall with a thud. A glass frame falls, shattering, and Cher yelps.

"Good move, Dipshit!" I shout, jerking him up from the floor with my free hand. "Break any more of Cher's belongings, and I will break *you*. Back to the couch!"

I shove him forward, and he hobbles toward the sitting room while I contemplate how much enjoyment I'm getting from the feel of Cher's feminine hand in mine. God, she feels too good. I've got it bad for this girl. But I don't know if I can trust her.

Besides, this is work.

I'm not used to deriving much enjoyment from work, let alone life. The idea of pursuing happiness is an anathema to the organization I was born into. Those at the top pursue power, not happiness. I know from experience that the former does not equal the latter.

Though I rose through the ranks at a young age, I found pursuing power an empty endeavor. At least with the position I've settled into within the company, I get to achieve a bit of justice in a world of corrupt systems. Most of my targets have it coming.

"Stay put," I order when Dipshit reaches the center of the couch, visibly sweating. As he should be. I want him fucking feverish enough that he spills his worst.

"I am your priest, little man. You are at the gates of fucking hell. Only a deathbed confession can save your soul," I say with cold eyes. I laugh when his face drops, turning pale.

"That's right, Dipshit. Except your fate."

I turn to Cher, still holding her hand. "How much was the frame worth?" I ask her, and she looks up at me like I've asked the oddest fucking question.

I stop her just inside the archway, tugging her close

enough that I can hear her breathing speed up. "I'm serious, Cher. I'll make him pay for that."

A tiny hint of a smile edges her lips as if she's intrigued. She isn't sure what to make of me, and she still hasn't figured out who I am. I am the shadow outside her window at night. The one she teases.

"It was a gift from my mom. I'm not sure how much—"

"Priceless." But I'm not just talking about the frame. "Don't worry. He'll pay with his life."

"I returned the money!" he protests from the sofa. "You got what you wanted, man."

"I want more," I say, eyes on Cher. "Where did you hide the girls, Dipshit?"

"I don't know what you're talking about!"

Liar.

"Let's test your theory, love," I say, clutching her hands behind her back in my one hand to where her breasts jut out further from the thin fabric of her dress. I dip my gaze along her parted lips before smashing my mouth into her and lapping her tongue like honey. She tastes even better than I knew she would, and when a tiny moan escapes her relenting mouth, the sound lingers in my ears like a little melody. I'm fucking enthralled by her.

I tug her forward, wrapping my arms around her waist. Her body goes rigid momentarily before relaxing under my embrace, my hard chest pressing into her soft breasts. I nearly forget we are not alone when I hear a sound from behind and glance back at her ex. His face is deep red, and his nostrils are flared with anger. Holy shit.

"Seems you were right, Cher," I smirk, but the half-smile doesn't reach my eyes. Tension is building inside me like a hurricane; there is only one way to let it out. But I know I should take my time—torture, if done correctly, is a slow process.

I trail my finger down her cleavage, gathering the tiny beads of sweat that have formed there before licking my finger. Fuck, she tastes good.

I'm only just started.

Her sweet taste lingers on my tongue as I pull my finger from my mouth. She attempts to glance at her ex but seems to catch herself and resist. She licks her lips as I hold her gaze and my hands slide down her ample ass.

"How far are you willing to go, Cher?"

She hesitates to answer. She can't resist glancing at him. "Did you hurt those girls, Jason?"

"Fuck you, Cherry!" he spits out, and if I weren't enjoying my arms around Cher's sweet frame, I'd fucking punch him for talking to her that way.

When her eyes return to mine, there is a note of determination in her expression.

"As far as it takes," she says quietly, and I wink approvingly. A plan quickly forms in my mind.

"Go sit in that chair," I tell her before picking up the cuffs and then the billy club. I'm going to put it to special use.

FOUR
cher

PIRATE IS all muscle and predatory purpose as he slowly stalks my way, and my heart viciously thuds in my ears at his raw, sexual power. He is, without a doubt, the scariest and sexiest man I've ever met. He makes me feel like my life is ending and beginning simultaneously, like this is one of those pivotal moments that will change me forever. There will only be the time before I met Pirate and the time after.

He said he's been watching me--for how long? How much does he know? My mind jumps to the shadow I've been dreaming about. Always there in the back of my mind. It began with a dark, mysterious shape outside my window when I was alone at night. I thought it was just the trees or my imagination until I saw the first pink rose, one of several.

Pirate lifts my hands above my head and cuffs my wrists.

"Ouch," I complain as they snap shut. Jason snickers.

"Shut your filthy mouth!" Pirate shouts at him.

"Too tight?" asks Pirate with a hint of satisfaction in his

tone over my discomfort. This may be about getting answers from Jason, but it seems Pirate wants me to pay for my associations, regardless of how little I know.

He lowers my cuffed hands into my lap. "You didn't answer my question, Cher." Black lashes form a dark ring around his eyes, accentuating his piercing blue gaze. His wavy dark hair, secured with a black headband, has sun streaks along the edges. It's easy to imagine him outdoors on a bike or a boat. A ship, even. *Pirate*. The name is fitting.

"They are very tight," I answer.

"*Good*. I wouldn't want to be too easy on you," he winks with a hint of charm in his stern eyes.

"Because of who my ex-boyfriend is?"

"This isn't just about him."

"Because of my employers?"

He nods. "They want you dead. I'm giving you a way out. You owe me. Understood?"

It's as I thought. But at least my punishment pales in comparison to Jason's. Over there, pathetically slumped on the couch. How could he hurt innocent girls? *How?*

Pirate goes to his bag and produces a rope, which he ties around Jason's feet. "Look, I gave you the money," Jason pleads. "Can't we just call it good?"

"Where did you hide the girls?"

"What girls?" he shrugs. "I truly don't know—"

"Shut the fuck up!" Pirate sneers in disgust. "You say another word; it better be to confess."

Jason huffs, his shoulders slumping. He shakes his head, saying nothing. Either he doesn't know, or he's afraid that admitting the truth will dig him a deeper hole. I'm not sure which.

Either way, I can't stand to look at him. I'd much rather stare at my captor, the *pirate*. He goes around closing blinds and curtains and turning off lights. He lights a large candle on the white mantel above the electric fireplace. Seeing him in the shadowy light reminds me of my stalker. My nightly visitor for many weeks. That shouldn't be a positive thing. Somehow, in my loneliness, it was. The pink roses helped. It was hard to imagine the mystery lurker wanted to hurt me. That's probably naive. Predators like to play with their prey. Lure them in before the kill.

Pirate suddenly peels off his shirt in the low light, and I gasp in awe. His entire torso is tan and solidly cut, like a statue of a Greek God—and those *shoulders*. His long, corded, tattooed arms hang languidly at his sides as he walks to me, pinning me with those sparklingly menacing eyes. I've never seen eyes like his, as blue and treacherous as the sea.

I take a deep breath, calming my nerves as best I can, but my heart races. Is he the one who has been watching me? I didn't stop it, didn't seal the blinds tight, or call the police. No, I encouraged it. I gave him a show and got off afterward because I was so turned on by something I couldn't see. But I knew it was something powerful. I sensed it in every fiber of my being. I wanted that dark shadow to want me so badly that it slipped through the barriers, forcing itself into my life. But I know it's just a fantasy! The real thing is nothing like the fantasy. The real thing is cruel, selfish, and full of pain. There is no pleasure to be had in a true violation—

"Oh, the things I've wanted to do to you, Cher," he drawls with that leather, dildo-like object in his hand.

My eyes widen in disbelief. "Since when?" I whisper. Was he referring to the short time span of tonight, or has he known me longer? His tone was weighted like he'd been building up to this moment.

God, is this him? Is this my shadow?

"Spread your legs for me," he says in a low voice that sends chills over my body. My jaw slackens. "What....are you going to do?"

He pulls a black strap from the pocket of his jeans. "If you promise to be good, I will only tie one foot to the chair."

I nod in compliance, reminding myself that this was my idea. To torture the truth out of Jason via his murderous jealousy.

Slowly, I spread my legs as he drops to his knees. I try to control my breathing as I process the inevitable. It all makes sense. He was watching me because he had plans—for me and Jason. This was all calculated, and I fell for it.

He removes my heels before taking my right ankle in hand, and then he fastens the strap tightly until I'm connected to the chair leg.

"Too tight?" he asks, but I don't answer. It's uncomfortably tight, but I know he wants it that way. This is punishment. I'm paying off a debt.

For years, I turned a blind eye to illegal practices that may have sometimes scammed innocent people, and now it's come back to bite me. If only I'd never met Jason. He introduced me to my current boss. Jason runs in shady circles. But that's just an excuse. I'm a big girl, and I could have walked away. I finally broke up with Jason, but I kept the job connection because it looked great on my resume and paid well. I was so close to being free. Just a little longer, and I could start my law practice. Do it my way—a fresh start.

"What are you gonna do to her?" Jason mutters from the couch.

Doesn't he remember what Pirate said? He wasn't supposed to speak unless he was ready to confess.

Pirate initially ignores him, letting him think he's gotten away with it. But after Pirate places the black object in my hand, he stands, suddenly lunging at Jason and punching him in the face. "Fuck!" cries Jason. Pirate responds by punching him in the gut. Jason grunts, "You fuck—"

Pirate punches him again. "Silence! You wanna know what I'll do to her, Dipshit? Watch, learn, and keep your fucking mouth shut! You talk *only* to confess. Nothing more. Got it?"

Jason nods, and Pirate returns to me as I clutch the leather. My palms are sweating nervously.

"Whatever it takes. Right, Cher?" he says in a low, deep, sexy voice that slinks between my thighs, making my panties wet.

Whatever it takes—my words. The truth is nothing would give me more pleasure than making Jason's skin crawl, even if I am all mixed up inside over what's happening. My body might be excitedly confused, but my brain hurts. My sense of reality is slipping.

Pirate grabs something from his bag before stepping between my legs with his hard, half-naked body. I trail my eyes along the prominent bulge in his jeans between his muscular thighs, swallowing thickly as heat floods my core at the thought of that beast coming out to play. I'm not sure I could handle it. That and... Well, it's been a while.

"That is a weapon, Cher."

It takes me a moment to realize he's talking about the object in my hands and not his big fat cock.

"But, I will let you use it as a toy. It looks remarkably like your vibrator. Don't you think?"

My eyes pop wide open as he finally confirms my suspicions. He is my shadow; come to life in the flesh! I blink at him stupidly as satisfaction gleams in his crystal blue gaze.

"I'll remove your panties for you, and you can try it out," he says, dropping to his knees before brandishing a switchblade. I gasp at the sight of it as he reaches under my dress, tugging at the silk. I bring my free leg inward as the undies reach my thighs. He grabs my panties in the middle, clasping them tightly with one hand. I yelp as he slices the knife upward through both sides of the fabric with his other hand. Candlelight glints off the sharp blade as silk falls.

"Shit," mutters Jason from the couch. He couldn't resist, could he?

Pirate shakes his head with a frown. "I'm just getting started," he snaps his head toward Jason with a ferocious glare that chills my bones. He raises the knife at him. "Want to know how this blade feels inside your veins?"

Jason shakes his head, mouthing, "No, no."

Pirate returns his gaze to me, and I squirm, wishing I could close my legs. My pussy feels exposed, damp, and vulnerable. He puts the knife under the chair before grabbing my wrists and freeing a hand as he leans into my ear. His hand comes between my legs, cupping my sex. "You're moist for me," he growls, sucking my lobe before biting it. "*Mm*. That makes you even wetter. Fuck, that's sexy, love."

He grabs my free hand and closes it around the leather before bringing my hand between my thighs. He guides my hand until I'm pressing the leather against my pussy, pushing the smooth round tip inside myself.

"Tell me who you think of while you fuck yourself, Cher," he whispers into my mouth while kissing me. Liquid heat makes my pussy cramp with need as I push the leather deeper, thrusting back and forth while Pirate sucks my tongue; his breathing gets heavier as I pant. I almost forget Jason is watching this; I'm consumed with Pirate's command over my body. His hand closes around my hand, and now he's the one thrusting the leather dildo, fucking me while lapping my mouth. He tastes as good as he looks and feels, overwhelming me entirely. I've wanted this. But I didn't imagine it would be with an audience.

"Tell me," he repeats, reminding me of those nights we spent separated by glass. His fingers replace the dildo, thrusting inside me while he brings his other hand between my thighs, circling my clit. "Tell me, love," he demands.

My head knocks back as I near the edge of orgasm, my face flushed hot. My heart speeds as he finger fucks me. Teasingly, he slows his pace to a stop, staring into my eyes. Oceans of blue lined in black, staring into my soul like a maelstrom, ready to suck me in. "Tell me, Cher," he whispers.

So this is to be my torture? I want him to finish what he started, but I don't want to admit the embarrassing truth. Tears flood my eyes as a subtle smile edges his masculine mouth. He's enjoying this.

"*You*," I mutter, humiliated as teardrops hit my cheeks.

"I thought so," he says before pulling his fingers from me. Did I say something wrong? I stare at him, confused.

He half-laughs. "You didn't think I'd let you get off that easily, love?" He slowly licks his fingers.

FIVE

pirate

EFFECTIVE TORTURE REQUIRES DISCIPLINE.

I won't admit to Cher that this is hard on me, too. I want to have her to myself without him watching, and I don't want to have to take my time. But I learned long ago that controlling my urges is rewarded in the end. I play the long game.

I remember my first lesson as a thirteen-year-old boy seeking revenge on the scumbag who molested my little sister. He worked inside the HO and thought he could get away with going after her. For a time, he was right. I told Mom, and she told Dad, and he reported it to human resources, but nothing happened. My parents were beholden to the system. Children are easily preyed upon when a system is run in this way.

So, I decided to take matters into my own hands. I followed the scumbag. Watched, waited, and finally, one day, I pounced. Beat the shit out of him and threatened to kill him if he didn't leave her alone. He told me what I wanted to hear to my face. But then he went behind my back and reported me. I was naive to think I had power back then. Turns out the scumbag was an essential member of the HO. I have some nasty scars from the slow, methodical torture I learned to endure. I kept myself calm by studying their methods; I knew it would be my future job someday.

Speaking of scumbags.

The one sitting on the sofa is bright red in the face, and I don't think it's just from the pain in his ankle. He can't stand me touching her, and I know another little secret of his. I wasn't the only one watching Cher over the last few months. He kept tabs on her.

I pick up the knife from under the chair and go to him. "*Why* did you do it?"

His brows shoot up. "I didn't do it!"

I shake my head. "Why were you keeping tabs on Cher?"

He stares at me dumbly. "I...wasn't."

Within seconds, I've got the knife at his throat, pulling his head back with my other hand.

"You'd think you learned your lesson not to lie to me."

"I-I don't know why," he whines as I press the blade into his skin, drawing blood. I trail the knife down, forging a crimson-colored river running the length of his neck.

"Stop!" pleads Cher. I pivot around to face her.

"I know why," she says, coming to his defense. "Because...he thinks he owns me. He's all about mind control. That's his kink," she explains.

I don't like the sound of that. I know what he does to females he thinks he owns. Maybe he planned to make Cher disappear like he did those missing girls.

Instantly, my knife is at his throat again. "*Nobody* owns, Cher," I grit.

At least, not her mind. I desire mastery over her body.

"I'll give you more money!" he pleads. " Just let me go. Name your price."

He doesn't understand me at all. "Let's get one thing straight. I make millions hunting down enemies of the HO. But that's not why I do it. I hunt for the love of the sport of catching scumbags like you."

He responds by crying pathetically. Heh. I know why. He realizes he can't weasel out of this, which is the scariest outcome he can imagine. There is nothing in that little psychopathic brain of his that's prepared him for this moment. Facing me, his priest, at the edge of his deathbed.

"Maybe he's been through enough now," says Cher from behind. The tinge of sympathy in her voice reminds me of her role.

After setting the bloody knife out of reach on a table, I return to her. I step between her legs, and my cock twitches, knowing full well what's hiding in plain sight under her dress. I gently cup her chin with my hand, looking into her eyes.

"Cher, the *enabler*," I whisper, watching my words cut into her mind, slicing away at her notions of innocence. Is that...*guilt* I see in her pretty brown eyes?

Her chin quivers as I run my fingers up her jawline before sliding my hand into her hair and palming the back of her skull. "Don't worry, love," I console. When I'm done with you, you will be a changed woman. I promise."

SIX
cher

LEANING BACK IN THE CHAIR, I try not to cry. I don't want to seem guilty. I don't want to do anything resembling Jason. Pirate has put me and Jason in the same boat, but we are different. I didn't know what he was up to, and I'll be damned if I am accused of things I've had no part in.

"I haven't spoken to Jason for months! We live separate lives," I explain. But that doesn't seem good enough for Pirate.

I feel like I'm drowning under the weight of his ocean gaze, darkened by shadow, like the Atlantic when hurricane clouds roll in, hellbent on destruction. He holds my face in his palm, promising to make me a new woman like he's some god. What does he want from me?

"Look at me," he demands when my eyes trail to the dirtbag sitting on the sofa. Why won't Jason admit what he did so we can move on with our lives? I think I've had enough now. Fantasy over. Reality is setting in.

"Okay," I say to Pirate, wanting to get this over with.

"Yes, Sir," he corrects.

I stare at him.

"Say it, love."

"Yes...*Sir*," I mutter, swallowing thickly under his command.

The way he traces the bones in my face while cupping my head with his other hand is alarmingly soothing. He is not my savior. I don't want to be saved.

He steps closer between my legs and leans his knees on the chair between my inner thighs, dangerously close to my naked sex —arousal clashes with defiance inside me. I've never felt so mixed up in all my life.

I feel strangely disappointed when he reaches down and unties my leg. "We're moving to your bedroom," he declares.

He grabs the bloody knife before yanking Jason up from the couch.

"Lead the way, love. I'm *trusting* you," he says, and I quickly think of what a reasoning victim might do now. I could try to run. Adrenaline courses through me as I contemplate my course.

The front door.

When I pass through the hall into the foyer, my eyes dart to the remaining vase on the accent table. It's the heavy, blue, and white twin to the now broken one from my dead aunt. I could throw the family heirloom at Pirate and try to get through the front door before he catches me.

But he's so fast, athletic, and strong. Seeing his body in motion when he grabbed me before lunging after Jason was like watching an action hero from a movie. But he's no hero. He's...a vigilante. I'm on his hit list. He's offering to save me. People want me dead. The only way out of this alive is through him.

Part of me wants to help him deal with my "Jason problem." I have a restraining order against him, but that doesn't stop him from harassing me at a distance. I've been afraid to date after what he did to my old friend, *poor* Billy. He was a good person. He didn't deserve to die.

But these aren't the only reasons I pass the vase without making my move.

I hate admitting this to myself, but deep down, something inside me wants to surrender to Pirate. To please him and atone for my sins. If that can be done.

For many weeks, I felt him watching me at night, and it's been a secret thrill I looked forward to after a long day at my soul-sucking job. Though I methodically locked the windows and doors every evening, I fantasized about him finding a way in after I turned off the lights. I wondered what he might do. Was he armed and dangerous? The terror in the mystery brought me erotic chills and made me hot with dark and twisted desires. I guess I'm fucked up in the head. Maybe I do need to be saved.

At least, I do need to get off this god-forbidden hit list. This isn't the kind of thing the police can help a girl with. This is mobster shit. I worked in law long enough to know how unsafe the average citizen is from the underworld once you're on its radar. I am, after all, an average citizen. So, Pirate's my ticket to freedom? Then, I have no reasonable choice but to stay aboard his crazy ship.

"Good girl," he says as I pass the entry and turn the corner into the next hallway. He delivered that pleasing affirmation as if he knew what I was debating. It makes me want to earn his trust even more. Get on his good side. Reap the rewards.

Like a blessing and a curse wrapped in a blood-red bow, his big, dark energy follows me inside my bedroom. And the twisted fantasy finally comes full circle.

SEVEN
pirate

THE WOMAN IS INTO PINK.

Her bedroom is grey with mauve accents, like the leather chair at her white vanity. I consider parking Dipshit there, but then he might bleed or sweat all over her pretty spot where she likes to sit to put on her earrings. When I think of punishing her, this isn't what I had in mind, and I don't want his fluids on her things or anywhere near her body ever again. The thought puts a sick feeling in my stomach.

I can't even stand seeing him in her bedroom, but like every grown-up, I must do things I don't like to reap the benefits. Discipline is rewarded in the end.

He hobbles forward, and I shut and lock the door before yanking him into the corner near the walk-in closet. I'm tempted to make him stand all night until his legs buckle, but he'll be less of a distraction sitting. Cher has enough trouble not feeling self-conscious with him watching. Knowing how uncomfortable it is for her and how anger-inducing it is for him makes my torture more bearable.

"Sit on the floor," I order, and he slides down the wall

with a thunk. I hogtie him, so I don't have to worry about his ass for a few minutes.

Cher averts her eyes while fidgeting with her hands at the center of the room. Countless times, I've imagined being with her here, sans the third-wheel spectator. She said he thinks he owns her, and I think she's right. I don't know precisely what makes Dipshit tick, but a man who preys on kids isn't the kind of sicko one can fully understand. All I know is I will enjoy stripping him of his claim of ownership. I want him to feel as pathetic as I know he is.

"Unbutton your dress, love," I order, and her brows raise. Her fingers twitch hesitantly, and I can tell she's breathing heavier now. Her eyes dart to Dipshit before returning to mine. She subtly shakes her head as her watering eyes plead with me not to humiliate her in this way. I suppose the act of covering her body with my own while fucking her with the leather dildo and my fingers was more intimate than this. Now, it's like she's exposed on a stage, ordered to commit the vulnerable act of undressing.

I dim the lights and then step toward her. "Imagine yourself on a regular night, love," I say in a low voice. "I'm outside. You're in here."

Her lips part as she glances at the window, imagining our nightly ritual. Her eyes return to mine, and I can tell she's getting up the nerve to confess her darkest little secret to me.

"What do you normally do on a night like that?"

"I...put on a show," she mutters, and I nod approvingly, enjoying the confirmation that she knew I was watching. And she liked it. But I wanted to make sure she didn't confuse me for that dirtbag slowly driving past her house every week, keeping tabs on her despite the restraining order.

So, I left little pretty clues. That slender, clear vase full of roses she keeps on her dresser proves this game could be real.

"*Who* have you been putting on a show for, Cher?"

When she lifts her fingers to the buttons of her dress, she shifts her body in my direction. The message is clear. She holds my gaze as she unfastens a button. "You," she whispers.

When I smile this time, I can feel it reach my eyes. It occurs to me that I haven't felt this in a long while. I've been like a machine, operating purely for function. But tonight, I'm fucking eager for satisfaction.

"Keep going, love," I say, encouraging her.

When she reaches the last button, I drape the black rope around my shoulders and set down my bag before going to her. I spread the top of her dress open, exposing her heavy, lace-covered breasts. "What did you imagine?" I ask, delighting in watching her mind race with possibilities. But I bet she didn't imagine *this*...

I grab each side of her parted dress and tear the rest of it from her curvaceous body in one swift, downward motion. She yelps; this time, when her skin is suddenly covered in goosebumps, my hands are there to feel it.

EIGHT
cher

I WANT to forget that Jason is in the room with us, but he's making huffing noises. I glance at him, fuming in the corner, and Pirate frowns.

"Stop looking at him."

My heart thuds in my chest as I try to focus on only one set of eyes--steely pale blue and closing in on me. I step backward until the back of my knees hit the bed. It's not like he told me to; he didn't even step forward. It's his *eyes* pushing me backward where he wants me.

He reaches up, and the hard muscles in his naked chest flex as he tugs the black rope dangling from his neck. He smooths it between his hands as he nudges his head at the bedpost.

"Stand there, facing forward."

I do as he says, my heart quickening as he approaches. Jason makes a thumping sound against the wall, and this time, when I look at him, Pirate grabs my chin. "Tell me what you imagined when I watched you last night."

I bite my lip, unsure how to find the words. Maybe...it's best to show him. I reach behind my back, unfastening my bra and letting my breasts fall forth before dropping my bra to the ground.

Undoubtedly, the deepening hunger in Pirate's expression turns me on, sending heat waves down my core. He steps forward, cupping my breasts with his large, strong hands as he smashes his mouth into mine. There is so much ravenous need in his kiss that I'm rendered to jelly as his tongue laps me. His hand finds my naked sex. "You're so fucking wet, love," he rasps before leaning down and sucking my tits, just as I imagined he would.

But I didn't imagine him biting, making me wince while keeping his eyes on mine as if trying to catch me in the naughty act of looking at my injured ex. There in my periphery, staring me down hatefully. But when Pirate suddenly thrusts his fingers inside me, and I moan, my eyes flick to the huffing anger in the corner.

Pirate comes to a sudden halt, his warm touch leaving my body. I'm standing here cold, wet, and naked before the bed as he stares down at me disapprovingly.

"I warned you, Cher."

"I'm sorry."

"Do you deserve a spanking, love?"

Thinking it will please him, I nod.

A hint of satisfaction flickers in his black-rimmed blue eyes before he goes to his bag. I glare at Jason while I have the chance. I want him to stop looking at me, stop watching us, and I hope he can see it in my spiteful eyes!

He shakes his head in disgust as if this is all my fucking fault.

"You bitch," he mouths at me, and Pirate cocks his ear.

Jason recoils, shutting his eyes tight, and I sigh in relief. I forget that the whole point is getting him to confess. He's supposed to watch and simmer to the point of exploding.

But it seems like this is a little more than that for Pirate and me. Fantasy has collided with reality in the most twisted of ways.

I return my eyes to Pirate just in time. He has a brown stick-like thing in his hand. *God, another weapon?* Oh, that's right. I agreed to a spanking.

"This is a *litupa*. Used by the South African police. I came across it on eBay. It's made of animal hide. Tapered. Perfect for whipping."

A strange laugh escapes Jason's mouth, and Pirate wastes no time lunging at him. "What did I tell you, Dipshit?"

He raises the whip into the air before striking down against Jason's ankle, making him cry out in pain. As much as I hate him, it's not easy to watch him being beaten.

"Where did you put the girls, Jason?" I say, hoping he'll finally divulge.

"I didn't do shit!" he shouts.

When Pirate turns around, my eyes are stuck on sniveling Jason.

"Naughty," scolds Pirate, grabbing my arm. "I told you to ignore him. He's no longer your problem. Turn around."

He doesn't wait for me to do so; he spins me around before grabbing my wrists and tying them above my head. I don't know if he plans to hurt me or fuck me, or both.

NINE
pirate

"SPREAD YOUR LEGS," I order.

Her plump, naked ass is mine for the taking, and all I want to do is pull my hard-as-hell dick out and ram my hips against her bouncing, thick ass while I fuck her juicy pussy. *But.*

I sigh, shaking my head. That would be rewarding her too soon.

She wants my cock. She's been wanting it badly. If she didn't want me to fuck her, she wouldn't have teased me through the window when she knew I was watching in the dark of night. Yet she took a dangerous risk—*anybody* could have been out there. She stripped her sexy body, exposing her luscious curves as she got off with a vibrator for the very man who was hunting her down to make her pay.

On paper, I check some bad boxes.

Hit Man.

Murderer.

Stalker.

Weapons expert.

She took a risk, but she got lucky. She has no idea how much I have to give. And *take*. I'm dying to show her.

I lift the whip in my right hand, smacking it against my other palm. Startled, she jumps, and I smile. This time when the leather whip makes the snapping sound, it's accompanied by a long, hard sting right at the center of her left ass cheek. She bonks her head against the bedpost with a yelp.

A red mark appears across the curve of her ass. I think for the sake of symmetry, she needs a matching one on the other side. I step slightly closer before lifting the whip and striking her other cheek, and this time, she grunts, bearing the pain much better.

"Good girl," I say, my eyes trailing to the clear fluid dripping between her thick thighs from her wet pussy. *Fuck, that's hot.* My cock is far too tight inside my jeans now; it isn't healthy. I unzip all the way, but even that is still too confining.

I pull my cock out as I come up behind her, letting my big fat erection spring forth against her ass. "Bring your legs together," I tell her, and she lets out a little moan as I thrust between her thighs, gliding my cock along the folds of her soft, wet pussy. The friction of my cock pushing between her thighs feels so fucking good, and by how much she's panting, I know the feeling is mutual.

"I think punishment made you even wetter for me, love," I say in her ear before sucking and biting her lobe. "Isn't that right?"

She nods, arching her back like a cat in heat.

"Have you been taking your birth control?"

"*Yes*," she pants urgently, like she'll die if I don't fuck her now.

"Do you deserve to be fucked, Cher? Or should I punish

you more? I've got so much I want to do to you. But time is short."

She clamps her thighs against my steely cock while thrusting backward. "Fuck me," she pleads.

I'm about to tell her *no* when she tilts her hips, causing the head of my cock to dip just inside her sweet spot, and all the blood in my body goes into fucking overdrive. My cocks throbs with violent need.

If I give her what she wants, she had better not think she got off too easily. I grab her hair firmly, forcing her head back until she whines. I raise my other hand and smack her thigh as I plunge myself into her heaven. I slap her thigh again, fucking her even harder, pounding her pussy like there's no tomorrow. My thick, meaty tip smashes against her cervix before I pull back, slowing my rhythm teasingly just as she seems to be near the edge of orgasm.

I grab her tit, thumbing her nipple as I slow-fuck her, gliding along her g-spot with my pulsing erection. When her pussy clamps hard around my manhood, I painfully force myself to stop. She cries out in agony before I finally resume fucking her at full force. When she cums on my dick, moaning so loudly it sounds like she's dying, a feral groan escapes me, and I lose my breath as seed bursts from me like a fucking super volcano. *Mm. I'm just getting started.*

TEN
cher

HE PULLS his big dick from my pussy, and fluids rush out of me. My arms hang from the ropes as I lean against the bedpost for support while catching my breath. He smacks me on the ass.

"Such a tight little pussy," he growls, palming my sex as blood rushes to my center. I haven't had enough yet.

His hand slides from between my thighs when his phone rings, leaving me.

God, he was so rough in how he handled me, and yet I've never orgasmed so hard in my life. He fucked me so hard that the bed frame crashed loudly into the wall, but there was another sound in the room. I was too busy being claimed by a Pirate to realize that the thumping noise from behind was coming from Jason.

"Knock that off!" orders Pirate, and I turn my head to see Jason repeatedly tapping the back of his head against the wall in angered frustration. His reddened face is twisted in pure disgust.

Did he watch Pirate's ass flexing as he rammed into me, or did he divert his eyes? Even if he had, there would be no escaping the moaning and groaning of our sex in the air, no escaping the scent of sweat and semen as our bodies furiously slapped together. My room hasn't smelled like sex in a long time.

Pirate taps his phone and zips his pants before tapping Jason upside the head. "What's wrong, Jay-Jay? You didn't like watching me get my dick wet inside Cher's delicious, juicy *cunt?*"

"I don't FUCKING WANT HER!"

Pirate laughs. "She was never yours to begin with."

I crane my neck, wishing I could be untied, and put some clothes on so Jason would stop glancing at my wet pussy and naked ass. That and having two men talk about me like I'm an object to be fought over while I'm tied naked to a bedpost is nothing short of humiliating.

How has my life come to this?

Not in a million years could I have predicted that the man bringing pink roses to my bedroom window would be the man to make Jason finally pay for his crimes.

"Just let me FUCKING GO!"

"I'm going to *kill* you."

Pirate's deep voice is so severe when he says the word kill that I have no doubt he knows the act intimately. I get chills at the thought of what he is capable of.

"Option B. *Confess.*"

"Can I please be untied?" I ask.

Both sets of eyes shift in my direction. Jason's hatred burns into me as if this is my fault. I rip my eyes from him. I have had enough of his face for one lifetime.

Pirate's phone rings, and he walks to the edge of the room instead of untying me.

"Stop looking at me!" I hiss after catching Jason's eyes on my ass like he wants to rage-fuck me.

He's violently jealous. He never could fuck me with genuine passion and get me off so good that I screamed in pain and pleasure. That wasn't us, and it never will be. He's a weasel, not a man. That must be why he's into underage girls. That I didn't know this eats at me.

But now it makes sense. He likes the advantage he has over them mentally. It doesn't make me feel great that I am somebody who dated him. I've been too busy pursuing my goals to worry about my habit of being in the orbit of weasels. Law firms are full of them.

Pirate called me "Cher the enabler." But I don't think he's being fair. I won't blame myself for Jason's crimes. That has nothing to do with me. I got a restraining order and tried to forget him.

"*Fuck.* Change of plans," Pirate says after getting off his phone.

He comes to the bed and unties me, and my wrists are as red and sore as my swollen pussy.

"You're letting me go?" says his nasal voice, hopeful.

"Change of location."

"*What?* Where you gonna take me, man?" whines Jason.

Noted that he said *me* and not *we*. Naturally, he's only concerned about his own ass.

"Cher, get dressed and pack an overnight bag."

"Where are we going?"

"To my place, love."

ELEVEN
pirate

I'M LOOKING FORWARD to being done with this punk, but my work here isn't done. I cover his mouth with tape before leading him to my work vehicle, a matte-black Aston Martin Vulcan, backed into the garage. The exterior house lights are off, and the shade of a large oak tree provides further coverage from neighbors.

"Lie down and hold still," I order before shutting the trunk. Modified to be street-legal, the former racing car's trunk is small, and he can't possibly be comfortable. *Good.*

But then again, I can relate to wanting open air. I would have preferred riding my Harley-Davidson motorcycle if I hadn't needed the trunk and a quiet motor. That would have made for a better night. The only thing good about this evening is that beautiful mess of a woman staring back at me with watery eyes, bright from orgasm.

God, I want to take her again. Right now. But no, I need to get the fuck out of here. Ignoring the twitch of my overeager cock, I lift the door open on the passenger side, assisting Cher into the black leather seat. Her mouth is taped, her hands are cuffed, and her duffle bag is slung over her shoulder, making it impossible to buckle her in.

I frown, thinking of a quick solution. This contract has run out of time. My boss just informed me that the plot has thickened regarding the case of my latest targets. This goes higher than the H.O., which means I have until midnight to report them dead, or the case is being passed to a privately hired outside hitman.

I unfasten Cher's cuffs before shutting the door.

Quickly settling into the driver's side, I start the engine. Cher mumbles from under the tape, and I glance at her.

Though she looks sexy, her mouth covered, and with pleading brown eyes, I'd rather see her pretty mouth and hear her voice.

I reach over and rip off the tape.

"Ouch," she complains, bringing her hand to her mouth.

I chuckle. "Don't even think about opening that door and jumping out," I warn as I exit the drive, quickly picking up speed.

"I'm not that stupid," she says, looking over her shoulder at the banging sound from the trunk.

"Can he breathe back there?"

"Somewhat," I shrug. "Maybe he'll do us both a favor and run out of air by the time I arrive at my place."

She frowns. "Where is your place?"

"Near the beach."

I watch the road with a sigh, taking the highway North from Boston. "I don't normally bring targets to my house. But...tonight, I have no choice."

"I'm just a nameless target, now? What is happening, Pirate?"

"I'm not killing you or leaving you to be killed. That's what's happening."

"But what does that mean?"

"It means that my boss isn't the only one who wants you dead. I'm taking you off radar."

"Oh *my god*. I don't understand how it's this bad. I'm just a legal secretary. It doesn't make sense!"

"It does if you understand the clientele of the law firm you've been working for. I bet one associate in particular—Dipshit back there—knew what he was getting you into when he recommended you to them."

"What, exactly?"

"The *mob*, Cher. You've been working for a faction of the Bratva crime syndicate. But deep down, you knew that, right?"

She gasps, bringing her hands to her mouth as if she does not even have a hint of a clue. How does this information not ring a bell with her? How is she this naïve?

"I mean...I knew they had some shady dealings with the mob, but—"

"They *are* the mob, Cher. One hundred percent. Your law office represents a vehemently loathed competitor of an important H.O. client. Do you understand?"

"So then...H.O. is mafia, too?"

"Not exactly. It rides a fine line. Hellfire Organization is a private security company and arms dealer."

I exit the coastal highway toward Salem, glancing at Cher. Her chestnut hair frames big brown eyes under knitted brows.

"Rides a fine line? Hiring a hitman is illegal."

"Depends on who is hiring and what for," I shrug. "Governments and corporations do it all the time."

"Then what's the difference between them and the mob?"

I smile. "Legitimacy. Other than that, not much. I was born into this, and I learned long ago not to try to find clean lines in a morally grey world. I focus on finding justice where I can, in my small ways."

"And large ways," she says, and I look at her for meaning. Her face is noticeably flushed, and she presses her lips together as if she regrets her choice of words.

"What precisely are you referring to, Cher?"

Her lips part, but she hesitates, the flush in her cheeks deepening.

"Are you referring to my cock?" I ask, and the memory of being inside her makes me instantly hard. "Not my usual means of interrogation. But I loved every minute of it. As did you, am I right?"

TWELVE
cher

"NOT TOTALLY," I lie, turning my head toward the view of the moonlit ocean.

Right now, I hate how damp my panties get thinking about what he did to me. Crossing my legs in defiance, I pull up the zipper on my pink velour sweat suit. It's not my first choice in clothing for a captive getaway, but I didn't exactly plan for this! I grabbed the first thing in my sweat-suit drawer. I should have gone with grey. Pink is peppy, loud, attention-drawing, and more so on a full-figured gal like me. Attention from prying eyes is the last thing I need right now.

Of course, my outfit isn't the only thing bothering me. If I were sane, I would consider my ability to orgasm while my captor fucked me a severe case of Stockholm syndrome. But it's more complicated than that. I'm not so innocent. I was turned on by knowing he was my mystery stalker.

But it begs the question. Did he know the pink roses would convince me this was an innocent game rather than a twisted, dark romance? I've never been so wrong or so confused in my life. I'm using so much brain power processing all this that it's hard to imagine what is coming next.

"Don't play coy with me, love," he winks, jarring me from my thoughts.

"Huh?"

"I think you lied when you said you didn't enjoy yourself."

"I said…not completely."

"Don't lie to me."

"You can't read my mind."

"I read your body. You were all in love."

"Under force."

"Ah, but that was an added benefit."

I puff out air. "If that's what you need to believe."

"Enough games, Cher. I have little to no tolerance for it."

When his cool eyes meet mine, there is a hint of a twinkle in the hardness, like a secret promise of pleasure wrapped in pain. I want to argue and tell him I'm not lying or playing games. But I also want to answer his question honestly. I did let a dirty joke slip from my mouth. He was merely calling me out on it.

"Yes," I sigh, cheeks slightly flushing. "I was referring to your cock, sir."

Fleetingly, the twinkle in his eyes deepens before his attention returns to the road.

"I was being relatively easy on you, Cher. You're used to weasels. I am far more man than you can handle. But I'm willing to…train you because…" he trails off.

"Train me?"

"Yes. Because I'm into you. *More* than a little."

My heartbeat jumps as I stare at him, mesmerized by his words.

"I thought...I had a secret admirer," I say. "But you were hired to kill me. So, why the roses?"

He shrugs. "I don't normally mix business with pleasure. But I enjoyed watching you. I...wanted to give you something as a reward and to ensure you didn't mistake me for *him*."

"Jason," I frown.

"Yes," he sneers.

I'm afraid to ask what he has planned for Jason, who has stopped thumping in the trunk. Is he alive? As much as I hate my ex, I wouldn't wish death on him. I can't believe it's come to this. Then again, I can't believe many things since Pirate entered my life two months ago.

After another exit and a few turns down dark roads, he speeds up a hill before entering a parking garage full of expensive, shiny motorcycles. The doors lift on both sides of his supercar. He comes around and offers me his hand, and when I take it, he pulls me into his arms so quickly that I gasp. His spicy, masculine scent and muscular, solid arms fully envelop me. It's overwhelming. I could get lost in him if I let myself, and that's a scary prospect. My life has already been turned upside down. I must cling to my sense of self and stay strong.

He holds me against his chest a second longer before letting me go. I wonder what he was thinking during that embrace. Is this all part of his plan, or is he improvising? The look in his blue eyes is conflicted, which makes me lean toward the latter.

He clears his throat, crossing his arms.

"I have rules for you to follow here. Trust doesn't come easy."

Loud banging and muffled sounds rise from the trunk, and I'm partly relieved Jason is still alive. But being alive means he'll be subjected to more torture. It almost seems more humane to rid this world of him while ending his suffering. Kill two birds with one stone.

"What about *him?*" I ask as Pirate turns, leading me to the garage door.

"What *about* him?" He shrugs, and my brows furrow with concern.

"I haven't decided," he sighs. "I should kill him."

"Don't," I plead.

Pirate tugs me suddenly closer, and a little yelp escapes my mouth. He clutches my chin between his fingers.

"Let's get one thing straight, love. I have a job to do. And I give the orders around here."

He pins me with a steely gaze that hints at anger. Not the hot-headed kind of anger that's hasty and tends toward outbursts. Pirate's anger is cold, slow-burning, and calculated. There is something fiercely unstoppable inside this man. He epitomizes danger and is not to be taken lightly.

"Okay," I say, and he releases my chin to caress the hair from my face.

"Please do not mistake my feelings for you as a bargaining chip on your part. You'll have to earn my trust."

His dead-serious tone is full of warning, sending goosebumps over my body. I think this man has been wronged before and is not messing around. I don't think he wants to hurt me. But I think he could be persuaded to do so if I'm not careful.

"Okay," I nod, swallowing thickly as a tear runs down my cheek.

* * *

He throws a sniveling Jason to the ground before an oversized, throne-like chair, wing-backed, red leather with skulls carved into a wood frame, like something you'd see on a pirate's ship. Beside the chair is a large model of a pirate's ship on display alongside a collection of old-world swords. More and more, I'm understanding how he got his nickname.

The statuesque man sits in his chair, proving it perfectly fits his impressive frame. He pulls the bandana from his head, and his dark hair falls along the edges of his face, accentuating his piercing blue eyes, striking cheekbones, and chiseled jaw with a chin divot. The man is a work of art.

"Three rules, Cher. Rule number one: You can only use the rooms I've permitted. All other rooms are off-limits. Rule number two: You do not leave this house without me. *Ever*. Rule number three: if somebody knocks on my door or rings the bell, you *hide*. Unless I permit you to show your face, you stay hidden when I have a visitor in the house."

I stare back at him, dumbfounded. Is this to be my new life? What kind of people does Pirate have as visitors? The kind that thinks I'm dead? How am I safer here than I was at my own home?

"How long will this last?" I sigh.

He raises a dark brow. "Having second thoughts?"

"I didn't ask for this."

"Don't blame *me* for your mistakes, love."

"I'm not!"

"I can see it in your eyes. If you want to earn my trust, be honest."

"I don't deserve to live like a prisoner."

"You made bad choices. But you're lucky I found you. Be grateful. I know I am." There is that twinkling charm in his pale blue eyes again. It's comforting when he smiles at me like that, even if he's speaking in riddles. He said he feels lucky to have found me.

Jason interrupts this would-be touching moment by sneezing and shooting bubbles of snot all over his face like a child. He raises his shirt and wipes himself.

"Get a fucking grip!" scolds Pirate. "One broken ankle and you'd think your life was over. I've scaled a wall in far worse shape than you. If you were truly dead, you would feel *nothing*. Is that what you want? Because I can make that happen in a heartbeat."

"No, fucking way, man! I'll do what you say," whines Jason.

Pirate shakes his head in disgust.

"I've got only one rule for *you*. Don't make me want to kill you sooner than I have to. See that big cage over there? Belonged to my pet tiger. It even has a bed, which is more than you deserve. Go make yourself at home and stay quiet as a fucking mouse."

Jason struggles across the grey stone floor, reaching the massive cage, which takes up the living room corner. He goes inside, fumbling to shut the gate before hobbling to the bed, where he collapses. He's too tired to notice that beside the cage are floor-to-ceiling windows overlooking an infinity pool with an ocean view. It's ironic. He is caged in the lap of luxury. Undoubtedly, a cliffside home with a view near Salem is costly. Being a Pirate pays well.

I'm his prisoner, too. What will he do with me?

There is a knock at the door, and Pirate snaps his head toward the foyer. "First test, Cher." The urgency in his voice fills me with nervous doubt. I have trouble understanding how I'm safer here than at home.

He points to the first door down the hallway, past a bar area, and my heartbeat quickens furiously as I run and hide, closing myself in what appears to be a guest bedroom. The space is minimally decorated in shades of grey and light blue, and a large conch shell sits atop a dresser—a beachy prison.

I lock the door, go to bed, and sit down, and my mind races with the possibilities of who could be visiting and why they aren't supposed to see me. I feel like a fugitive on the run—the kind the police don't know about yet, but the mob does.

I focus on the muffled male voices. Is it another mercenary? A friend or work associate?

Why else would Pirate insist that I hide? Whoever is visiting, Jason is out there for them to see. Why doesn't he have to hide? Pirate must truly have different plans for him. I don't know his fate, but it can't be good. Pirate hasn't killed him yet, though. *God, what has come of my life?*

Bratva? I'd be lying if I said I hadn't heard the term before, tossed around at the office with weighted significance. I just hadn't put it all together in my head, or didn't want to, maybe a little of both. Denial is a tricky thing. Being a legal secretary is even trickier. On the one hand, you are privy to all kinds of inside information.

On the other hand, it's none of your damn business. So you learn to handle the work from a mental distance, like a banker dealing with other people's accounts and money. It's not your business to know where the money truly comes from. In this way, it's easy to look the other way.

I put my ear to the door, trying to listen. Silence now. Did they go outside? I sit on the bed, jumping at the sound of the tap on the door. I hold my breath as the door slowly opens, and the delicious scent of hot food wafts. My stomach growls.

"Hungry?" half-smiles Pirate, and I bite my lower lip with a nod.

"Very."

"Follow me," he says.

He's taken off his shirt, and the muscles in his back are a sight to behold as I saunter across the living room like a gladiator between fights. He stops and locks the cage gate before leading me outside, where food packages are on a table near lit hedges and several lovely, potted plants. The lit swimming pool shines blue in the moonlight.

"Did you really have a tiger?" I ask as he opens the enchiladas and side dishes and arranges them before two chairs facing the starry-skied ocean view.

He nods. "His name was Jin. I fucking loved that crazy cat. I sent him to a zoo when he got older, where he could have a better retirement. I visited there often before he died."

"I'm sorry," I say, sitting in a padded chair at the wrought iron table.

"Don't be. He lived a long, healthy life. I wish I'd had the time to take care of him later, but my job is demanding, and I didn't trust a sitter with him for more than a few hours at a time."'

There is that word again. Trust. *Who* does this man trust? Anybody?

"You've been a mercenary your whole life?"

"More or less," he shrugs, pointing at my food. "Do yourself a favor and dig in. You'll need your appetite."

"For what?"

His blue eyes darken, making my body clash with alarm and desire.

"For *me*."

I press my lips together. Under ordinary circumstances,

this might be considered a date. But this situation is far from ordinary, and I'm too hungry to think.

So hungry that it takes effort to eat politely. The enchiladas are no doubt tasty, but my brain is chewing in unison with my teeth over thoughts about what Pirate may have planned for me. Sure, he made me orgasm harder than I ever had before, but he wasn't easy on me.

He said he plans to *train* me. What the hell does that mean?

"Good?" he asks, and I nod, wiping my mouth. I take a drink of water.

"Will *he* get to eat?" I ask, hoping I won't get in trouble for caring.

Pirate looks at me with a cold, blank expression. "Depends."

There is that predatory calculation in his eyes again. It's a rare gift to have the ability to be so cold and yet still human. He's more human than Jason could ever be.

"Enjoy your meal," he says in a low, almost melancholy tone.

The way he watches me think makes me self-conscious, and I distract myself by eating. We eat silently, and each time he looks up at me from his plate, his expression is thoughtful and conflicted. I don't think he's made up his mind about me yet. He said I needed to earn his trust. He wants to trust me, and I find that flattering.

I also haven't made up my mind about him. But I don't think he's a happy man. I get the feeling he secretly wants more out of life. There's almost a repressed longing in his eyes. Or maybe I'm just imagining it, hopeful that there is more to this twisted trauma-bond between us. I don't know.

"You said you've been a mercenary more or less your whole life. What do you mean by that?"

He wipes his mouth and takes a swig of water.

"I was born into it."

"So your father was a mercenary or military?'

"Military, yes. Mercenary, no. He was a biker. The Hellfire Club started as a motorcycle club, and my old man was a full patch member. He was one of the loyalists who stuck around when the H.O. went corporate, and money was no longer small-scale and under the table. Hellfire merged with a mercenary arms company, and the rest is history."

"The Bratva is an enemy of your company?"

"Certain members are."

"Like the members of my firm."

"Correct."

"Are they all...dead, now?"

A pointed look enters his eyes, and I know the answer.

"Certain members of your firm have been taken care of. But I don't have all the details. I was tasked with two lower-level members."

"Does the H.O. always kill off its enemies?"

He shakes his head. "Not when it can be avoided."

I glance at his Olympic-sized infinity pool overlooking the sea.

"I guess it pays well," I smile.

He nods. "Indeed, it does."

"And does it make you happy?"

His brows furrow. "Odd question."

"Is it? I'm just wondering if you like your job. That's all."

His eyes dip to my lips. "Some days, I like it more than others."

He stands, holding out his hand. I nervously take it, but his firm, warm hand wrapped around mine is a nice feeling, even if it shouldn't be. Under the guise of protection, he's removed me from my home, my life, my sense of identity. I should hate him, not love him. I *could*. Love him. That's the scariest part of this whole thing.

He leads back inside, where Jason is snoring. I shake my head at the sight of him in that tiger cage. He's injured, probably in a lot of pain. It's difficult to feel an ounce of sympathy for him, given the suffering he has caused—god, I can't even think of all that right now—the missing girls. I already know he's capable of murder. Eh, it's too much to bear in an already overwhelming situation.

I sit on a leather sofa while Pirate takes a phone call. He glances between Jason and me, and butterflies fill my stomach. Is he making or breaking a deal? After all, this man was hired to kill us both. He hates pedos, but he has a thing for me. The woman he was stalking turned out to have a kink for spying eyes.

Yep, that's me. Embarrassing but true.

Thirteen Pink roses—that's how many I collected from him before he showed up inside my house with Jason. I kept them all in the same vase. Half of them are dried, wilted, and a paler shade of pink but still preserved in a tilting, bell-like shape. I think the wilting rose represents lost love. But what if that love was lost to begin with? Every moment with Pirate feels like sailing toward a distant shore, my old life fading in the distance. Reality is no longer grounded but floating at sea.

"Wake the hell up!" he shouts at Jason, and I jump with a yelp.

Pirate slams his phone on a table before rattling the cage loudly.

"That missing girl was found *dead*. No doubt, *you* are the fucking cause. Time to die, asshole," he rumbles, pulling his knife out and flicking it open. It isn't a little pocketknife; it has a very long blade.

"WAIT!" I shout, panicked, and Pirate turns to me, his grey eyes as fierce as a wolf. He looks at me like I've interrupted his kill. For which the punishment is to be killed.

"I give the orders, Cherry Coleson," he grits, jaw clenching.

Wide-eyed, I shake my head. I can't watch a murder happen. What the hell do I do?

He turns away from me and opens the gate. Jason jumps backward as Pirate steps forth, the blade at his side. Jason backs himself into a corner, balling up like a scared child. This is the man who killed a girl? Did he do that?

"Can't we just...*torture* him more?" I cry out, desperate to stop this from becoming a blood bath.

Pirate stands there broad-shouldered and towering over a cringing Jason. "What do you think, Dipshit? Should I fuck your ex-girlfriend in front of you some more? Or should I just fucking kill you? How about...*both*."

He turns around, and Jason shocks me by lunging at Pirate's back with a giant bone in his hand. Just as Pirate turns around, Jason slams the bone against Pirate's neck. Pirate doesn't flinch; he squeezes Jason's hand until he drops the bone.

Pirate grabs his shirt and drags him forward, parking him at the front of the cage. He smacks him upside the head.

"You move. You *die*. Where is the other girl?"

"I promise, I don't know, man!"

"BULLSHIT!"

Pirate locks the cage before disappearing into the hallway.

"Quick! Call the police!" urges Jason.

I put my palms in the air. "I don't have a phone!"

Pirate reappears with a big silver bowl. He opens the cage.

"What...are you gonna do with that?" Jason flinches as Pirate lowers the bowl onto his lap. Jason looks down.

"Popcorn?" he says, surprised.

"That's right, Dipshit. Enjoy the fucking show. Triple X rated for your viewing torture."

THIRTEEN
pirate

WHEN I TURN AROUND and catch Cher looking at Jason, I shake my head at her.

"That rule about not making eye contact with him applies here, too. Take off your shirt."

She hesitates briefly before doing what she's told. As much as she hates him watching us together, she'd rather that than the alternative. So, I'm letting her have her way. Maybe this will motivate that sicko to tell me where the other girl is. Then, I can finally rid myself of his filth.

When she drops her shirt to the floor, I delight in the bounce of her heavy breasts through the nude lace bra and the way they shade from pink to red in the cool air, hardening into suckable cherries.

Ignoring the tinge of regret I feel over sharing this moment with that rat in the cage, I reach down with my free hand and unfasten my military belt before pulling it off.

I stick my knife between my teeth before wrapping the belt around Cher's eyes and head. She stands motionless with her arms at her sides as I tighten it at the back. I grab the knife from my mouth.

"Can you see, Cher?"

"No."

I trace my tongue along her lower lip. "Good. Forget about him and focus on how I make you *feel*."

I raise the tip of my knife, sliding it just under her bra strap, and she shudders as the dull back of the cold metal blade touches her skin.

"You came so hard last time my dick was inside your wet pussy. It made me wonder. Have you ever gotten off that good before? Be honest."

She hesitates a second when I flick my wrist and slice the tip of the blade through the strap, making her yelp as the fabric falls, exposing her full, supple breast.

She sharply inhales. "No, I haven't."

Didn't think so.

I trace my tongue around her nipple before sucking and biting it. Her breathing is suddenly audible, and I notice her mouth is slack when I look up at her.

Sliding the blade under her other strap, I pause. "Seems to me like you are turned on by *danger*, love. Yes?"

Her chest heaves under the feel of my knife resting on her chest, and I lower my hand, slinking beneath the fabric of her sweatpants until I find her pussy. Just as suspected, she is deliciously wet for me.

"Answer me, baby."

"I guess so."

"You guess so? That's not an answer," I say, slicing her other strap with one quick flick of the blade.

She gasps as the other breast spills forth, and I lower my mouth, sucking and biting until her nipple is firmly bright red. "Take off your pants," I order, lowering my knife to my side as she bends and tugs.

She stands there in nothing but black silk panties, and I trail my gaze along her curves, pausing on her thick, sexy-as-hell thighs. The memory of her jiggling thighs and bouncing ass as I fucked her from behind flashes into my mind, making me instantly rock hard. *Mm. I need more of that.*

"Those panties must come off," I demand, but when she lowers her hand to her waist, I tell her to stop. "I will do the honors. But first, I want you to answer my question properly."

I peel off my shirt and grab her by the waist, luxuriating in the feel of our naked chests pressed together, her pillowy tits smashed against my hard, muscular chest. "Answer me, Cherry baby."

"I...never thought about it before."

With our bodies tightly together, I slide the blade along her hip bone and under her panty line.

"But you know that I'm right," I tell her. "You liked me watching you. That was risky behavior. You didn't know who I was. And when I busted into your house and finally tied you to your bed, your pussy was dripping wet for me."

I slice the blade outward, cutting away at her panties. She doesn't yelp or gasp this time, but her breathing gets loud, and her chest heaves against me.

"I was rough with you when I fucked you. You came all over my dick in a heartbeat. Ramming myself so deep inside your hot cunt, I filled you up. You couldn't get enough. Admit it, love."

"When you put it that way, yes," she mutters before I flick my blade again, slicing another strand of fabric from her hip. I reach down, testing her pussy with my other hand. *Oh, fuck.* My girl is drenched. She's so ready to be fucked by me I can hardly contain myself. My dick is so swollen with need now, it's painful.

I feel hasty as I slice the remaining fabric from her hip. Startled by my sudden onslaught, she yelps, but that only makes me more urgent. I fucking *love* the sound of her yelping.

I flip her around. "Reach out your hands to the chair."

She bends, grabbing the upholstered arms while her panties still cling to one hip.

Unzipping my jeans, the weight of my erection springs forth as I pull aside the fabric still clinging to Cher, exposing her ass and right between her thighs, her beautiful vulva, pink and moist and supple for the taking.

Setting my knife on the table beside the chair, I clutch her thick thighs in my hands as she spreads her legs, arching her back.

"Do you want me to fuck you hard, love?"

She nods, and I instantly thrust my cock between her thighs, pumping myself inside her wet heat. Her pussy wraps tightly around my dick—*oh...fuck...yes-s-s.*

She pants and moans as I ram my hips against the soft flesh of her ass cheeks. I push harder, and she arches her back, matching my thrusts like a good girl. My urgency builds quickly, fucking her more deeply with each thrust. I reach around her thigh with one hand, cupping her swollen pussy as my fingers find her clit. I fucking love the feel of her sweet, little sensitive spot between my fingers, caressing her there while I fuck her. Her moans get louder and louder as she nears the edge. This makes me insane, and I groan as I fuck her harder and deeper.

I grab her hair tightly in my hand, bringing my mouth to her ear. The tip of my cock hits her cervix, spasming with release as she tips over the edge. I lose my breath, coming hard deep inside her to the sweet sound of her moaning.

My lips find her ear again. "I'm *all* the danger you'll ever need, baby."

FOURTEEN
cher

JUST AS MY heart pounding in my ears starts to quiet, I hear the rattle of the cage. Then I remember. We aren't alone, and this isn't just the best sex I've ever had with a man so wrong he's right. For a fleeting moment in the throes of orgasm, I felt like I was his—just him and me. But now, it's back to reality.

Pirate pulls the length of his thick cock from me, smacking me on my sore ass before releasing his grip on my shakey thighs. He hands me something. A towel.

"Turn around and sit," he orders, catching his breath.

Thankful for the towel, I spread it over the leather chair before falling back into it. The cage rattles again, and I lift my hand to the belt around my eyes, turning my head toward the sound.

Peeking at Jason from under the fabric, I catch a glimpse of a man I barely recognize. His face is red and twisted into an ugly scowl. I've never seen him so miserable. His eyes are full of hate.

My eyelids feel itchy from the fabric, so I pull the belt from my head while I can.

Jason spits in my direction. "You fucking *whore*."

"Fuck you, Jason!" I hiss.

He puffs out air, then spits on the ground.

I shake my head in disgust. "Did you do it, Jason? Did you hide that girl? Did you hurt her?"

He drops his gaze to my tits, and his mouth slants into a crooked smirk. I get this visceral urge to go over and smack him across the face. I'm not usually a violent person.

"I'm just getting started," I smile. "I could let him fuck me all night and make you watch. Or you can tell him where the girl is, and this ends. It's that simple. Stop being pigheaded!"

His eyes dart around the room like he's considering his options.

"The only way out is through admission, Jason. Where is the girl?"

The hate returns to his dark eyes, and his mouth cracks into a villainous snarl. "You'll never find her," he hisses, and my stomach drops. I stare at him with a lump in my throat. *Pure. Evil.*

"You make me sick," I cry, and he snickers as if this is his revenge on me. It occurs to me that maybe Pirate was right. Perhaps he should put Jason out of everyone's misery.

Suddenly, I regret taking off the blindfold. It was to help me ignore that piece of shit. Instead, I'm sitting here naked in this leather chair with a wet pussy, and thoughts of violence.

Then again, I just orgasmed so hard; it's shocking. God, Pirate has the thickest cock, and he wields it like a pro, and the way he adeptly caressed my clit while he ruthlessly fucked me—I have *never* been fucked so hard. I've never come so hard.

But how will this end? I wish I knew.

"Dirty, dirty, *whore*," Jason spits again, shaking the cage with a rageful gaze. He's finally showing me the unfiltered version of himself, which chills me to the bone. I think he'd kill me if he had the chance, just like he killed my friend and probably that poor, innocent girl.

I divert my eyes from him, crossing my legs and covering my breasts with my arms. He's dead to me. He's Pirates' problem, not mine.

"Nasty, disgusting *cunt*," he continues. "Piece of *TRASH!*"

Pirate appears in the hallway with a phone to his ear.

"The kids are fighting," it sounds like he says, which digs deep under my skin. Did he really say that? His lumping me in with Jason makes my skin crawl. It's insulting. Sure, we both worked for Bratva, the connection between us. But we are not the same in any other way. I must have heard him wrong.

As he approaches, Pirate holds out a black robe, tossing it to me.

"Put that on. I don't want Dipshit deriving enjoyment by looking at you. He's only allowed to see you when I'm fucking you."

I take the robe with a frown. I'm done doing anything in front of Jason, but I won't say it aloud. He still needs to confess. I frown at Pirate as he watches me cover myself with the soft, oversized robe.

He cocks his head, studying my face. "What's wrong, love? Didn't I fuck you good?"

I sit in the chair, crossing my arms and saying nothing.

His eyebrow slants. "Pouting, huh? I suspect this has something to do with *him*. I can't leave you two alone for five seconds—"

"Do *not* equate me with that bastard!" I snap, and Pirate stares at me, surprised.

He leers at Jason as if he's to blame for my outburst, and with the flick of his fingers, the blade of the knife appears at his side. He approaches the cage, and Jason's eyeballs bulge as he shuffles backward on his ass.

"Not like this!" I cry out.

"Too much blood? I'll use a gun, then."

Pirate sighs in frustration as he turns around and faces me, shirtless and menacingly beautiful in his towering, muscular stature. But did he say what I think he said? Is he just pretending to regard me as more than a target? Is it all a calculated game in which I'll be discarded after he gets his confession?

"He *is* going to die, Cher. The sooner, the better."

"What about me?"

"I will keep you safe."

"As your slave?"

He smiles darkly. "You will have to earn my trust. I can keep you and *not* fuck you. But I don't think that's what you want, love. Is it?"

FIFTEEN
cher

HE'S NOT WRONG, but...

I'm suddenly embarrassed to admit it. I shouldn't be into him, just as I should never have played games with his shadow or offered myself up as a form of pain inflicted on Jason. What was I thinking? This didn't even lead to an honest confession. What is the fucking point, now?

I wouldn't be in this position if I had never gone against my instincts and dated Jason. Yeah, I did all these things that led to this moment, and now I'm stuck in a conundrum. Wanting Pirate may be just as wrong as wanting him to like me in return. But that's the tricky part.

He knows I want his bittersweet medicine as if I need it for survival. In a way, I do. The same man holding me captive is the same man keeping me alive. Hired to kill me. Then, saving me instead. That is, if he's telling the truth about his intentions toward me.

"You going to answer me?" he says with a cocked brow before reaching into a mini fridge at the bar. He sure doesn't let a girl off the hook. I'm pathetically temporarily distracted by how his jeans hug his muscular ass as he bends down.

"Well?" he says, standing.

How can I admit to my captor that I'm along for the ride? Not that I have a choice.

But I do have a choice in how I feel about it.

I'm grappling with this as Pirate brings two water bottles, hands me one, and then chugs the other. I bet Jason is dying of thirst. I've never been a believer in actual torture. Dying of dehydration fits that bill. I am part of an evil man's torture, and I can't feel good about it, even if he deserves it.

I look down at myself with a sigh. This robe smells like the man who just hungrily consumed my body—is it wrong to crave the scent of him so damned much, and the feel of his body commanding mine as he fills me up inside, violating me like a dark dream?

I look up, and Pirate watches me intently as if he wants to pick my brain. He's so thoughtful and conflicted, and maybe that is because he has been lying to me. Maybe he did plan to kill me all along.

His blue eyes lock with mine, and the cold twinkle in his gaze gives me chills. Icebergs lit by the sun may sparkle, but that doesn't mean they have any warmth inside them. He smiles softly.

"Don't worry," he says, as if reading my mind. I want to cling to this glimmer of hope, this small comfort. But I can't let myself fall for a stupid illusion. I won't survive if I can't outthink my captor. I'm at his mercy and have never felt so out of control. It could feel liberating if I truly trusted my life in his hands. He says that bad people want me dead. But what if that is just what he wants me to believe?

"What are you thinking?" asks Pirate, seeming genuinely interested. Does he care, or is he just a good liar?

I shake my head, puffing out air. Spilling my heart out won't keep me alive, but continuing to show him I'm vulnerable might. I need answers. Proof that he's telling the truth.

"How will I..." I trail off, allowing the tears to well up in my eyes.

"How will you what, love?"

"How will I ever...start over?"

He nods at me as if that is a valid question. Then he walks over and reaches his hand to me, and when I give him my hand, he pulls me from the chair into his naked chest. He runs his thumb down my jawbone, and my breathing thins under the tingling power of his touch.

He kisses me once. "Follow the rules."

He kisses me again. "Earn my trust."

He gently sucks on my lip. "Can you do that for me?" he whispers.

Tears flow down my cheeks as he peers into my eyes. I want to believe that he is as straightforward as he seems.

I nod at him. "And then what?"

He brushes my hair from my face. "Then, I will help you start over."

SIXTEEN

AFTER CHECKING that the house is secure, I turn down all the lights and lock my bedroom door before showing Cher to my suite's bathroom. She can take a hot shower while I prepare the bed.

I commonly sleep and work odd hours, often on my laptop, processing case files and doing intel research. So, I may not be here to babysit her all night. Until I can trust her, she must sleep tied to the bed via hospital limb restraints. At least, that's my excuse. She doesn't know I have cameras all over the house.

I pull the restraints from a duffel bag. I keep a few sets on hand for interrogation purposes, which are usually conducted at a private storage facility. Luckily, I had a spare pair here.

Bringing targets to my residence is a risk I've never been willing to take, and changing my protocol is not a habit I intend to keep. This is an unusual situation that I could not have predicted. Everything changed the night I spied on Cherry Coleson.

I waited until after nightfall, about an hour after she got

home. I'd planned to get a quick close-up to snap some pictures, but I watched her longer than intended. I *liked* watching her.

Watching Cher didn't feel like work because I enjoyed it too much. Then, after I tapped on her window one night and left a pink rose, we reached a turning point. At first, she looked stunned. I half thought she might call the police. But instead, she returned to her room with a vase.

Now, it was my turn to be stunned.

I was a mere shadow to her. She toyed with the mystery of that shadow, letting me see far more of her body than I'd intended, far more than I needed to conduct my surveillance. She fed into my fantasy just as I fed into hers. She made me covet her more than I should.

Playing with shadows is dangerous business.

Knowing what she knows now, she might choose otherwise if she could turn back the clock. But it's too late.

She's mine.

I could have carried out my mission and killed her, or I could have left her for the hitman that was inevitably coming in my stead. But I didn't. She got lucky.

When she exits the bathroom, she is wearing my black robe. The clothes she had on when she arrived are still on my living room floor, as is her luggage.

"Can I please get my things?" she says. Her tone and manner have been different since I left her alone with Dipshit.

I shake my head. "You aren't free to move about the house alone yet. I'll get them in the morning. You don't wear clothes for sleeping."

Her eyebrows lift. "Together in this bed?"

"For a few hours. Or you can sleep in here on your own.

But if you get thirsty or need to use the bathroom, I might not hear you call my name from the other room."

She looks at the restraints attached to the bed, seeming to get my meaning.

"Do you want me to sleep here with you, Cher?" I ask. She frowns, seeming conflicted.

"What is it? What did he say to you that was so upsetting?"

"It wasn't what he said as much as what *you* said."

"When?"

"On the phone. It sounded like you said 'the kids are fighting.' But I thought I was a secret. That, and...you equated me with *him*."

"Yes, you are a secret. No associates of mine know that I've brought you here."

"Then who was that?"

"Well, I was speaking to my Mom."

"Your *Mom* knows...?"

"About my work? Yes. She's a survivor of a lifetime married to the H.O. She's in protective custody now."

"From the H.O.?"

"No. From bad guys who might target her to get to me."

She glances at the bed and then tightens the robe around her waist. She's still feeling unsure.

"I didn't mean that comment about the kids the way it sounded," I explain.

"How would your mom have interpreted that?"

I nod, getting her meaning. A strange feeling washes over me. Why does she care what I say to my mom? It's the response you might expect from a legitimate girlfriend. I haven't had one of those in years.

"Yes, I was talking about two targets. But she knows..." I trail off. I hadn't planned on divulging everything I said to

Mom. But I don't like how Cher is looking doubtful about me. Trust is a two-way street. But it's more than that. I care because she cares. I wasn't expecting to give a shit what Cher thinks. But I do.

"My mom knows me pretty well," I explain. "She knew something was up with me at the first mention of your name. My tone gave it away."

"Gave what a way?"

I wasn't planning on admitting this to her, but here goes.

"That I'm into you. More than a little. Mom knows it's not like me to mix business with pleasure. I've always been stoic, not making much time for my personal life. But...you make me want to change that."

"I do?"

She tightens her lips like she's holding back a smile, but I can see in her eyes that this is good news. Maybe only because she thinks it means I'll keep her safe and alive. She's not wrong, but I'd like it to be more than that. I've admitted enough for now, though. Can't have her thinking she has more leverage than she does. No matter how much I'm into her, I need her to prove herself. There are limits to my affection.

I won't keep what I don't trust.

Seeming satisfied, she goes to the bed and slips out of the robe before climbing in. I meet her there to fasten the cuff around her left wrist. The strap is attached to the bedpost and is long enough to allow her to move in her sleep. Next, I fasten her left ankle to the longer strap attached to the bottom of the bed.

I pull the sheet and blanket up to her waist, and she grabs on with her right hand, pulling them up above her chest.

"I'll be in the shower," I say before stripping off my jeans. My hard-on springs out. *Damn, son.* After so many years of interrogations, I never knew that tying somebody up could turn me on. But this is what it's like for me with Cher.

Her eyes dip to my manhood, and her lips part, followed by a noticeable rise in her chest. Maybe before I shower, I should…

"What do you *want*, Cher?"

She bites her lip. "I want…to know your real name."

This catches me by surprise. "Why does it matter?"

"You know mine," she says.

"I know many things about you that you don't know about me. That's the nature of how we met."

"That can't change? I can't know you better?"

"Trust and information are intertwined, love. I give neither easily."

She frowns, and I sigh, looking down at her.

"I'm going to start a rewards program with you. In exchange for my earned trust, you will be rewarded certain freedoms and information."

"Okay. How do I start?"

Her eagerness is ticklingly cute. I repress a smile. All I want to do right now is pull the blanket from her and claim her in my bed. But I need to give her a chance to prove herself to me.

"I could have tried to run," she offers. "I mean, at my house. But I didn't, not just because I was afraid. I…wanted to play along."

"For revenge?"

She nods. "Jason's been a problem in my life. You seemed like a solution. But that's not the only reason. I…"

she sighs, cheeks flushing. Whatever she's trying to say, she's embarrassed about it.

"Wanted to please me?" I offer.

When the pink in her cheeks deepens, and she nods in confirmation, my dick gets even harder.

As I pull the blanket down, followed by the sheet, the draft causes her nipples to perk. My mouth salivates, and my cock pulses in eager anticipation. I want to see her front side bounce this time.

I grab her legs, parting them before sliding her free leg upward into a bent position, allowing me full access to her glistening pussy. I climb between her thighs on my knees.

"I'm glad you shared this with me, Cher. After I fuck you, I'll reward you with some information."

Hiking her free thigh, I slide my steely shaft over her soft folds before striking her damp pussy with the head of my cock, and thrusting myself hardness inside her softness —*mm...fuck-yeah.*

"You're fucking perfect," I thrust deeper and deeper as she moans.

I lower myself, sucking on her her bouncing tits while I pound my hips against her clit. My big dick spasms, swelling stretching her pussy to accommodate every ounce of my cock as I pump inside her.

She matches my thrusts with her hips, and her free hand clutches the muscles flexing in my supporting arm as her nails dig into my skin with a moan. She's already so fucking drenched when I release a torrent inside her to the sound of her nearing the edge—*oh...fu-u-ck...grr.*

I fuck her slow, deep, and hard as I finish coming to the delicious sound of her orgasm. Her clinging pussy begins to relax its hold over my cock as I kiss her, lapping her mouth and feeling like this woman is something I didn't know I was missing in life. Damn, I can't get enough of her. The sound of her breathing and the feel of her heartbeat fills my ears as I suck her lip. I get this feeling like this is all I need.

I study her smile like it's a work of art. I promised her information for good behavior. Before I have time to second-guess myself, I can feel the regretful words slipping from my mouth.

"My real name is Bastion," I rasp before pulling myself from her body.

SEVENTEEN
cher

I WATCH him in the moonlight.

He looks less edgy when sleeping, and his handsome face is relaxed.

His wavy, dark hair hits just above his shoulders. His face alone could make him a model in a men's magazine, let alone his muscular, statuesque body. *Bastion.* His real name is Bastion.

I earned his trust enough to get that out of him. Now, if I can get him to stop tying me up—at least when I sleep. I rotate slightly on my hip. The straps are long enough to sleep on my side or back, but turning over on my belly is impossible. Luckily, I'm not a belly sleeper.

I heard Jason yell something in the other room a few minutes ago. That woke me, but it wasn't enough to wake the sleeping giant beside me. Bastion-the-pirate has burned many calories in the last twelve hours—wrestling with Jason, binding and transporting him, and wrestling with him more.

Then there is the workout he's gotten with me. Lord, have mercy.

His words circle in my mind. He said he'd never brought a target to his home before. That it was risky to do, that he wouldn't make a habit of. He did it for me and has kept Jason alive this long because of me. But that won't last. He plans to kill him. He also plans to keep me safe. But I must earn his trust.

When he wakes, I need to discuss the issue of my friends and family, who will soon realize I'm missing. They will call the police unless they don't hear from me via text, our typical communication method.

Would it be a good thing if they reported me missing?

The police would conduct an investigation, and they would learn about my work connections to the mafia. They would tell my parents. My disappearance would be ruled suspicious. My parents would be overcome by grief, and they would want to go to my home and look through my things for clues to my whereabouts. What if the hitman hired to kill me showed up and hurt them? Killed them?

No, this is a terrible plan! I must get permission to send out texts and let everyone know I'm taking a little vacation with a new boyfriend nobody knows. Yeah, that's what I'll say.

Bastion opens one eye, looking at me. He reaches out and puts his hand on mine.

"Close your lids," he whispers, then falls asleep with his hand still on mine. His hand feels protective, and part of me hates this attachment I already feel for him. It can't be healthy. I've had some fucked-up relationships in my life, but never anything as insane as this.

My attachment started back when he was still a nameless mystery.

But I was convinced the shadow tapping on my window was the strange, beautiful man I had caught a glimpse of one night. Tall, broad-shouldered, athletic, and leaving my yard just before the whole thing started and before the first rose. I watched him walk, and I fell in love with his swagger. Even from behind, I knew he was something special.

When my shadow came at night, I imagined that strange man. His dark hair, broad shoulders, and that purposeful, powerful swagger. Who wouldn't want a guy like that stalking them? Call me crazy.

In retrospect, I might not be alive if I hadn't played along the way I did.

I watch my pirate, Bastion, sleeping in the moonlight, trying to decide if he would have killed me otherwise. Has he killed other women? Women like me who got entangled with the wrong people?

He says he was born in hell, as in the Hellfire Organization. This is what he knows, what he's good at. He must have worked hard to climb up the ranks. Speaking of...

I have a bar exam coming up. I've worked my ass off to get to this point, and my law career is only a test away—another thing I must discuss with...what do I call him? I think Pirate is his work name, and that is how he identifies. But I want to get to know Bastion. I doubt he wants me to call him by his real name around Jason. He seemed to regret telling me at all. But when we're alone together, I'm going to try.

"Cherry," he mutters in his sleep, closing his hand gently around my wrist. This simple act warms me as I close my eyes with a yawn. Nobody calls me Cherry. But it rolls so nicely off his tongue. Maybe we can strike a deal with what we call each other.

I'm thinking of that as I doze off, his hand still clasped protectively around mine.

EIGHTEEN

pirate

"I'VE GOT a new investigative contract that may interest you, Pirate."

I glance back at Cher before exiting the room. The tantalizing image of her beautiful body in my bed is overshadowed by the dirtbag passed out and drooling inside my pet tiger's old cage.

"I'm listening," I tell Connor with a scowl as I exit onto the patio before shutting the sliding door.

Today, I plan to get rid of the pedophile so I won't have to see his pathetic face anymore. Once he's dead, Cher will no longer worry about him like she does. She may feel guilty for helping me, but she can't blame herself for his death. That task will fall to me, and I will bear no burden.

Though most of my contracts don't require killing, there have been enough, starting with the man who gave me my nickname. After what he did to my mom, he thought that boarding a superyacht and heading out to sea would keep me away. I appeared suddenly on deck with a jagged bushcraft blade in hand. He called me a fucking pirate before I slashed his throat from ear to ear and fed him to the sharks.

"It pays twenty thousand. You'll have to travel to Miami for a few days. I know you love a good ride on the open road."

"Not in the mood to travel," I sigh, stretching my free arm overhead before reclining in a lounge chair by the pool.

"Since when aren't you itching for a change of scenery? *Shit*. Is it a girl? Well, bring her the hell along, son."

Matter of fact...it is. But I won't tell him that, especially considering she is supposed to be dead.

I sigh, flicking my hair back while running my hand along the stubble on my chin.

"Send the specs to my email, and I'll review it," I say.

"Of course. One more thing. You left something behind at the Coleson girl's house. Tanis sent a picture of it to the H.O. Antique weapon. I knew immediately it belonged to you. The weird thing is, he said it was sticky and that the leather smelled faintly like pussy. Did you have yourself a little fun on the fucking job?" he laughs heartily.

I shake my head, pissed off that I left that behind. "All due respect, but shut the fuck up, sir."

He snickers. "Well, it got me thinking. You took a liking to Coleson, yes?"

I don't like where this is going.

"What of it?"

"Just confirming you finished the job."

"She wasn't the important player in this."

"Meaning?"

"Meaning that Jason Fischer was the main liability. She was ignorant and didn't know much about the Bratva operation."

"Mm-hm. But you did her in, right?"

"Why do you care so much? They wanted her to disappear. Done."

He sighs, long and drawn-out.

"You're keeping her, then?"

"I don't like the fifth degree. It's not like I need the money anymore, and I have little tolerance for bullshit."

"It's never been about the money with you. You work because it's what you do. You are a *machine*, Pirate. Born and bred. An asset to the organization for that reason. You've never kept a personal life; it would get in the way of your purpose."

"So why would I change my habit now? Send the email, and I'll get back to you by tomorrow."

"Will do."

Irritated, I toss my phone on the table. He knows me too well. I've been in this game for too fucking long.

Why change now? Good question.

I peel off my clothes and jump into the pool. I should hurry and rinse off and then check on that sexy woman tied to my bed. She's the reason things are suddenly different, and it feels like I'm somehow on a new trajectory. It's unnerving. But I must keep in control. Control is my middle name. I let that slip, and I'll lose myself. I can't and won't let that happen for her or anybody.

NINETEEN
cher

I WAKE to the tickle of his lips on my foot.

He's hidden under the sheet as I squirm my free leg. He grabs that ankle firmly in his hand while focusing his mouth on my tied leg. I don't like to be tickled, so I continue to resist. But the more I resist, the more firmly he squeezes my free ankle in his strong hand. *Ouch.*

With a sigh, I stop moving, and he relaxes his grip.

A trail lingers from his soft kisses, reaching my upper thigh. God, that tickles, too. I reach my free hand down, pushing on his head. "*Stop.*" But it's only half-hearted. My pussy eagerly knows the reward at the end of this soft torture.

But then again, I'm so damn thirsty; my throat is paper dry, and my eyes are itchy.

"I need *water*," I croak with a cough, and he stops. But I can feel his hot breath on my inner thigh as he lingers a moment before sliding out from under the sheet.

He stands beautifully shirtless, his sculpted, tanned torso a sight for sore eyes. The tattoos on his arms are tropical and exotic: a tiger peaking predatorily between ferns, a black sail with a skull and bones on it, and the letters H O scrolled in cursive. This organization he works for isn't just a job to him. It's his identity. How can any girl ever compete with that?

He turns and grabs a bottle of water from the edge of the nightstand.

When he turns to face me, our eyes lock—and there it is! That charming twinkle surfacing like a polar sun seems to be what I live for these days. Knowing it's fleeting, I gaze at him while I drink.

"How does a shower and breakfast sound?" he says, and I smile with a nod. But then, the worries occupying my dreams last night move to the front of my mind, and I frown.

"What is it?" he says, sitting on the bed.

"I have to tell my family and friends that I'm away, or they—"

"Yes, I've thought of this. You can contact them today."

I sigh in relief, and he takes my hand.

"Is that it?"

"Well..." I look away briefly, listening for *him*.

Pirate—*Bastion*—shakes his head at me disapprovingly.

"Even with a wall between you, you still obsess over him!" He yanks the sheet from my body. "I'll get him off your mind," he says firmly.

His threat makes my heart speed up as he lowers his black sweatpants, exposing his thick, hard erection.

"That's what you want, isn't it, love? To learn to forget him?"

My lips part, and I faintly nod. I can't deny it's true.

"I'm going to keep punishing and claiming you until I've fucked all the memory of that weasel from your body and mind. Until it's only me who occupies the dark corners of your heart and soul."

His words reverberate through me as he climbs between my legs and spreads my thighs.

"Your pussy needs breakfast, too," he rasps, licking his lips as he grabs his thick cock in hand, pumping it twice until it swells red with veins. Blood floods my core as my pussy aches with need.

"But I'm not giving you what you want quite yet," he teases. He inches forward on his knees until that thick beast is before my mouth.

"I want you to suck my balls before I put my cock inside your pretty mouth."

He scoots closer, and I duck my head, sucking his balls into my mouth and enjoying the manly taste of him and the way he growls in the back of his throat.

He grabs my hair in his hand and guides me upward before sliding the tip of his cock past my lips. He's already so swollen that my mouth can barely contain him as he thrusts, grazing along my teeth.

"Good girl," he rasps, thrusting deeper until I gag on his fullness.

Pulling out, he lowers on his knees before grabbing my thighs and gloriously shoving his cock inside my wanton pussy. He clutches my throat with one hand while he fucks me, deep and hard.

I'm instantly panting, my heart beating in my ears as his pelvis slams my clit, and each forward thrust of his powerful hips fills me inside with his tumescent morning erection—*oh, god, yeah.*

I'm burning hot near the edge of release, and my thighs clamp as my pussy spasms around his swollen cock. Grunting, he grows more urgent, and his hand tightens around my throat as he pounds into me.

I clutch his hand around my throat as I climax with a moan. He groans deeply, coming hard inside me before his grip loosens on my neck, and the rhythm of his thrusts slows to a stop.

He pulls out, catching his breath as he unties my ankle and my wrist, freeing me from the bed. But I know that my freedom is both temporary and conditional. For the foreseeable future, I'll be proving myself trustworthy.

He helps me from the bed and leads me to the shower, turning on the hot water. "I'll be back in a few," he says, walking off.

"Thank you, *Bastion*," I say, and he abruptly stops. He turns back; his brows pinched over a conflicted gaze as if he half regrets sharing this part of himself with me. His real name. Not his earned mercenary name, but the name his parents gave him when he was born.

But he can't put the genie back in the bottle.

"Enjoy your shower," he mutters before leaving me.

TWENTY
pirate

PACING THE ROOM, I wait for Cher to finish her shower.

I stop at the window, running my hand along the curtain's edge as I process the strange sound of my name on her lips and the soft feel of her delicate throat still lingering on my palm from when I necklaced her. My hand fit perfectly around her neck, tight enough to feel her racing pulse. But choking her while fucking her was more than I could bear.

The way she knocked her hips forward, sending me deeper inside her—I've never come so hard before. Just when I thought I was done spasming inside her, her delicious pussy finished me off by swallowing my dick whole. Her moans reached a cacophony. I bet that dirty bastard heard us loud and clear, but the thought of it doesn't give me much satisfaction.

With a sigh, I look out at the tree tops descending downhill. I've given her a bit of privacy so she can shower. It dawns on me the ironic nature of taking her captive. In doing so, I've made myself a prisoner, too. Even with

Dipshit locked inside my tiger's old cage, I can't move about freely. At least, that is, not when I don't have Cher tied to the bed. As sexy as fuck as it may be, I can't keep her bound 24-7. But what if she does something stupid and tries to free her ex?

Adding to this complication, I can't resume my work outside the house until Dipshit is out of my hands for good. He must be dealt with. He'd be dead by now if it weren't for Cher. At first, I thought her resistance to my hurting him was due to her still having feelings for him. But the repulsive look she gets when his eyes meet hers makes me think otherwise. It seems her humanity drives her to care about someone as lowly as him. A fucking pedo, no less. I cannot relate to Cher's compassion, yet part of me admires it on some level.

Also, she pointed out the need for me to let her contact her family. I must allow her to check in with them before they report her missing and instigate police action. Her concern was how her family might be told she was presumed dead, and how distraught they would be, added to the danger of them becoming targets by going to her house, which is under watch by elements of the Bratva mob.

Her family needs to know that she is alive and away from town for a bit, on vacation. Speaking of vacations, I'm unsure about taking Cher to Florida with me. This current arrangement cannot be sustained. I must devise a longer-term solution to the difficulty I've created. Cher is supposed to be dead. As is that ex-piece-of-shit boyfriend of hers. But I've chosen to take Cher under my wing, and now I must mitigate the consequences as much as possible.

Besides all this, the thing weighing most on the back of my mind is how hard it hit me when she called me Bastion. To say I have mixed feelings about it is an understatement.

Nobody calls me Bastion anymore, save a few family members. I've been married to my work for so long that Pirate is the me that I know. Pirate is damn near immortal. Bastion is merely human, a relic of my past.

Why did I share this with her? So she could use it against me? No. That's a silly thought. A name can't have power like that unless I let it.

Still, hearing it from her lips stung. It felt like I bled a little inside, the name twisting like a summer rose with sharp, cutting thorns. I realize that this woman is more trouble than I predicted, and I have this nagging sensation that if I don't keep control, she could ruin me, breaking down what I've built.

I shake my head with a laugh. That will never happen. Control is my middle fucking name. She thinks I've been tough on her. She has no idea how tough I can be. Pray, she doesn't have to see that side of me.

TWENTY-ONE
cher

WHEN I EXIT THE BATHROOM, I'm not expecting to be alone. I glimpse his back as he shuts the door behind him, leaving me. He didn't like me calling him Bastion; that much is clear. I don't want to push my luck by calling him something he doesn't like.

So, Pirate it is.

Relishing in the private freedom of the moment, I'm happy to see my bag sitting on the dresser. Pirate is a thoughtful man. I suppose that comes with him being so calculating, but it sometimes feels like more than that, as if he enjoys thinking about me.

I slip on a pair of black silk panties, a matching bra, jeggings, and a pink-and-white striped blouse. I don't know why I bother wearing my black leather flats as if I'm going somewhere. But it feels nice to get fully dressed. I even put on the few items of jewelry I managed to pack before we left my house in a rush—a pair of rose-gold earring studs and a matching rose-gold bracelet.

Perhaps if I dress the part of a lady, he will treat me as such and not just his idiotic captive who he enjoys fucking.

Maybe that's being harsh. He did, after all, tell his mom about me. Or that he's into one of his *targets*. But I guess in his world, that's sweet talk.

Curls—that's what I need! I grab my curling iron from my tote bag and head to the bathroom to plug it in when I hear screaming—*Jason*.

Dropping the curling iron, I rush from the room and into the hall, where I see Pirate pulling Jason like a child by the ear through the living room and into the garage. Again, he's left me alone. If I genuinely wanted to get out of here, I could find a phone and call for help.

Deciding the smartest thing to do is to continue earning his trust, I follow his path into the garage, where I see him close the trunk. He opens his bloody hand when he appears in front of his sports car. I blink at the battered chunk of flesh comprising the center of his large palm. It takes me a moment to realize that it's Jason's ear. Shit, it's his *entire ear!*

I raise my hands to my mouth with a gasp, slowly backing away.

"Oops," Pirate shrugs.

"What the?" I stare at him in shock. I'm so in shock that I let out an awkward laugh.

"Easy mistake," he says, bursting into laughter.

I shake my head in disbelief. "What?"

"It only takes seven pounds of pressure to pull off a human ear," he explains, sobering me.

"Why is he in the trunk, Pirate?"

"See that short shovel in the corner," he points, and I turn my head. "Put it in the backseat while I get my go-bag and lock up."

With shaky hands, I follow his instructions. When I open the car door, I see a blanket across the backseat, where I put the shovel. *Oh, God, is this happening? Is Pirate about to kill and bury Jason?*

I open the front door to see if the keys are inside, contemplating making a run for it. The garage opener is in plain sight, attached to the sun visor, but I see no keys. When I hear Pirate coming, I rush to the other side and get into the passenger seat.

"Where's your luggage?" he asks, surprising me.

"Huh?"

"Guess I forgot to tell you to bring it. Go get your things, Cher."

"Okay. Where are we going?"

"Errands. Time is pressing."

I nod, hurrying inside. I grab my bags and shove my sweatsuit inside before returning to the car. Though he pulls the car quickly from the garage and speeds down the road, the tires make no sound. The car hugs the road as he adeptly veers around each curve of the hill in descent.

Bright morning sunshine crowns the horizon over the big blue sea as Pirate cracks the windows, letting the cool, ocean breeze in. It's the kind of day that makes you want to be outside, walking in a park or on the beach, not racing away with an earless criminal stashed in the trunk.

I catch Pirate in my periphery, glancing at me, and I shift my attention to him with watery eyes.

"I don't want to be an accessory to murder."

"Don't be afraid," he says.

"He's going to die?"

He returns his eyes to the road, entering the highway Southbound.

"Yes," he says.

"We were supposed to...I was going to tell my family today—"

"Yes. I've brought your phone. We'll take care of that once we get to the airport. You can tell them we are going on a little vacation to Miami. If they happen to track your phone location once it's turned back on, it will confirm that you are in Florida."

"I doubt they would do that. We only speak every month or so. No reason to worry yet. My parents probably don't even know about the phone tracker."

"That would be the wrong kind of information to tell a serial killer who has abducted you, Cher."

I stare at him. "I thought I was earning your trust."

His cunning blue eyes briefly lock with mine.

"You are."

He sounds almost melancholy when he says that.

"And...what about you, Bastion?"

His brows furrow, and he goes quiet, except for a heavy sigh that lingers. The man is troubled, and I seem to have something to do with it. If I'm careful, I can wield this to my advantage. I'm not the only one earning trust here. I still don't know what he has planned for me long-term.

He drives silently, and I let myself get lost in the scenic views, enjoying myself until we pull off onto a lonely dirt road—the road forks, ending at a small white house surrounded by wooded acres.

"Is this yours?" I ask, and he nods.

"One of many. Get out of the car, love. Follow along."

I now know he has my phone in this vehicle, and I'm thinking of this as he pulls a groveling Jason from the trunk. I could find my phone and call for help. But then, his earlier warning interrupts my thoughts. That the Bratva was hunting me, but they think I'm dead. Dead equals no longer hunted. If I'm rescued by the police and resume my old life, I'm a dead woman walking.

"Get the shovel and walk toward the house," he orders. His tone is grim, and I know it isn't just the road ending in this neck of the woods. Jason's time is ticking.

"I'll give you all my fucking money, man. Just let me go," whines the dead man.

"I don't want your filthy money. Now, walk!"

I glance back at a hobbling Jason. Pirate taps him in the ass with the tip of his boot. "Faster!"

I hurry my steps, stopping when I reach the house.

"Go around back," orders Pirate, and I follow the stone path between trees until I reach the backyard with a small stream running through it. Branches crunch as a deer takes off running.

It was peaceful out here until we showed up.

"Over there, where that hole is," orders Pirate, and I look around until I see a recess in the ground just beyond the stream.

I navigate a haphazard path of larger stones to cross the water before arriving at a small, narrow ditch.

Pirate shoves Jason, sending him tumbling downward. When Jason hits the bottom, he's motionless at first. Then he lifts his head, spitting out dirt.

"Admit what you did to that girl, and I might let you live," shouts Pirate before taking my hand in his as he stands by my side. We both watch Jason settle into a sitting position at the bottom of the hole.

"Okay, okay. I...took her. I took her, okay? Just let me fucking go."

"Took her where, Dipshit?"

"To...to the motel, for sex, and—"

"Where did you take her after the motel?"

"I...she...wasn't breathing, so..."

"Where did you take her!?"

"To...the dump. In a...duffel bag. I-I tossed her in. Please, let me--"

"Oh, god," I gasp in horror over what he's done. I hold my hands over my face as a pile of dirt hits him in the head. He spits with a moan, looking up at Pirate holding the shovel.

"Okay, there's more!" cries Jason as more dirt hits him square in the face. "I stashed the other girl in a fucking trash can."

"Monster!" I scream, feeling sick in the stomach as the bitter taste of bile hits the back of my throat. Holding back puke and tears, I stare at the evil worm covered in dirt beneath my feet, down in a hole where he belongs. We have a horrible confession, and this man should be going to jail.

But Pirate hasn't other plans.

I watch in numb shock as Pirate quickly removes earth along the edge of the ditch, lowering its height by slicing away measured chunks in a circular motion. It isn't just dirt he drops on Jason, but rocks. Big rocks.

I'm so consumed with rage over what Jason did that I do not shed one tear when his muffled, garbled pleas finally turn to silence beneath what has become his grave. There is comfort in the quiet finality of his absence. Only after Pirate covers the burial site with hay and branches and a small iron bench, do I realize what I've done. "I'm an accessory to murder," I mutter.

Pirate dusts his hands in a satisfied way before coming to me. He takes my hand, and when he looks into my eyes, his expression is softer than I've seen before. He doesn't look like a murderer; he looks disarmingly peaceful.

"You are *innocent*, love."

I shake my head. "I'm *not*."

"You didn't come here willingly, and you didn't help.

This was my doing and mine alone. Now, we have to hurry."

"But…where to?"

"We're going on a little vacay, just like you're about to tell your parents."

I glance again at the fresh grave before Pirate takes my hand, leading me back to the car.

"Exactly where are we going?" I ask, trying not to freak out. Jason is dead now. Dead and gone. I can't believe I just saw that.

"To somewhere with palm trees. I think you need a break."

"I think so, too."

"Margaritas on the beach and a ride on my boat."

"But you still haven't told me where that is."

"To the Port of Miami, love. We have a plane to catch."

TWENTY-TWO

EN ROUTE to my private airplane, dust rises from the dirt road in the background where the body is buried. With a frown, Cher watches the scenery out the window, her thoughtful silence weighing on my mind. I could do without her mournful energy.

Usually, I feel satisfied after the rare occasion of killing, but it seems she's robbed me of that. It's not that I feel guilt or regret regarding taking out a murderous pedophile. It isn't him, his death, that is bothering me; it's *her*.

The irony of her situation has become blatantly clear to me. Rescuing Cher from the fallout of the Bratva crime ring has only brought her closer to crime. I may have saved her, but I'm no saint, and my lifestyle is anything but wholesome.

Her robbing me of my moment feels like revenge for what I have stolen from her. Before I came along, she was a legal secretary who had the misfortune of seeing too much —the wrong numbers and names on paper. But she lived a comfortable life. She spent her days tucked away in a tidy office, her nights in the safety of her private bungalow, where she studied for the bar exam.

But then, unbeknownst to her, things got sticky in the background. Her office became a target, and everyone in it. She wasn't that important in the scheme of things, but they wanted no trails left behind. The order was served. She would be killed along with her boss and his associates. Hellfire got hold of the boss, and dealing with the lesser players was up to me.

Because of her, I didn't follow orders this time. Because of me, she is alive. She played a seductive role in that outcome, gambling by flirting with danger, putting on a show in her bedroom window for me, her secret admirer.

We played a little game and got stuck together, for better or worse. But is there another way?

I look over at her, studying the silken tendrils of chestnut hair running along her cheekbone, which point to pouty lips. The memory of kissing, sucking, and biting those soft, sexy lips and the feel of my manhood penetrating her mouth is fresh in my mind. The woman makes me feel like an addict. But I want to punish her for robbing me of my post-kill satisfaction.

I sigh, resenting her power over me while pondering my options. Do I want to take her to Miami with me? What other choice do I have?

"Where would you go, Cher?" I ask, and she turns her head toward me, confused.

"If I let you go," I explain.

The distance between her raised brows and jaw widens in disbelief.

"I..." She clears her throat. "Not the police. I'd probably be arrested."

"Possibly," I agree. "You could cut a deal. Rat me out."

She stares at me. "I'd rather do it another way. I'd like to go home--"

"*No.* That isn't safe yet. In time, this will blow over. You won't be on the run forever."

She nods, sighing with tears in her eyes.

"I can't go to family or friends," she sniffles. "I'd be worried about endangering them. But I'm a little fish in a big pond; I can't see how the bad guys would find me."

"You are a little fish that got caught in a net. This put you on 'the bad guys' radar. The good news is, they think you are dead. You'll soon be forgotten."

She presses her lips together, visibly holding back tears. When she looks at me, something has changed in her eyes.

"Where do you fit into all this, *Bastion?*"

My jaw tightens, clamping down over the sting my real name brings.

"Why do you cringe when I say your name?" she asks gently.

I shrug, turning my attention back to the road.

"It's an old name. The old me. Dead and buried."

Or so I thought. Hearing it from her awakens something inside me that I honestly didn't know I still had access to after all this time. But I can't stand it. It feels like a false hope, a lie to taunt me into believing that life could be different.

"That name...takes me back to when I still believed in fairytales. You can't understand."

"I want to understand," she says, and I glance at her. The earnest, heartfelt expression in her bright brown eyes softens the sting a little, and I shake my head with a sigh.

"What's the fucking point, love?"

"If we're going to be stuck together, I want to know my captor."

"I'm not your captor anymore. You're free to go. I want to be rid of you."

"Fine, then let me go," her voice cracks, knowing that isn't an easy option.

"Nah. I won't let you die," I whisper.

"Why not?"

"Because. I'm on your side, Cherry."

"But I thought..." she trails off.

"You thought I wasn't on anybody's side? That I'm all about my work. No feelings. Just a fucking robot."

"Something like that," she shrugs.

"You aren't wrong. I am a machine for hire. It's what I'm good at, it's what I do. But... You remind me that I'm still a human. For better or worse."

"You resent that?"

"Yes."

Her brows pinch with confusion, and I hate how she makes me want to explain myself. I sigh, shaking my head as I drive.

"Just because I resent something, doesn't mean it isn't good for me," I admit, already regretting it.

I ignore the thoughtful weight of her eyes upon me as I light a cigar, listening to her stifled cry. Surely, she's overwhelmed. I've brought her into my world, and it can't be easy.

Part of me wants to stop the car and kiss away the tears. I laugh at myself for having such a sappy urge. I must focus on getting to the airport promptly. My eyelids are heavy from lack of sleep, and I look forward to a long-overdue sleep on that private airplane.

She wipes her tears and drinks from the water bottle. When the weight of her stare finally nags at me, I look over.

"Thank you for helping, Pirate. I won't use your real name anymore if it angers you."

"Not angry. Just... Bastion is the name given to me by a woman who didn't yet know what was coming for us. I... became Pirate the day I killed the man who gave her permanent scars and left her nearly dead."

"That's terrible. You've...had a hard life," she says as I turn down the airport road, blinking my tired eyes.

"Is what it is," I shrug, dialing the code on the gate before entering. I turn left, driving around back to the open hangar where the pilots wait. "The seats fully recline for sleeping, on my plane," I say, changing the subject.

When I stop the car, I look at Cher, who has a bewildered expression.

I reach out and take her hand without thinking. I give it a little squeeze, enjoying the sensation.

"What is it, love?"

"This is your plane?"

"Yes. I own it."

Her eyes widen. She knew I was wealthy. But she didn't know how much.

I get out and go around, helping her out of the car. Her expression hasn't changed. "Why can't you just walk away from all this? You don't need the money."

I smile at her naivete, pulling her into my arms. She doesn't understand organized crime. It isn't a lifestyle you walk away from, no matter how wealthy. I'm in too deep. But all I'm thinking about now is how deep I want to be inside her body and mind.

"I've made my bed, love. Now, I'm sharing that bed with you and intend to take *full* advantage."

TWENTY-THREE
cher

LIKE AN IMPRESSIONIST ARTIST trying to capture a fleeting moment, I cling to the memory of his body all over mine as I study the changing colors in the skyline out the airplane window.

I can't believe I'm arriving in Miami with Pirate aboard his private airplane. For one, it's gorgeous...

The late-day sky is deep blue with a single, pink cotton candy cloud. White yachts line the calm blue waters. The sun drops a little lower, and suddenly the skyscrapers along the beach are smattered in irregular patterns of light, black towers with gold that imitate the streaking sunset behind. It occurs to me that you can't watch the sunset over the beach on the West coast of Florida; only the sunrise. But from the sky and water, the skyline glows along the cityscape as darkness seeps around it. Yeah, it's beautiful, but... God, what the *hell* am I doing here?

Staying alive, but it's more complicated than that.

Turning from the view, I study his handsome face. Pirate. Bastion. Jekyll and Hyde? I'm slowly getting to know the man I've been enthralled with since he was only a shadow, a dangerously sexy threat. I played with fire. But will I get burned?

It's hard to think ahead, and impossible to plan. I've always been a planner and an organizer. But my existence has been upended. I am in his world now, biding my time. After the unthinkable happened—after he killed Jason—he seemed to have second thoughts about keeping me captive. Said he wanted to be rid of me, but then he wouldn't let me return home. Too dangerous. For now. Until the bad guys forget me, which should be soon enough, I'm just a pawn on a board of real players. But enough time needs to pass to convince them that I'm dead. Then I can be free. But will I be? How can I return to my old life after what has happened? I feel I'll never be the same again.

For one, I don't have a job to go back to. Everybody I worked for is dead. But changing jobs is the least of my problems. I stood and watched my ex-boyfriend be murdered. How will I live with that?

Sighing, I gather my hair aside and fasten my seat belt as the pilot announces landing. Pirate opens one eye. When he sees me, the satisfied lift of his sexy mouth makes me crazy inside. I like pleasing him, and I like how that goes both ways.

When we began our twisted interrogation of Jason, Pirate didn't have to concern himself with my feelings. But he seemed so aware of how I was feeling, intensely attuned to me. The way he deeply studies my expressions and the look in my eyes. That intensity plays itself out full throttle when he's commanding my body. He makes me feel like he's been just as obsessed with me as I have been with him. Starting with him stalking me.

This unhealthy obsession has led to this point, but it's

so much more than I could have ever bargained for. I'm in over my head, but I think so is he.

He broke his own rules because of me, like sharing private information. He regrets sharing his actual name. The first time I said, *Bastion*, he cringed. His shoulders tensed, and he breathed deeply through his nose before leaving me. The second time I said his name, he was a tad calmer. He even briefly gave me some insight into his past. But it wasn't much. It still feels like he is more comfortable being my shadow, knowing far more about me than I do him.

I suppose that's what he's used to. Being in the background, being in control, and having intel on others. He doesn't like that going both ways. At least not with me. Not yet.

Part of me wants to get closer. Part of me is scared as hell.

I expect him to feel relaxed when he wakes and his chair lifts—quite the opposite. Whatever moment of relief I saw in his blue eyes after he came hard inside me is gone. He looks as if the world's weight is on his shoulders, reminding me that this trip isn't what I told my family it was. A mere vacation. No, this is *work*.

"Do you...regret bringing me?" I ask just before the plane hits the runway.

He looks at me, running his hand through his mess of dark hair.

"What's done is done," he shrugs, his tone heavy.

Is it because he killed a man? No, I don't think so. He's done it before, and he said he has no regrets.

"Just get your things," he orders, unbuckling his seat belt before the plane has come to a complete stop.

"My bag is right here," I say, feeling the sting of his dismissive tone.

"You might not have enough clothes," he says, glancing at the tote bag as I lift it from the ground. His thoughtful observation softens the blow.

"How long will we be here?"

He shakes his head. "As long as it takes."

"So, I'll do some shopping," I smile, trying to be positive. I don't know when I'll see the rest of my wardrobe again, nor anything else at my abandoned home. Every day since my abduction, I've thought of new things I'm missing and wish I had brought, like my favorite hand cream and my other purse.

"Are we staying at a hotel or do you have a place here in Miami?" I ask as we exit the plane.

"I've got a place. Maybe not what you're expecting."

"What could I be expecting? I know nothing about... your life."

"You know some," he says, his tone softer than before.

He studies my eyes a moment before reaching his hand to my face. The caress of my chin between his fingers is soothing.

"But you want to know *more*. Don't you, love?"

Butterflies flutter madly in my chest as he reads my reaction. It's like he enjoys putting me on the spot. I press my lips with a nod as the edge of his mouth lifts.

"Come on. Let's go," he half smiles, taking my hand.

When we descend the steps, a black SUV is waiting.

I expect the driver to take us into the city, but we coast along the beachfront highway until the sky rises and falls back, and a natural area with palm trees and mangroves appears.

"Biscayne Bay," the driver says, motioning toward the sea. I gaze across the bright blue waters, landing my sights on a narrow island in the distance.

I want to ask about Pirate's job and where we are going. But he probably doesn't want to talk about that in front of the driver. So I watch the changing scenery in silence. When Pirate claims my hand for the second time today, part of me hates how good it feels.

Since he came into my life, he has terrified and comforted me nearly every hour of the day. So what the hell is this between us? I can't wrap my mind around it. I highly doubt that a normal or healthy relationship can come from these twisted circumstances. All I can do, for now, is play along and make the best of things until I'm free again. If I'm going to be in captivity—or *protective custody*—I might as well enjoy what moments I can. Right now, his big, strong hand holding mine feels good.

He winks at me, nudging his head toward the window. I follow his gaze to where boats are docked along a pier.

"Black Point Marina. That's where I keep my ship."

My eyes widen. "Your ship?"

"A sailing yacht, to be exact."

"We're going boating?" I smile, liking how this feels less like a mercenary work trip than a real vacation. The driver pulls into the marina.

"After we settle in, I can take you for a spin."

"You mean we're staying—"

"Aboard my ship, yes."

He seems to take satisfaction in my surprise. Now I know what he meant when he said his "place" might not be what I expected. So, the Pirate has a ship. He continues to live up to his name.

JASMINE P. DANE

...to be continued...

Note: before being released to retailers, the subsequent books in this collection will continue exclusively as WIPs @ GothikaBooks.Com

book boxes!

Need more dark romance in your life? Check out *the* leading dark romance book box service...

Books + Merch for fans of Dark Romance, Dark Fantasy & Horror! We've got all the tropes, triggers, and toys! Currently ON SALE. Visit: **Dark-RomanceCrates.Com**